"Can you help me?

Mel didn't answer. He concentrated on the scuffed toe of his work boot. "Can this wait until next month or next year?"

She crossed her arms over her chest. "I won't be here next year."

He shook his head. "None of my business if you want to keep running away from home."

Her cheeks colored and he knew he'd struck a nerve. He'd had no intention of firing any weapons, but it had been a very long day.

June cocked her head and studied him. "You don't ever wonder if there's something else out there for you—something outside of Starlight Point?"

He shook his head again.

"You want to stay on this merry-go-round your whole life? Working all year getting ready for a summer of twelve-hour days?"

Mel glanced at the dusty wall clock. "Fifteen hours."

June sighed, uncrossing her arms. "Some things in life you only get one solid chance at," she said. "Apparently you don't get that. Nobody seems to."

he flung the shop door open and disappeared the night.

Dear Reader,

Thank you for visiting Starlight Point as you read *Carousel Nights*. Can you imagine inheriting a summer resort and amusement park? It sounds like great fun and hard work to me. I love an old-fashioned theme park with a carousel, cotton candy, roller coasters and the sound of the waves on the shore.

This is the second book in the Starlight Point Stories miniseries. The first book, *Under the Boardwalk*, followed Jack Hamilton, the oldest of the Hamilton children, in the first summer they inherit Starlight Point. In *Carousel Nights*, middle child June Hamilton struggles with a tough choice: continue the Broadway career she always wanted, or come home and devote herself to Starlight Point? A summer romance she left behind years ago sweetens and complicates her decision. The third book in the series will be available in December 2016 and follows Evie, the youngest member of the family, as she finds her place at Starlight Point.

This is my eighth published novel, and they all take place in the summer and by the water. I love sunshine and waves because they are fleeting, like the first rush of falling in love. For me, writing about July days and the sparkle of the blue water makes them last all winter long. I hope reading *Carousel Nights* puts summer and love in your heart.

Thank you for reading my book. I hope you'll visit me at amiedenman.com, follow me on Twitter, @amiedenman, or send me an email at author@amiedenman.com.

Happy summer, wherever you are!

Amie Denman

HEARTWARMING

Carousel Nights

———

Amie Denman

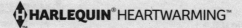

Recycling programs
for this product may
not exist in your area.

ISBN-13: 978-0-373-36801-3

Carousel Nights

Copyright © 2016 by Amie Denman

Printed in U.S.A.

Amie Denman is the author of eight contemporary romances full of humor and heart. Born with an overdeveloped sense of curiosity, she's been known to chase fire trucks on her bicycle and eavesdrop on lovers' conversations. Amie lives in Ohio with her husband, two sons, a big yellow Labrador and two cats. She believes everything is fun: especially wedding cake, show tunes, roller coasters and falling in love.

Books by Amie Denman

Harlequin Heartwarming

Under the Boardwalk

Carina Press

Her Lucky Catch

Visit the Author Profile page
at Harlequin.com for more titles.

Carousel Nights is dedicated to my parents, who encouraged their four daughters to be anything they wanted to be. Thank you for your unwavering love and for taking us on all those vacations that sparked our curiosity and imagination.

CHAPTER ONE

I SURE AM far from Broadway. Right back where I started.

For June Hamilton, standing on the stage of the Midway Theater was pure nostalgia. She had danced her first semiprofessional steps here during the summers. But she had no intention of dancing her last ones on stage at her family's amusement park. Her legs were still good for six or seven seasons of New York City, and she still had a dream to chase.

"Thank you for spending your summer at Starlight Point," she said. The performers gathered around her shifted even closer. "You'll dance your legs off doing five shows a day, but the experience you'll gain can take you anywhere."

"You've been on Broadway for ages, right?" a girl with a tiny waist and a movie-star face asked.

"Hey," June said, narrowing her eyes but

smiling at the girl. "Only a few years, and I'm going back for the fall season. After I transform this theater and the Starlight Saloon into standing-room-only attractions."

She had one month until the two theaters at Starlight Point opened for the summer.

Today she and her stage manager, Megan, would begin a marathon of rehearsals and performances. The new crop of college-aged performers gathered on stage at the Midway Theater, leggings and loose sweatshirts ready to come off so they could dance.

June handed a shop broom to one of the guys. "Do you mind knocking off some of the construction dust?"

The young man smiled, perfect white teeth giving him a showbiz gleam. "Didn't know I'd be dancing in a work zone," he said, taking the broom and heading downstage.

"Life of the theater," June said. "You never know what you're getting into."

"It's all good. I'm happy to have a summer job."

"Sorry I'm late," Megan said, coming through a back door onto the rear of the stage. "I was battling my computer files and uploading practice music to my phone." She headed for a small set of speakers propped on a cardboard box. "I love the show you've put together," she continued, fumbling with a cord and searching the back of the speaker for a place to plug it in.

"Everyone loves Broadway, especially people who are willing to take a break from spinny rides and cotton candy," June said, smiling at the six-months-pregnant stage manager, who still managed to look like a dancer despite her protruding belly. "At least I hope so."

"You brought the glamour home," Megan agreed. "I have no idea what we'll do next year when you're back to your day job."

June walked to the front of the stage. The seats were all empty, but she felt the magic anyway. She always had. She faced the rows of seats and the midway wall of the theater where the marquee hung over glass doors.

June breathed deeply, raising her arms and stretching. She imagined the excitement, music, costumes and applause. More than anything, her feet wanted to spell out a routine on the floor that would have the audience wishing for three sets of eyes to take it all in.

But she had a lot of work to do before one patron filled a seat. When June had agreed to come home for the summer and take a hiatus from dancing on Broadway, she'd exacted an agreement from her brother, Jack, and sister, Evie. They had to let her update the old theaters. It was their second year running Starlight Point after the unexpected death of their father. They'd had bumps in the road, major and expensive ones, but ramping up the live shows would be a return on investment.

As she stood on the stage, breathing in theater air and listening to the clicking of tap shoes behind her, June wished she could fast-forward to opening day with a hundred people soaking up the great Broadway revue show she'd sketched out.

"You're smiling," Mel said.

She hadn't heard him come in. *How long has he been there?* He stood near an exit door at the side of the house five rows back. Mel Preston. Tall. Blue work shirt with Starlight Point over one pocket and his name over the other.

She already knew his name. And plenty of other things about him.

June had left Starlight Point seven years ago, when she was eighteen, to attend college in Manhattan and begin her Broadway career.

She didn't regret striking out on her own and leaving the family business to the rest of the family. But she did have one tiny regret.

Okay, one six-foot-three regret.

"Of course I'm smiling," June said. "Theater is my life." She spun on her good leg and tapped out a short rhythm with her foot.

"Even this dinky theater?" he asked, walking down the middle aisle.

Her heart rate sped up with each step he took.

"Careful," she said. "I know the owners of this place and I could have you fired."

Mel sat in one of the hundreds of empty seats. He leaned back, a travel mug of coffee in his hand. *He's staying?* June needed to concentrate on her rehearsal, and Mel divided her attention with his mere presence.

"How have you been, June?" He sat as if he were a ticket-holding patron waiting for his entertainment. Asked the question as if they were high school classmates bumping into each other at the bank or the grocery store.

June had been home just over a week and she'd somehow avoided a reunion with Mel. But Starlight Point only covered a few square miles. If she was planning to be home all summer, she had to find a way to tune out the way Mel made her feel, even after seven years. *Maybe I'll turn the music up very loud.*

"I've been fine," she said with a business-casual tone she hoped would convince at least one of them. "Busy. I'll tell you all about it when I get my shows open."

"I heard you're staying all summer."

June nodded, unsure if Mel considered it a good thing or a bad thing she was staying all summer. Her two goals of recharging herself and the theaters did not allow room for reviving a romance she'd left on the table. Not that Mel's tone or posture suggested a return to old feelings. He was busy, too, the head of maintenance at Starlight Point. If he'd already seen her plans for renovation on the Midway Theater and the Starlight Saloon Theater, he was probably ready to drive her to the airport.

"Why did you decide to come home?" he asked.

Why did he want to know? She could tell him to mind his own business...but it was a fair question.

A question she'd been dodging since she'd announced she was coming home. In the competitive world of Broadway, she'd only admitted the pain in her knee to her closest friends. And there was no reason to acknowledge it to Mel now. Especially since it already felt better after weeks off the stage.

"I came home to revitalize these theaters," she said. "I do own a third of Starlight Point."

Loud music poured from the small speakers behind her.

"Sorry about that," Megan said, "trying to find the right track."

June broke eye contact with Mel. He could stay and watch if he wanted to, but she had work to do. She could certainly keep her composure. After dancing in front of thousands of Broadway fans, keeping her heart and mind on her career should be as easy as learning to two-step. She turned to her waiting dancers.

"I made copies of the order of the numbers for you. I'll grab them."

June crossed the stage and dug through her lucky duffel, a high school graduation present from her parents. She'd stuffed her shoes and dance clothes in it for years, hauling it along to her Broadway debut in *Oklahoma!*, her chorus role in *Hello, Dolly!*, her crazily costumed role in *Cats*, and her most recent performance in *Pippin*. In all those shows, she'd been a background dancer. Her next ambition was to get a larger role where she could sing and dance. The front of the stage—that's where she wanted to be.

She handed out copies of the program and sat at the piano.

"Let's do a read and sing-through," she said. "I'll play since it's easier than stopping and starting the sound track."

The six male and six female performers sang through the pieces culled from a dozen or so Broadway shows. Typical audience members would recognize nearly all the songs, and June hoped the combination had just the right energy and appeal for the amusement park crowd.

"Ready to try the first dance number?" she asked, rising from the piano and stacking the music on top.

Her breath quickened just thinking about dancing and she pulled off her hoodie, tossing it toward the side of the stage and taking a quick look to see if Mel was still there.

He was. She should not care either way. Didn't he have work to do?

June waited, tapping her toe in anticipation

while Megan fiddled with the music on her phone.

"Wish I could dance," Megan said, "but I'm barely surviving morning sickness as it is. Slow movements are my friend right now."

June smiled sympathetically. "I thought morning sickness was supposed to go away after the first few months?"

"Apparently not for everyone," Megan said. She finished searching the playlist and looked up. "Ready?"

Spin, step, step, hold, dip. June moved with the dancers, letting the energy of the stage and the familiar music take her back to the time when she never thought about her knee, never took a cautious step waiting for the slice of pain. When she was happy just being a dancer.

She wanted to keep going, but the song ended. Megan thumbed a button on the player and the silence was broken by the dancers' quick breathing. A moment later, applause from the lone audience member reminded June *he* was still there.

June walked to the front of the stage, signaling the other dancers to join her. They held hands and did an elaborate stage bow. Mel stood, continuing his applause until the dancers dispersed to the rear of the stage where they'd stowed their water bottles and cell phones.

"Glad you liked it," June said to Mel.

"What's not to like?"

She smiled. Despite the four rows of seats between them, he could probably hear her heart racing with adrenaline and endorphins. It was the dancing, her love of the theater. What else would it be?

She focused on the ramshackle catwalk and the back wall, which sported faded posters and a series of cables and spotlights older than she was. There was so much work to do in the weeks before her show opened. Too much.

"I'm glad you asked," she said, "because I have a long list of jobs that have to be done before anyone lays eyes on this theater or my show."

Mel nodded. He put his hat on and stepped into the aisle. The way he moved, tugged on his hat...it was as familiar as her mother's voice in the kitchen or the feel of her father's hand holding hers. The father she had lost while she was off dancing toward her dream. If she could go back, would she do anything differently?

"You're not leaving right now?" June asked.

"Work to do."

"I was hoping to talk to you about some construction I need."

"Out of time," he said, his words matter-of-fact.

"You had time to watch us rehearse for half an hour."

"And it was great. I always knew you'd be a success," he said.

June crossed her arms. "What's that supposed to mean?"

Her voice, combined with surprisingly good acoustics, bounced off the back wall just as Evie and Jack entered the theater. They paused, probably trying to accustom their eyes to the dim lighting.

They had either the best or worst timing in the world.

"What's up, Mel? Is June ordering you to make this place look like Times Square?" Jack asked.

Evie elbowed Jack and Mel chuckled.

"She's trying. I interrupted their rehearsal and now I have to get back to work. The Kiddieland helicopters will be grounded unless someone troubleshoots the control panel.

Opening day wouldn't be the same without them."

He sent one long look at June and slid out the side door, opening a brief rectangle of bright sunshine.

"Still rehearsing? Want us to come back later?" Evie asked.

Behind her, June heard Megan rounding up the dancers and having a quiet conversation with them about blocking and potential props. There would be a million small decisions to make, but a big one was right in front of her.

"I'm glad you're here," she said, carefully sitting on the edge of the stage and scooting off. "We should nail down our plans for final improvements here."

Jack and Evie exchanged a look. "That's why we're here, but I'm not sure we're going to make your day."

June shrugged. "I was having a great day until about five minutes ago. Unless you tell me we can't shape up these old theaters in the next month, I'll live."

Jack sat in a theater seat, his long legs protruding into the aisle. He dug in his pocket and pulled out a sandwich bag full of cookies. He bit into a star-shaped sugar cookie and held out the bag.

"Want some?" he mumbled, mouth full.

"You're stress-eating, Jack. It's not even lunch and you're hitting the sweets."

Evie sunk into a seat in the row in front of her brother. "Better than drinking before lunch."

"That's next," Jack said. "We're bleeding money and none is coming in."

"The park's not even open yet," June protested. "Stop panicking."

"We have to be conservative with the little capital we have," Evie said. "We're looking for places to cut."

"Don't look here. This theater anchors the whole front midway. If it's closed or cheap-looking, guests will notice." She rested her hand on a seat back. "Bankers and investors will notice."

"Can we get away with closing the Starlight Saloon for the year?" Evie asked.

"Are you kidding? My steampunk Western show is going to put the Wonderful West on the map. I can guarantee it will bring people to that part of the park and make them stay. They'll get elephant ears and tacos while they wait for the train. You can't afford to make that area into a ghost town. Kids love the shooting range and parents can get a cold beer and catch a show."

"But the kitchen—" Jack began.

"Sucked last year, but we—you—got by. We can serve prepackaged food and drinks. Chips, cookies, cold bottles. No kitchen required."

"It would be easier to just—"

"No." June cut off her sister. "We can do this. Even if we have to work night and day until opening. Remember how you two ran around like the sky was falling last year on the day the vendor boycott and the bankers' visit collided? Everyone pulled together. Augusta, Mel, the maintenance staff, a few other poor suckers I recruited. We got through it. Starlight Point survived. We can do it again this year. Especially since—" she lowered her voice with a quick glance at the stage, where the dancers and Megan were absorbed in their plans "—we have no choice."

"Should've been a drill sergeant. Or a cheerleader," Jack grumbled.

"I'd rather dance. The costumes are much

better. Right now, I'm getting back to work.
This old place is going to shine if I have to
scrub the floors myself."

CHAPTER TWO

A WEEK LATER, Mel Preston parked at the maintenance garage, which was tucked out of sight behind a fence, trees and a roller coaster. Just as he had since he was sixteen, he buckled on his tool belt and picked up a clipboard with the day's work orders. As a young summer employee, he had changed lightbulbs, greased brakes on coasters and cleaned up messes. A dozen years later, he was the head of maintenance, writing and following his own work orders.

Usually.

He frowned at the plans on his desk from a local architect. Starlight Point had its own planning and design team ensuring continuity and maintaining a sense of history at the park. Why June wanted to hire an outside architect to design the facades for her theater upgrades was an irritating mystery.

Mel tossed the plans into the back of a three-

wheeled cart and drove through the open gate
onto the midway. Some members of his crew
were picking up limbs that had fallen in last
night's spring thunderstorm. Old trees lined
the trail through the Wonderful West, a quaint
and relatively quiet respite from the coasters,
flashing lights and games of the front midway.

He parked and surveyed the Starlight Saloon
Theater. From the boards on its plank porch
floor to the rustic marquee still advertising last
year's Western show, it was old and familiar.

A dented silver spittoon rolled out the front
door, bounced down the steps and came to rest
by his foot. June stomped onto the porch, hot-
pink shirt matching the color in her cheeks.
She lugged half a countertop bar behind her.
When she saw Mel, she let go of the prop and
straightened, her chest heaving with effort.

"Bring me a Dumpster?" she asked, her tone
hopeful.

"Not yet. Working on it."

June sat on a barrel-shaped chair and tapped
her foot. "I've waited patiently for a week."

"Patiently?"

"Well," she said, a half smile appearing. "I
have waited."

"Theaters aren't the only things that need

attention before opening day," Mel said. "They don't even open the first couple weeks of the season."

Mel propped his foot on the spittoon. He wanted to stride onto the porch and ask June why she was always running away. But she was like a bird taking handouts in a park. If he made a sudden move or got too close, she'd head for the nearest tree.

"I do have a project for you," she said.

"Does it come with breakfast?"

"You don't want to eat out of the kitchen in this theater. I don't know how it passed inspection last year."

"It didn't," Mel said. "So we only served drinks at this show. With all the bigger fish to fry after your dad passed away, we let a few things go."

As Jack's best friend and an unofficial member of the Hamilton family, Mel knew firsthand that Starlight Point had flirted with bankruptcy. When Jack opened the books after his father's fatal heart attack, he found a mess that had taken years to accumulate. It would take years to clean up, but Jack and Evie had gotten a strong start last summer.

June fished a rubber band from her jeans

pocket and gathered her long light brown hair into a tight ponytail. Although only two years younger than he was, June looked like a lost little girl sitting on a barrel in front of the empty saloon.

"I don't think I ever got to tell you how sorry I was about your father's death," Mel said.

June met his eyes. "You did. You were at his funeral."

"The whole town of Bayside and anyone who ever worked at Starlight Point was at his funeral," Mel said.

"I remember talking to you." She smiled and her whole face softened. "You brought me a tissue and a glass of iced water."

Although the entire Hamilton family was shocked at Ford's death, June seemed to take it the hardest. Maybe that's because she felt guilty about not being around the past few years. Was that why she decided to come home this summer?

"Least I could do," he said.

"And you've been there for Jack," she said, standing and moving closer. "When he took over last spring, he needed a good friend."

"We all do."

June crossed her arms and leaned back on

a porch post. She stared at her feet for fifteen seconds while Mel counted silently. He recognized the grubby work boots she'd had for years. She'd worn them as she helped around the park in the off-season until she went away for college. He remembered every tool she'd ever handed him and each ride she'd accepted in his cart. The owner's daughter and his best friend's sister who'd always been around.

"Can you tell me why the main electric switch won't turn on in this old theater?" June asked, adopting a neutral, businesslike tone. "I have to finish cleaning in here and I need to keep working when it gets dark or I'll never get it all done."

Mel had never doubted June's dancing ability, but he wished she wasn't using it to sashay a wide circle around him. There was no question it was better that way. Better to pretend that summer seven years ago and that kiss had never happened.

He picked up his clipboard. "Don't think that's on my orders for the day," he said, trying to keep his tone light. "I'm supposed to run electrical diagnostics on the Sea Devil, fix the organ's circuit board on the Midway Carousel, and call the state inspectors about the ride li-

cense for the Skyway cars. Boss won't like it
if I get diverted."

June snorted. "You *are* the boss."

Mel smiled. "I love hearing you say that.
How about once more?"

"Very funny."

"It *is* funny. Because you, Jack and Evie are
in charge of this place. I just work here."

He swung one leg into his cart, turning his
back on June.

"Hey," she said.

Mel tensed, wriggling his shoulders in his
blue work shirt, the tag grating the sensitive
skin on the back of his neck. He turned toward
June and fought a grin. She looked hopeful
and bossy at the same time. Close to the six-
foot mark with long, slim arms and legs, she
reminded him of Jack. Her green eyes flecked
with brown and her full lips made Mel remember she'd briefly been his girlfriend. Until
she'd left for college and left him cold.

"I can spare a half hour," he said. "But you
have to help. The wiring in there hasn't been
updated during my lifetime, and the conduit
runs up high over the stage." He strode over
and stopped in front of June, eye level with her

on the elevated porch. "It's going to be a real pain in the neck," he said.

June laughed, stepped back and shoved through the swinging saloon doors.

IF SHE WANTED to revisit a time when her insides didn't flip whenever Mel Preston came into view, she'd have to go back about a decade. The first time she'd seen him was at her older brother's seventh birthday party. Even then, his sandy hair and blue eyes combined with a giant smile had set him miles above Jack's other friends. When high school rolled around, she'd started to realize just how much she liked him. Now, at six foot three, Mel was easily head and broad shoulders over other men. Except Jack. June's older brother and Mel had competed for vertical supremacy throughout high school until Jack finally edged Mel out by one inch during a late-teen growth spurt.

Gradually, over the last decade, their easy relationship had heated, tempered, flared, cooled and simmered. But never jelled. It didn't have a chance to because June couldn't give up her dream to tap her toes on Broadway. The two live theaters at Starlight Point with their creaking floors and seats were not enough for her then or now.

How ironic that she was standing in one of those theaters and trying to make it sparkle. *Temporary*, she reminded herself.

She tilted her head to see Mel balanced on a ladder ten feet over the stage. Only his worn work boots were visible from her angle. A screwdriver clattered to the floor, almost clobbering her on its way down.

"Sorry about that," Mel said. "Can you toss it back up here?"

"I'm a bad throw," she said, picking it up. The handle still held Mel's heat.

He chuckled. "I know."

"Hey," she said. "I was only ten and you guys were twelve. Big difference. And I didn't want to play baseball anyway but you were short a player."

"That was my first time replacing a pane of glass," Mel said. "I did okay and your parents probably never would've known if Evie hadn't told on us."

"Too young to know better," June said. "She was only six or seven."

June tossed the screwdriver up but missed

by several feet, causing Mel to overreach and almost fall off the ladder.

"I better come get it before someone loses an eye," Mel said.

He backed down the ladder while June crossed the stage to retrieve the fallen tool. Her back to him, she said, "Your son's about six, isn't he?"

"He'll turn six this summer. Starts first grade in the fall."

She turned to face him as he stepped off the bottom rung, a flicker of silence between them.

Mel jerked his head toward the upper catwalk without taking his eyes off June. "Think that old catwalk for the lighting will hold my weight?" he asked. "I don't know if it's been used in years."

"I hope so. My shows include lots of lighting. Maybe some special effects."

"In the Wonderful West? Seems out of place," Mel commented.

June rolled her eyes. "What you know about theater would fit in your back pocket."

"Maybe," he said, taking the screwdriver from her outstretched palm, "but that's where this goes. Lucky for you, I know about electricity."

June watched him climb one rung at a time. When he reached the junction box ten feet up, he put a small flashlight between his teeth. Although full daylight outside, the theater was dim.

"I've gotta follow this line," Mel said. He climbed another five rungs and eased onto the narrow metal catwalk that hugged the theater on three sides. Ancient spotlights were mounted beneath it and cables snaked over and under it.

"Seems solid," Mel said. "I'm going down to the junction box in the corner. I have to see where we have spark and where we don't."

Good idea, June thought, following his progress as he crawled along the back wall. She held her breath when he slid across a gap between missing supports. When he reached the corner, the flashlight between his teeth threw patterns of light on the wall as he banged at something metallic.

"Any luck?" June called.

"Just…" The flashlight clanked onto the steel catwalk, rolled off and crashed onto the floor near June. The light went dark.

"Shouldn't have opened my mouth," Mel said from the darkness above her.

"My fault," June said. "I asked you a question."

"You can make it up to me by digging through the toolbox on my cart and finding me another flashlight."

"Be right back."

June headed for the daylight streaming through the front windows. Mel's cart had two toolboxes and she had to dig through both before finding a large industrial-looking flashlight.

Inside, Mel's long legs hung over the side of the catwalk fifteen feet up. He swung his feet like a kid waiting for his third-grade girlfriend on the playground.

"Can I convince you to bring that up here?" Mel asked.

"I could throw it."

"I haven't got a death wish. Just come up the ladder and I'll crawl along the catwalk and meet you at the top."

He didn't wait for an answer. She knew he wouldn't. June had worked at Starlight Point until she was eighteen. During the off-season, she'd tromped around handing tools to maintenance men after school, climbing the emergency steps on coasters and taking any challenge. When she was old enough to officially work, she'd sold popcorn until she finally convinced her parents to let her dance on stage. Although her parents owned the amusement park, they made their children work regular summer jobs. It was a great way to see Starlight Point from the inside out, and all three of them had earned reputations as hard workers.

Mel had every reason to think she'd scamper up the ladder, flashlight in hand, like she would have done in the past.

But the shining aluminum faced her like a demon.

Her heart rate accelerated as she placed one foot on the bottom rung and pulled herself up with her free hand. One rung down, at least fifteen more to go. Maybe she could do this. *Jumper's knee. That's what her doctor had called it. If she stretched, did her exercises, and avoided stairs and high-impact jumps, it would get better.* She'd been taking it easy, keeping her movements small and not telling a soul. She felt stronger, ready to take on these theaters and get on with her life.

She sucked in a breath and steeled herself for another vertical step.

Pain streaked through her right knee when she put her foot on the next rung and tried to pull herself up. Agonizing pain. Ladders were not on her therapy plan. A wave of nausea hit her and sweat chilled the back of her neck. She dropped the flashlight and grabbed both sides of the ladder. She stepped backward to the floor, fumbling for the light, afraid to look up. Back on both feet, the pain subsided and she took a deep breath.

"What are you doing?" Mel asked.

Trying to pretend everything is just fine. "Picking up the flashlight," she said tersely. "What does it look like?"

"At this rate, it'll be dark before I even get started. That's an expensive light, so be careful with it."

"Sorry," she said, eyeing the ladder and trying to think of a graceful way out. Her heartbeat pulsed through her neck and hammered in her ears. She risked a glance up. Mel lay full length on the catwalk, his chin propped in his hands. Waiting for her.

But that was a mountain she was not climbing today.

She parked the light at the bottom of the ladder. "If it's so precious, you better come get it yourself," she said. "I'm going back to work in the prop storage room."

She walked slowly and carefully away, willing herself not to show a trace of weakness. Would Mel let her off the hook? The catwalk overhead groaned and the ladder behind her creaked as Mel started down it.

"Don't know when you became such a princess that you can't help a guy out," he said.

June counted to thirty, numbering her steady steps to the storage room door. She closed it, sat on a box and elevated her leg on a dusty plastic hitching post. She was still sitting there staring at years of props in the gray light from the solitary window when the overhead fluorescent lights buzzed on. She waited, listening, until Mel's cart started up and drove away. Rubbing her knee, June tried to quell the panic in her chest. If she couldn't dance, she couldn't go back to Broadway and the roles she had already sacrificed so much for.

CHAPTER THREE

EVIE SAT AT Jack's desk, staring at his computer through her green-rimmed glasses. Three years younger than June, Evie was generally sweet, except in her ruthless devotion to accurate accounts. And her attitude toward the architect June had hired to fancy up the two live-show venues.

"The money is one thing. But I don't see why we should pay his hourly rate when we already have our own planners," Evie said. "And how much do you think we can really get done on the facades when the park opens in a week? It's nuts."

Jack, who was standing by the window, raised one eyebrow at June. His look said *you're on your own with this argument*.

June wasn't asking for the moon and stars. She just wanted the theaters to look like they hadn't been designed by the same person who'd imagined the cheeseburger stand.

Something a little more modern—even a new paint scheme and lightbulbs would be better than nothing.

"Fresh blood," June said. "Our planning guys will just come up with the same old same old."

"So?" Evie asked. "Same old ensures continuity. People like the old-fashioned aura. Even if you don't."

"News flash," June said. "Change is good."

June crossed her arms and leaned against the large window beside Jack. He'd finally moved into their father's office over the winter. Last summer, he'd kept the smaller office next door out of a combination of shock, grief and respect. Moving into this office—rich with their father's history, his big wooden desk, awards and mementos from years in the business—was a sign Jack was growing into the job of CEO.

"I refuse to be the grown-up here, if that's what you're thinking," Jack said. "Just because I'm the tallest and smartest of the three of us."

Evie breathed loudly through her nose and stared down her older siblings. When had she gotten so opinionated? Evie had always been the nice, sweet one. Hadn't she? June had been away for seven years, and in that time Evie had gone from fifteen to twenty-two. Practically a lifetime.

"Fifteen hundred bucks so far and all I've gotten out of him is an argument," Evie said.

"You argue with people?" June asked.

"I'm doing it right now."

"That's different," June said. "We're related. And what the heck is wrong with doing something new around here? You opened the Sea Devil last year. A multimillion-dollar roller coaster is a pretty big deal compared to what I'm suggesting."

Although it was by choice, June felt like a third wheel when she had meetings with Jack and Evie about Starlight Point and its future. The small profits last year had been split three ways. This year's profit would be split as well, even though it'd certainly still be modest as they worked to convince the bankers to extend the loan.

June wanted to earn her share, small though it was. And theater was the best way she knew how to do that. Better shows could mean more ticket sales. They might bring local pass holders across the Point Bridge a few more times each summer to see the shows, and locals spend money on popcorn, elephant ears and soda.

"The Sea Devil was Dad's idea," Jack said. "He started it, he just didn't get to finish it."

"Are you saying you wouldn't add new rides in the future?" June asked.

Jack exhaled slowly, staring out the second-floor window at the front section of the midway. "I'm saying I wouldn't go *that* big, especially if it practically bankrupted us. Not anytime soon."

"Our plan for this year is good," Evie said. "Small improvements that guests will notice. New paint, a few new facades on buildings—"

"Like both theaters," June said.

Evie went on as if her sister weren't even there. "Restroom upgrades, new safety belts in the children's rides, new signs on the Point Bridge. But we're not breaking the bank."

"Unless the bank breaks us," June said.

Jack waved at someone outside and then turned back to his sisters. "If we made it through last year, we'll make it through this year. The bankers liked what they saw last summer even though we had very little time to do anything. We have a solid plan. And one of our owners is now a CPA with more money sense than the other two of us put together."

"Hope it helps," Evie said.

"Credibility," Jack said, "helps make up for the fact another one of the owners is a Broadway dancer who never sticks around."

June narrowed her eyes and threw a pencil at him. The elevator outside Jack's office dinged.

"Mom," Jack whispered. "And she's got Betty with her. I just saw them outside."

Virginia Hamilton zipped into the room. She pulled a red wagon behind her and parked it by Jack's desk. The brown, black and white dog snoozing on a blanket in the wagon opened one eye, yawned and went back to sleep.

Evie rolled over in Jack's chair and stroked the dog's ears. "Betty smells good today," she said, smiling at her mother.

"Just picked her up from the groomer. She rolled in something dead on the beach yesterday," Virginia said. "How's it going here in the war room with one week before the big opening?"

Jack groaned loudly. Evie rolled back to the desk. And June looked out the window, thinking about big openings she'd been part of before. Opening day at the park every year through her eighteenth birthday. Opening night of four major Broadway productions. She was getting to be a pro at pulling a show together.

The elevator dinged in the silence and Mel ambled in.

He stopped. His eyes met June's and held for a heartbeat until he shifted to the oldest member of the family.

"Sorry," he said. "Don't mean to interrupt. I just came by to see if Jack wanted to get some lunch. I need a break from trying to figure out how water got into the circuit boards of the Silver Streak over the winter."

June hadn't seen Mel since he'd turned on her lights at the Starlight Saloon. She'd heard through Jack that Mel was rewiring the entire theater before he'd allow even one extension cord to be plugged in, so she'd avoided the Saloon for a week, focusing on costume and prop designs instead.

"Gus is bringing lunch," Jack said. "She's coming over anyway to get her three bakeries ready to open."

"I hear she's working up some new creations for this summer, themed pies and turnovers," Mel said, wiping a fake tear and using a tragic voice, "I love your wife."

Jack punched Mel's shoulder. "There's probably enough lunch for you, but no way am I sharing dessert."

"I can live with those rules," Mel said. He dropped to one knee and made kissing sounds to Betty, who hopped out of the wagon, threw herself at him with embarrassing abandon and rolled over for a belly rub.

Virginia cleared her throat. "While we wait, I thought we could talk about my STRIPE program this year."

June turned back to the window, staring outside. Every year, Virginia muscled someone into running the Summer Training and Improvement Plan for Employees. Every employee had to participate and learn a specific skill such as conversational French, water rescue, ballroom dancing, knitting. In the past, the program had been mandatory. Last summer, it had become voluntary. But it was still an onerous task for whoever Virginia chose to be the STRIPE sergeant.

"Any ideas?" Virginia asked, enthusiastically. "What should the STRIPE topic be this year?"

"I'm off the hook," Gus said, coming through the door with a cardboard box filled with paper bags and drinks. "I taught hundreds of people to decorate a birthday cake last summer. I'm still recovering."

"And you were wonderful," Virginia said. She cleared a space on Jack's desk so her daughter-in-law could set the box down.

Jack approached the food, eyeing the bags but avoiding direct eye contact with his mother. June smiled at his pathetic attempt. If he thought cowering would save him, he was in for a surprise.

"How about kayaking, Jack?" Virginia asked. "The lake is one of our best assets, and you're such a good rower. You'd be great."

"Sorry, Mom, too busy. And I don't know where we'd get dozens of practice kayaks."

"Don't we rent those on the hotel beach?" June asked. "I thought we had thirty or forty kayaks."

When their mother turned her back, Jack stuck his tongue out at June.

"Evie," Virginia said, turning to her youngest daughter, "no one can doubt the importance of managing money. You could teach practical bookkeeping. How to balance a checkbook. Perhaps the wisdom of investing at a young age." Virginia's face lit up. "Stock tips!" she proclaimed.

Evie took off her glasses and cleaned them meticulously until her mother moved on to her next target.

"June," Virginia said, approaching June's hiding spot by the window. *Great, she thinks I'm going to teach them all to dance. Maybe I should tell her about my bum knee instead of keeping it a secret. I could use a great excuse for getting out of the STRIPE.*

"How about teaching piano lessons? Wouldn't it be wonderful if everyone could play something nice like *Für Elise* or *Happy Birthday* on the piano?"

June blew out a sigh. Teaching two thousand summer employees to read music and play the piano with both hands would be worse than teaching the tango. "You can't play the piano, Mom, and you're perfectly fine."

"I'd be better if someone would teach me to play."

"Sorry, no time," June said, eyebrows raised in innocence. "Choreography, costumes, blocking… The theaters are a huge task. Huge. Plus, I may have to take a short-notice trip to New York for auditions at some point. Can't guarantee I'll be here on the class days. You'd have to hire a substitute teacher. Could get pricey."

"It might give you a purpose," Virginia insisted. "Make you feel like you're part of the team."

June felt her cheeks heat. She wondered when the guilt trip would start. *Jack and Evie were devoting their lives to the family business. Why wasn't she*?

She could explain in one sentence. *She didn't want to.* She'd never made any promises and she had a right to her own career—a career she hoped would soon step beyond dancing into lead singing and acting roles. She had no plans to give that up.

"I don't need a purpose. I have my own life. I've already given up my summer to be here. If that's not enough for you, I don't know what you want."

June saw Evie's face flush, probably mirroring her own. Augusta focused on handing out lunches. Jack dug into a sandwich.

Only Mel appeared willing to get in the middle of the family volley.

"Simple electricity," he said.

Everyone turned to stare at him. *What is he doing?*

"Electrical circuits," he said. "Basic wiring."

More staring.

He accepted a sandwich and a drink from Virginia, smiling and asking, "Don't you think it would be a good idea for people to learn something about voltage and current? Maybe wire a switch?"

Virginia swished her lips to the side. "You mean for a STRIPE topic?"

"Uh-huh," Mel said.

"Don't most people hire an electrician?" Jack asked. "Like you?"

"For big jobs, yes," Mel said. "Same reason they go to a bakery for big or fancy cakes." He nodded at Augusta who gave him a two-eyebrows-raised look of skepticism.

"But you can make birthday cakes at home," Mel continued, "and you can do a lot of wiring on your own, too."

Why was Mel arguing to be in charge of the STRIPE when he'd probably spent the last decade dodging the event? He had to be out of his mind. Everyone in the office was looking at him as if he'd just announced an elegant tea party in the maintenance garage.

"I don't know," Virginia said. "Electricity can be dangerous."

Evie laughed and rolled her eyes at her mother. "Water-skiing was dangerous, Mom. The water rescue thing two summers ago was dangerous. Even the conversational French got pretty dicey when some of our locals tried it on the international workers we hired that year."

"That was not my fault," Virginia said. "French is a very romantic language."

"Sounds like voltage is the safe choice this summer," Mel said. "Can't cause an international incident with that, and I'll make sure no one gets electrocuted."

Virginia sipped her drink and stared at Mel. "Do you think you could teach hundreds of summer employees about electricity?"

"I'd need plenty of help," Mel said. "Some of the other maintenance guys are really good and all of them know at least something about electricity. But I still need volunteers. Guys I can get, but I'd like females, too. It's good evidence there's no gender bias in wiring a circuit." Mel grinned, catching June's eye. "Women can handle sparks just as well as men can."

June wanted to be mad at Mel for trying to

be a hero. But she couldn't. Because she was
the one he saved. She had no idea why he'd
thrown himself on the STRIPE grenade, but
she had a feeling she was going to find out.

CHAPTER FOUR

OPENING DAY WAS PERFECT. Blue sky, a forecast of 75 degrees and a tiny breeze off Lake Huron. The typical first-day crowd was a combination of roller coaster fanatics, families with little kids anxious for their turn on the helicopters and bumper cars of Kiddieland, and locals who'd had enough of long winters in Michigan. Folks who wanted to smell and feel summer.

The newly improved loudspeakers played theme park music. Food vendors sent heavenly aromas to lure guests in.

Perfect. Except for one thing.

"We need a parade," June declared. "Floats, music, live performers."

Evie and Jack exchanged a look. "I knew we shouldn't have let you conduct the ceremonial gate opening," Jack said. "The excitement went to your head."

June giggled. "It was exhilarating. I thought

the pack of preteens would break a speed record as soon as I declared the Point open."

"There's a certain cachet to being the first in line at the Sea Devil," Jack said. He cracked his knuckles. "I already rode it twice yesterday, but I won't tell the coaster fanatics. It'd burst their bubble."

"I haven't been here on opening day in seven years," June said. "I forgot about the adrenaline."

"I'm glad you're here this year," Jack said. His expression sobered and he slung an arm around both his sisters. "We're in this together."

Evie leaned into the hug. "I know," she said. "I miss Dad the most on days like this."

June felt tears prick her eyes and nodded, not trusting herself to speak.

Standing off to the side and watching guests stream through the gates, June, Evie and Jack did a paradoxical combination of holding their breath and deep breathing.

"Off and running," Evie said. "If we made it through last year, we can make it through anything."

They watched parents with strollers moving at the back of the pack. Older people with no

ride-crazed kids dragging them forward saun-
tered along. They'd be the first to notice new
paint, signs, different offerings in food and
merchandise. Everyone else was headed for
the queue lines, ready for a coaster fix after
a long winter.

June kept her eyes on a couple roughly
her parents' age, holding hands and looking
around, pointing things out to each other.
Laughing. Really noticing the sunshine and
the flowers planted in a pattern that would
look best from the Skyway cars above. She
wondered how many years they'd been coming
to Starlight Point. Maybe they'd met here when
they were teenagers and had already raised
a family, coming to the Point every summer
and making albums of memories. Her vision
blurred and her eyes stung a little. She shook
it off. For all she knew, it was their first date
and they'd met on a seniors gambling bus tour.

"A parade would be perfect for the midafternoon doldrums," June said. "You know. Three
o'clock when the buzz wears off a little and the
sunburn starts stinging. Kids get all cranky
and parents are looking for a mood-changer.
They could line up for a parade."

"I thought they were going to fill the seats

in your theaters. Soak up the air-conditioning," Jack said. "A parade is the opposite."

"No, it isn't," June said. "It takes the show to the people. Live music, costumes, dancing. Maybe we could have a banner made up, advertising showtimes in the theaters."

Evie and Jack glanced at their sister and returned to counting the guests streaming past.

"Everyone loves a parade," June added.

Evie shrugged.

"Maybe next year," Jack said. "If we're lucky, you'll forget all about it."

"I'm serious."

"That's what I'm afraid of."

"How hard would it be to jazz up the high school band thing that's been going on for years?" June asked.

Every summer, high school bands from all over the state applied for a day at the Point. Band members got free admission in exchange for two performances. They played the national anthem at the front gates at park opening and marched through the park at some point in the day. Decent deal for the high school kids, probably hellish for the chaperones and a vague return in live entertainment for the Point.

"We standardize the time of their marching performance—say three o'clock every day—and add some other stuff," June said.

"Opening day fever has gotten to you," Evie said. "It's a lot of adrenaline to handle, and I forget your immunity is down. You probably think you can do a triathlon right now."

"Or at least name all fifty states and their capitals," Jack said.

"Everything seems possible on opening day," Evie said. "It's the family curse. It makes us commit to a lifetime of insanity, one hundred days at a time. And then spend the other two thirds of the year wondering what the heck we were thinking. It's a Vegas-wedding way to spend your life."

"But you love it," June said.

Evie smiled and waved to a little girl shoving an umbrella stroller with her doll in it. "Of course I do. I'd be crazy not to."

"And you love my idea of a parade."

"Maybe," Evie said. "I'd have to see how it looks on paper."

"I'll take a picture of it going down the midway and email it to you."

Evie cocked her head and blew out a long

sigh. "You can't just pull something like this out of your hat."

"Sure I can. It won't be that hard to put together a float, get some of my dancers to ride along and entertain, maybe a banner. I just need a theme and I'm good to go."

"But—" Evie protested.

"Listen. I own this place," June said, smirking. "I can pull this off if I want to."

"One-third," Evie said. "You're not even a simple majority."

Jack ran a hand through his hair and loosened his tie. "If you want a controlling interest, you can have my share," he said, heading straight for Aunt Augusta's bakery on the midway, a beacon of sugary hope under a pink awning.

"How does he stay so skinny?" June asked.

"He's in love," Evie said.

June and her sister stood side by side watching hundreds of guests continue through the front gates. From their position on a small raised bandstand, they could also see over the front ticket counters to the Point Bridge, where cars waited at the toll booths. Sunlight flashed off windshields, and the line of vehicles stretched all the way to Bayside.

"And how about you?" June asked. "Anyone you've got your eye on?"

Evie shook her head. "I'm married to Starlight Point right now. I'm trying to get the red ink and the black ink to pick out china patterns together."

"Might do you some good to get out of the office every day. You might meet people. Maybe around three o'clock?"

"Nice try."

"I'd let you wear a sparkly sash and carry the banner," June said.

"I think I'll stay in the office and be the adult in charge."

June raised her arm and did a perfect beauty pageant wave, nodding and smiling at her sister.

"You're perfect for the job," Evie said. "You've got more drama in one arm than I've got in my whole body."

June laughed. "Someday, that's going to change."

"You mean you're going to give up the stage?"

"Nope," June said, "I mean you'll get in touch with your inner drama queen one of these days."

"Doubt it," Evie said. She glanced at her smartphone and tucked it back in her skirt pocket. "You can have two thousand bucks to get your parade going. That has to cover float, costumes, everything. It's the best I can do."

"I'll take it. I might even do it for less and spend the rest on a spa day for us."

"Rain check on that until November."

"No good. You'll be insane by then and I'll be in New York."

Evie shoulder-hugged her sister. "I wish you'd stay. No matter how expensive your plans are." She smiled at June and started to walk away.

"Evie," June said, stopping her sister. "Which columns are the good ones—red or black?"

"Depends on how much fun you're having," Evie said, laughing, and then she turned and headed toward the corporate office behind the midway games.

"WHO THE DEVIL made this mess?" Mel thundered. It was almost ten o'clock at night. Mel would've gone home hours ago but rides shuttered for six months didn't come to life without some kinks. Opening week was a maintenance challenge every year. That's why his son, Ross, spent the week before and the week of opening "on vacation" at his grandparents' house in Bayside. Without their help, Mel didn't know what he'd do.

Without a beer, a shower and at least five hours of sleep tonight, he was on the verge of stealing one of the bumper cars and wreaking havoc on the Point Bridge.

The last thing he needed now was a mess in his maintenance garage. Someone had rearranged rolling tool chests, moved a lawnmower, turned on every light in the place and dragged an ancient maintenance scooter from its personal graveyard in the far back corner. Clanking and voices led Mel to the other corner where one of his most trusted year-round workers—Galway—was shoving a big box of stuff on a two-wheeled cart.

"What are you doing?" Mel yelled.

Jack stepped out from behind a tall rolling tool chest. "Plotting your overthrow," he said. "I've just made Galway here the head of maintenance. Gave him your corner office, key to your personal bathroom, everything."

Mel kicked a tire resting against a steel post.

It rolled across the floor and whacked Jack in the leg.

"He can have it," Mel said. "I'm going home. Someone else can clean up this mess."

"Any idea how long it's been since that old beer truck ran?" Jack asked, completely ignoring Mel's outburst and pointing to a shadow in the far back corner.

"Two hundred years," Mel said, his mood steadily worsening. "Heck if I know, it's been at least ten since we sold beer in those trucks on the midway. Don't even know why we even have one of them around anymore."

"I think it's perfect," June said, her voice emanating from inside the boxy truck. "Needs some work," she added.

"What's going on?" Mel asked. He could already guess he didn't want to hear it. Especially if it involved June. From what he'd seen in the weeks she'd been home, it was obvious she hadn't changed much. She was just as beautiful. Her smile was just as wide. And her ideas remained way up high in the sparkly and expensive clouds.

"June wants a parade," Jack said.

Mel rolled his shoulders and cracked his

knuckles. *That beer and shower might as well be on Mars*. "What's the occasion?"

Galway locked his tool chest, pocketed the key, glanced over his shoulder and quietly left the shop. Mel couldn't blame him. If he could lock up and leave, he would. But he didn't own the place and he was stuck listening to some harebrained idea involving one of the old beer trucks. On a pickup truck frame for maneuverability, the beer trucks had served gallons of the cold stuff for years on the midway. A sliding glass window on the side made it easy for guests to walk up and indulge.

"A daily parade," Jack explained. "Afternoons. Down the midway, through the Wonderful West and out the back gate."

"You twirling a baton and leading it?" Mel asked Jack.

"Nope. You are."

"Kiss my butt. I'm going home."

The back doors on the long abandoned truck creaked open and June looked out. Her hair was pulled back, but several chunks of it slipped out and framed her face, flushed with energy and sunburn.

"Plenty of room in here for sound equipment," June said, her voice vibrating with excitement. "We could put a speaker on the roof for days when we don't have a high school band lined up."

Mel felt the air change the moment her gaze swung to him. He wasn't foolish enough to think she brightened because of any reason except one: he was key to getting things done around Starlight Point. And she had a project in mind.

"Hey, Mel," she said.

Mel crossed his arms and leaned against one of the many steel posts supporting the roof of the maintenance garage. "Happy opening day, June. I can't believe you're not dead on your feet."

She smiled. "I'm used to long days on my feet. Staying up late. Broadway, you know." She ended her explanation with a tiny shrug.

It was far more endearing than he wanted it to be. He pictured her for a moment, a brief flash where he saw June singing and dancing under bright lights, electrifying a crowd of thousands.

And now she wanted a parade.

"Long day," Jack said. "Think I'll go home and let you two work this out."

Mel flicked a glance at his friend but didn't

say anything. Jack didn't need his permission to leave. But Mel wished he'd stick around and help him fend off June's ridiculous request.

Walking slowly toward the beer wagon, Mel heard Jack's receding footsteps, and the shop door clicked closed.

June stood in the back of the piece of junk she apparently hoped to make into a parade vehicle. Mel didn't give a darn if she was standing in Air Force One. He was tired. Exhausted from the maniacal ecstasy of opening day. There was a chicken potpie in his freezer just waiting for its five minutes in the microwave.

"You're out of your mind," he said, his voice low and controlled. "Doing a parade every day on top of however many shows is nuts."

"Ten," she said. "Six in the Midway Theater, four in the Starlight Saloon."

"Whatever. It's still crazy."

June sat on the floor of the truck, her legs dangling off the back. "I've done crazy things before," she said.

They were alone in the shop. Maybe this was the time to ask June if their summer romance seven years ago meant anything to her, or if it was just one of the crazy things she'd done. Suddenly, Mel remembered their awkward dance at her senior prom. He saw scattered moments as if a slow-motion movie were playing, filled with images of them together and not together. Like two magnets with the same polarity shoving themselves backward. If their charge ever reversed...

But it wouldn't. June always had one foot out the door, the other one right behind.

"Can you help me?" June asked.

Mel didn't answer. He concentrated on the scuffed toe of his work boot. He heard her sigh and shove off the back of the truck. Feet in green sneakers appeared right in front of him.

"Can this wait until next month or next year?"

He hazarded a glance up. She stood, arms crossed. "I won't be here next year."

"I know."

"And..."

He shook his head. "None of my business if you want to keep running away from home."

Her cheeks colored and he knew he'd struck a nerve. He'd had no intention of firing any weapons, but it had been a *very long* day.

Instead of looking angry, June cocked her head and studied Mel.

"You don't ever wonder if there's something

else out there for you—something outside of Starlight Point?"

He shook his head.

"You want to stay on this merry-go-round your whole life? Working all year getting ready for a summer of twelve-hour days?"

Mel glanced at the dusty wall clock. "Fifteen hours."

June sighed, uncrossing her arms. "Some things in life you only get one solid chance at," she said. "Apparently you don't get that. Nobody seems to."

She swung around and flung the shop door open, disappearing into the night and leaving the parade issue on the table.

"Yes, I do," Mel said in the empty shop, an echo his only answer.

CHAPTER FIVE

DRESSED IN HER dancing clothes and running her troupe through a scene, June only heard her cell phone ring because there was a break in the music.

"Trouble at the Silver Streak," Evie said. "Can you run over and see what's going on?"

"I'm in rehearsals. This show opens in seven days."

"Sorry. Jack and I are interviewing candidates for the open accounting and finance position. The Silver Streak is right behind your theater so I hoped you could run over and see what the big deal is."

June sighed. "I'll pin on my name tag and go see."

Two Starlight Point police officers got there ahead of June and the first-aid staff. One of the officers, Don Murray, had been there since before June could remember. Large and stoic, he was a mountain in uniform at the entrance

gate of the Silver Streak. He gave June a meaningful look and nodded toward the turnstiles
behind him. The dual system of turnstiles
counted guests who entered the queue lines
on the midway and those who made it all the
way through the line to the loading platform.
*Maybe comparing the numbers was interest-
ing for someone like Evie.* If she did compare
them, the numbers were not going to match
up today.

The first-aid scooter, obnoxious horn beeping, pulled up behind June and one of the firefighters got out, shouldering a first-responder
bag. The tall firefighter, Martin, nodded at
June and spoke in a low voice, "Dispatch said
there's a leg stuck in the turnstile. No idea how
something like that happens."

"Is it bad?" she asked.

"We'll see," the other firefighter, Curt, said.
"We called Maintenance as soon as we got
here. Probably need help taking apart the turnstile."

A boy who appeared to be fifteen years old
raised his head when June and the two firefighters walked up the steps to the loading
platform. Lanky and blond, the kid wore the

summer uniform of basketball shorts and a
Pistons T-shirt.

The Silver Streak was silent, summer workers standing around watching the spectacle.
The boy whose leg was trapped grimaced
in pain while two ride operators held him in
the air above the three-pronged silver arms
of the turnstile. His leg was twisted at a terrible angle.

June's knee hurt just looking at the kid's
leg. *There's no pain like knee pain.* Before she
could ask the boy what happened, the rear entrance of the Silver Streak opened and Mel
strode through. His long legs flashed and he
carried a huge tool bag slung over his shoulder. He made brief eye contact with June and
the two firefighters and drilled in on the mechanical problem.

"Did you try to jump over it?" Mel asked
the kid, a reassuring smile on his face.

"Uh-huh," the boy replied.

"Looks like you almost made it, but I don't
recommend trying it again."

*Why on earth would someone try to jump
over a turnstile? Boys.* The kid was paying
for his stupidity now, though. *And how did he
get stuck like that?* Apparently, his foot didn't

clear the arms of the silver turnstile as he tried to jump it. His shoe hooked, the arms locked, and he was trapped.

"My knee is broken," the boy whined.

"You can't really break your knee," Martin said. "But that's gotta hurt."

Martin slid an arm under the skinny teen and held him up. Both ride operators scooted back, obviously happy to be relieved of the sweaty and miserable victim of the turnstile.

"I'll hold him up if you can slide the leg out," Martin told his partner.

"Can't. The arm locked a notch back and the angle..." He didn't finish the sentence, but June knew what he meant. This was going to be a painful lesson for the kid, and he would never want to look at a turnstile again, much less jump over one to impress his friends.

Mel knelt and examined the boy's leg and the mechanical operation of the machine. He wiped sweat from his brow. June imagined him racing to get here in the maintenance scooter, which was probably parked under the platform. Starlight Point was surrounded by a road informally called the outer loop which offered multiple gates into the park. These gates were always locked and used only by maintenance and security, but they provided quick access when necessary without driving vehicles on the park's midways. Only the onsite fire department drove on the midways during park operating hours, and only if it was really necessary.

"I think we can get his leg out if we take it apart," Mel said. "I brought a bunch of tools."

"You can't take my leg apart," the kid cried.

"No," Mel assured him. "We're taking the machine apart. I don't cut up legs. Not in my job description."

June glanced around, hoping no one was taking cell phone video or pictures of this. Ride closed, line empty, upset friends and armed security standing by. Two girls and one boy, probably friends of the kid locked in the turnstile, stood on the platform talking to one of the ride operators and watching anxiously. *At least they don't have their cell phones out.*

"What's your name?" Mel asked the boy as he knelt underneath him and started to remove the weathered blue metal shields on the turnstile.

"Jason."

"First time at Starlight Point?"

The boy shook his head. "We live in Bay-side and come all the time."

"First time jumping over a turnstile?"

Jason shook his head and lowered his eyes. His flushed face got even more red.

"First time not making it over?" Mel asked.

Jason nodded and made eye contact, a tiny smile breaking through the pain on his face.

"Thought so. Were you trying to impress one of those girls over there?"

The kid looked down. "I feel stupid."

"Don't," Mel said. He pointed to a scar above his eyebrow. "See this? I got it trying to impress a girl. I don't even want to tell you how."

"Did it work?"

"She didn't even know I was alive. Story of my life," Mel said.

June stood silently listening to their conversation, impressed by Mel's ability to put the boy at ease. *He must be a wonderful father.*

"We'll get you out of here," Mel continued, "but you'll have to trust me and work with me."

"Have you ever done this before?" Jason asked.

"Not exactly, but I did get a Matchbox car

out of the garbage disposal at my house. My son thought he'd never drive that car again, but it turned out fine. Just a few scratches on the fender."

The kid didn't respond, just hung there miserably while Mel used a wrench to remove more bolts from the turnstile. With the shields off, June could see the guts of the machine. A series of gears and levers. She was glad Mel knew what he was doing.

"We all have a few scratches on our fenders," Mel continued, smiling at the boy. "Gives us character."

June was sweating. The boy was sweating. Mel appeared perfectly calm.

One of the firefighters held an ice pack on Jason's knee.

"It'll cool us both off," he said. "And make it easier to slide you out of here."

This is my family's park, June thought. *I should know what to do.* But she didn't. She leaned close and spoke in Mel's ear. "Is there anything I can do to help?"

"Not at the moment. You can do the paperwork later." He raised one eyebrow at her. She was so close she could see the tiny lines around his eyes from hours working outside in the sun. "Lots of paperwork," he added.

"Thank you for knowing what to do," June said quietly.

Mel moved his head and his hair brushed her cheek. "It's my job," he said.

He worked silently a few more minutes. Roller coasters, happy screaming and carousel music formed the background, but the loading platform at the Silver Streak was silent. Everyone was waiting for Mel to tell them their next move. June stepped aside and called Jack on her cell phone, giving him a quick overview and assuring him it was under control. She expected him to show up at any moment and was surprised when he didn't, even after another ten minutes went by.

Jack was trusting her to handle this.

And she was trusting Mel.

June walked over to talk with Jason's friends and the ride operators who were in a clump on the edge of the platform.

"I'm sure Jason will be okay," she said. "We have our best maintenance man unlocking the turnstile and two firefighters standing by to help."

Jason's three friends looked relieved. The ride operators looked nervous.

"Did you see this happen?" June asked the girl whose name tag identified her as Jessica.

"Yes."

"Good. I'll talk with you later." She turned to the three friends. "I'm guessing you saw it happen also?"

They nodded. Their expressions were tight, body language rigid as if they were being questioned as accessories to a bank robbery.

"It's not a crime to show off for your friends and hurt yourself," June said. "At least I hope not. I just want you to write down what you saw so we have a written record. That's all. We'll work on that together later. Right now, getting Jason's knee out of the turnstile is our number one priority."

She patted the girl on the shoulder, smiled and returned to where Mel was working. She knelt next to him.

"Thanks for calling me your best maintenance man."

"I thought it would inspire confidence," she said. "It does for me."

She touched his shoulder as she leaned close

to view his progress, and heat burned her fingers through Mel's blue cotton shirt.

"I'm going to release the spring and hope it doesn't make this thing snap around," Mel said.

"Is this going to hurt?" Jason asked.

"Not if we do it right," Mel said.

One of the firefighters wedged his leg against the free arm of the turnstile to control the movement. Mel slowly released the spring while June held her breath. One look at Jason's tortured face made her want to protect him, but all she could do was count on Mel.

The spring let go and the arm of the turnstile unlocked and moved, allowing the two firefighters to lift Jason free.

Although Mel's expression remained the same, June noted the long slow breath he let out.

"There was a lot less pressure with the car in the garbage disposal," he said to June as the firefighters placed Jason on a gurney. "Ross shed some tears, but I fixed that with ice cream."

Maybe it was the incredible relief of freeing the guest from the turnstile without, she

hoped, serious injury, but June felt a rush of…
something…for Mel.

"Want to get some ice cream?" June asked.
"I owe you, and I'll buy."

Mel laughed. "I'm on the clock."

"Maybe later this afternoon? I'm going to
meet this young man and his friends at First
Aid and see what we need to do next. Starting
with calling his parents, getting X-rays, and
filling out reports. I may need your input on
those reports."

"So, it's a working ice-cream date?"

June smiled. "It's hot. Good ice-cream
weather."

Mel cocked his head and said, "I'll meet
you at Tosha's at four thirty if I can bring a
guest. If Ross finds out I had ice cream without him, it'll take me weeks to earn back my
super-dad status."

"REMEMBER YOUR MANNERS, ROSS," Mel said.
"Please and thank you."

"Can I get strawberry?" Ross asked.

"One scoop."

"Only one?"

They walked up the beach path to enter the
park by one of the side gates. Like his father,

Ross was lanky, with sandy hair and blue eyes. He also had Mel's easy smile and gait.

Instead of working until at least five o'clock as usual, Mel locked his big steel desk in the maintenance garage at a quarter after four and headed to the Lake Breeze Hotel to retrieve Ross from the employee day care center.

"We're guests, and guests can't be greedy and ask for seconds. Besides, I don't want you to ruin your dinner. I'm making mac and cheese and dogs tonight. Your favorite."

"Will Uncle Jack be there?"

Mel smiled. "I think he's still working. His sister is buying us ice cream today."

"Uncle Jack has a sister?"

"Two. You've met one of them a few times, Miss Evie, but this is the one you don't know."

"What should I call her?" Ross asked, swinging his dad's arm as they stopped at the turnstile. Mel let go of Ross's hand to dig his wallet out of his back pocket, but the white-haired lady at the beach gate waved him through. Summer employees might need proof of Mel's employee status, but Janice had worked the beach gate for ten years, ever since she gave up schooling first graders in Bayside.

"Riding rides tonight, Mel?" she asked.

Mel shook his head. "Quick ice-cream stop on the way home."

She smiled. "Good for you. The heck with ruining your dinner. Life is short."

Ross smiled and waited until they were several steps away. "Dad," he whispered. "That lady said life is short, but hasn't she been alive a really long time?"

Mel chuckled. "I think that makes her an expert. And don't say things like that when other people can hear."

"I won't. So what do I call her?"

"Her name's Janice."

"Not the old lady, the ice-cream lady."

Mel hesitated. It wasn't much use figuring out an official name for someone Ross would probably never get to know very well. Even though he spent most of his summer days at the Point, Ross wasn't likely to cross paths with June.

"If she's Uncle Jack's sister, can I call her Aunt Jack?" Ross asked.

"Her first name is June," Mel said, suppressing a laugh. "How about Miss June?"

Ross shrugged. "Okay."

Mel held Ross's hand as they passed Kiddieland and turned toward the front midway, where many of the food vendors filled both sides of the avenue. Guests stopped at Bernie's Boardwalk Fries, Hank's Hot Dogs, Aunt Augusta's Midway Bakery and Tosha's Homemade Ice Cream on their way into and out of the park. Aunt Augusta also had a location in the Wonderful West and the Lake Breeze Hotel so guests could get their doughnut and cookie fix wherever they were. Tosha had borrowed the idea and opened a second ice-cream stand on the beach this year.

Judging from the lines, all the vendors were doing brisk business. Mel hoped the steady crowds he'd seen so far would keep up all summer and help his friends get their amusement park out of financial trouble. Jack and Evie poured their souls into Starlight Point. And June? She poured her soul into whatever she was doing at the time. At least, she seemed that way to him.

This summer it was the live shows and theaters at Starlight Point. But it was only for the summer.

June was waiting for them, chatting with Tosha over the front counter of her ice cream stand while summer employees in cheerful hats and aprons worked the window.

"Here they are," June said as Mel and Ross came up.

Tosha grinned broadly. "There's my best customer," she said, pointing to Ross. "Are you having strawberry?" she asked.

Ross nodded.

Mel cocked his head and focused on Tosha. "The kids love it when you bring them ice cream, but you should let me pay you. It has to be putting you into bankruptcy."

She laughed. "Not at all. I take ice cream to the day care because I love it. And Jack Hamilton always pays."

"My brother?" June asked. Both eyebrows raised, she laughed out loud. "I had no idea he was such a softy."

"He has a serious sweet tooth, so he understands," Tosha said. "I also think it's his way to get back in my good graces after last summer's squabble over the vendor contracts." She shrugged. "Water under the bridge. What's the special occasion today?"

"I owe Mel. He was a real hero when a guest got his leg stuck in the turnstile at the Silver Streak," June said.

Mel's neck burned under the collar of his work shirt. Taking apart a turnstile did not exactly make him a hero. Ross squeezed his hand and smiled at him. "You're a hero," his son said.

"I was just doing my job and Miss June is just being nice," Mel said.

June knelt so she was eye level with Ross. "I'm June Hamilton," she said. "I've heard nice things about you but we've never met."

Ross stuck out his hand as his father had taught him. "I'm Ross. I'm five and I can write my name."

June smiled. "I can write my name, too. And it has four letters just like yours. Did I hear you like strawberry ice cream?"

Ross nodded.

"Then that's what I'm having." She glanced up at Mel. "How about your dad? What's his favorite kind of ice cream?"

"Chocolate chip. He eats chocolate chips right out of the bag when we go to Grandma's house," Ross said. "Grandma doesn't know."

Mel wanted to crawl into a crack in the concrete. He'd have to talk with Ross about revealing personal information to relative strangers.

June stood up and smiled at Mel. "I eat frosting out of the can when I'm truly desperate," she said.

"What makes you desperate?" Mel asked. He had no idea why he'd asked and was afraid of the answer.

June's smile faded and she drew her eyebrows together.

"No idea where you put all those calories," Tosha said. "Skinny as you are, you must dance them all off. Wait here and I'll make up three cones for you so you can skip the line."

Thank you, Tosha, for changing the subject.

They collected their cones and sat at an umbrella-covered table. June filled Mel in on what happened with Jason the turnstile jumper. After a precautionary trip to the emergency room in Bayside, she explained, it appeared there was no serious damage. Some swelling and tenderness, but he was fifteen and he'd heal fast.

"Do you think his parents will sue?" Mel asked.

June shrugged. "They didn't seem inclined, but you never know. I hope not. I don't think we were negligent, and we certainly did everything we could to help him. Thanks to you."

"My grandparents have a cat," Ross said.

Mel rolled his eyes at June.

"I like cats," June said. "Back in New York

City, where I usually live, I got to be in a show where we all pretended to be cats."

Ross frowned. "Don't you live here?"

"No. My work is in New York City."

Ross nodded. "Like my mom. Her work is somewhere else in some city. We never see her." He balled up his napkin and headed for the nearest trash can.

"Sorry," June said.

"Not your fault," Mel replied. "Facts of life."

Ross came back and slid onto his seat next to Mel.

"Dad is making mac and cheese with little hot dogs cut up in it for dinner," he announced.

June smiled. "That sounds wonderful."

"He'll make some for you if you come over," Ross said.

June met Mel's eyes and held them for a moment. Mel broke the contact and ruffled his son's hair. "We should get going, buddy."

Ross bounced up and Mel stood. "Thank you for the ice cream."

"My pleasure. It was nice meeting you, Ross."

Ross nodded vigorously, apparently out of polite conversation.

"See you tomorrow," Mel said. He took

Ross's hand and headed for the marina gate, where his pickup was parked with the other year-round employees' vehicles. Maybe it was the ice cream, but something sat like a cold lump in his gut.

"She's nice," Ross said, swinging his dad's arm as they walked to the truck. "And she likes strawberry ice cream just like me."

Mel helped Ross get his seat belt buckled around his booster seat.

"We should get a cat," Ross said.

Mel sighed and climbed in the driver's seat, wishing somebody else was cooking dinner for once.

No one ever signs up to be a single parent.

CHAPTER SIX

JUNE UNLOCKED THE doors at the Starlight Saloon Theater and swung through them. Dust swirled in the shafts of early-morning light that came through the windows.

There's no way this theater will be ready in less than a week. Her performers, yes. The costumes, probably. The venue? Sigh.

She heard a truck pull up in front. The park wasn't open until ten, but trucks drove all over the midways ferrying supplies in the early morning. June stepped outside. It was the delivery she'd hoped for.

Mel Preston, in maintenance blue as always, unloaded rollers, brushes, seven gallons of paint and two short ladders onto the porch of the Western-themed saloon and dance hall.

"Good luck," he told Gerry, a summer worker dressed like Mel but probably just old enough to drive. "I think you're going to earn your minimum wage today."

"I'll have help, right?"

"June Hamilton's in charge of this project," Mel said, gesturing to June, who was already picking up cans to haul inside. "You'll have to ask her."

June paused and smiled at Mel. "You could stick around and help us if you want."

Mel raised an eyebrow and leaned against the side of his blue maintenance pickup with Starlight Point in white letters on the door. "Cleaning and painting this old barn is not on my list for the day."

"I could offer ice cream."

He shook his head, chuckling.

June crossed her arms over her chest. "You'd probably nail the doors shut if it were up to you."

He nodded. "It would be the easiest thing to do considering I have to finish running about ten miles of new wire in there."

"So that's today's plan? Should we wait up?"

Mel laughed. "That's a three-day plan for a team of electricians."

Was it really a three-day job? This theater was scheduled to open on Saturday. And today was already Monday. Maybe she should have stayed in New York for the summer.

"Better get started, then," she said cheerfully, hoping there was a chance Mel was exaggerating.

Mel reached through the open window of his truck and picked up a clipboard from the seat. He flipped through several papers, studying them. June suspected he was stalling for some reason.

He finally tossed the clipboard back through the window. "The wiring supplies have been delivered. I'll have to grab them from the warehouse, but I might as well start today. Having Gerry here is good because he can give me a hand pulling wire if I need it." Mel smiled at Gerry. "You might end up learning to be an electrician. That's how it happened to me."

When Mel drove off, June headed inside to tackle the kitchen area of the saloon. Getting a drink—or anything—from this kitchen would involve a major flirtation with a health-code violation. No wonder Jack and Evie had chosen to close the kitchen last year. Scrubbing and rewiring might earn a passing grade from the health department later in the week, but it would not be easy.

Nothing was easy.

Mel claimed he had a serious wiring job, but she had work in spades, too. Ramping up the sleepier part of the park with her high energy steampunk show was just what the Point needed. People would come for the show, and then stop by the food stands, games and shops before boarding the train or walking up the trail to the front midway. A great return on investment in the Wonderful West would make Evie and Jack happy and prove the value of quality live theater.

Not that they really doubted the need for live shows and the power of their draw. But June felt like they doubted *her*. They never said it out loud, but they treated her like a hummingbird they'd caught in a net.

"What do I do first?" Gerry asked.

June turned to consider the saloon. She walked to the control panel behind the bar and flipped a master switch. Lights—courtesy of Mel's quick repair job last week—buzzed on throughout the room and over the stage.

"Lights. Awesome," Gerry said. "I was afraid we'd be painting in the dark."

"It's old, but not totally in the Dark Ages," June said. "I heard you had some painting experience. That's why I asked for you. I could sure use the help."

"Yep. Painted houses with my dad the last two summers. He does interior painting in the winter, exterior in the summer."

"He'll miss having your help this year."

Gerry nodded and looked at his shoes. "I know. But I just didn't want to work in the family business another year. Thought it would be fun to branch out a little."

June smiled. "I think we're going to get along just fine."

MEL ROLLED HIS shoulders and ran a hand through his dusty, disheveled hair. The good news was that someone—at some time—had run some new conduit in the Starlight Saloon. That meant he could tie into it and not spend the next three days trying to battle an ancient wiring schematic. Making this theater usable for the summer wouldn't be the major undertaking he'd expected. Throughout the day, Gerry had pitched in between painting walls and muscling junk into an outside Dumpster.

The bad news was that the job was only three-quarters done but he needed food and a shower too bad to continue.

At seven o'clock, he gave up and loaded his tools in his maintenance truck. He had to put in an hour's worth of work at the garage and then it would be lights out. Although it wasn't his parents' usual day to keep Ross, he'd called them hours ago to pick up the boy from day care at the Lake Breeze. They were used to such calls during the operating season. Ross was probably curled up on his grandpa's lap right now watching television. Reruns of old black-and-white TV shows. *Lucky kid.* If Mel got out of here before it was very late, he'd pick up Ross so he could sleep in his own bed.

The hour in the maintenance garage stretched to three, courtesy of a mess made by one of the new hires and an emergency call to a food stand with no power. The food stand was in the Wonderful West, which had just closed. Employees and security guards were sweeping the guests toward the front, so Mel drove his personal truck along the vacant midway, hoping to make a quick fix and head straight home.

The restaurant's power problem was an easy fix, a tripped breaker. Mel headed for his truck, pajamas and bed becoming more inviting by the moment. He could almost taste the leftover pot roast his mother would have waiting in plastic containers.

However, as he drove past the Starlight Saloon, he noticed a light on inside. He stopped and got out of his truck, cursing whoever left the light on—probably June.

It was definitely June. Because she was still there, alone on stage. On her knees working her way across the stage with black matte paint. Mel paused in the doorway, watching as she rolled paint onto the floor.

"You've put in a long day," he said quietly, afraid to startle her and end up wearing a bucket of paint.

June laid the roller in the tray and sat back. "You have, too," she said. She used the inside of her elbow to brush stray hair off her cheek. "I thought you were headed for food and a shower three hours ago."

"I was, but I had to do some cleanup in the maintenance garage. Where's Gerry?"

"I sent him home after you left. He worked hard today, and he seemed happy to leave." June smiled. "I think maybe he had a date. Or he was starving."

"When I was his age, I was always starving," Mel said.

"And did you always have a date?"

He laughed. "With a cheeseburger." He fumbled in his front shirt pocket. "Speaking of which..."

"Don't tell me you have a cheeseburger in there."

"Nope. Mini doughnuts from the vending machine. I can't bring you one, but I can toss it."

"Risky. I'm not a great catch."

Mel grinned. "Lucky for you, I'm a good throw. Can't miss."

He fished a mini doughnut from the half-eaten package and tossed it carefully to June. She caught it left-handed and popped it in her mouth.

"Impressive," Mel said.

"Had to," she mumbled, her mouth full of doughnut. "My right hand is full of paint."

"I've never doubted your talent."

June chewed slowly, keeping her eyes on Mel. "But you've doubted other things about me," she finally said.

He shook his head. "No."

She resumed painting, only a quarter of the stage to go before she backed out a stage left door. Mel pulled up a chair at one of the many tables in the saloon. Unlike the big theater on the front midway, this one didn't have orderly rows of pull-down seats numbering in the hundreds. Instead, high-top tables were surrounded by four chairs and scattered around the floor, each of them with a view of the raised stage. The room had an old dance hall feel, like in a Western movie.

"Think I need an audience for this?" she asked.

"Just keeping you company and waiting to offer you a ride home."

"You don't have to do that," she said, her tone implying he was not unwelcome.

"I'd like to help paint, but there's only room for one in that pattern you've got going. Wish I had a cold beer in my front pocket I could toss you next."

She laughed. "Now, that would be risky. Either I'd miss and splatter it everywhere, or I'd catch it and not give a darn if I finished this job tonight."

"Could finish it tomorrow," Mel suggested.

June shook her head, never slowing with her roller. "My big plan is to give this all night to dry so we can walk on it tomorrow—at least a little bit—as we continue bringing this stage up-to-date. I ordered some big props and they'll be in tomorrow or the next day, and I assume you don't want to store them in Receiving or Maintenance."

"You're right about that."

"Well, when you're one-third owner of a struggling amusement park, you have to use your head." She glanced up and grinned. "Otherwise you'll have your back against a wall."

"You'll probably be glad when you get to the wall—then you can go home."

"Almost there," she said.

"You're not going to be able to walk tomorrow after kneeling all this time," Mel observed.

She glanced up sharply. "What do you mean?" Her tone was almost confrontational.

"I just mean a job like that is a knee killer," he said. "I pawn off those jobs on the young guys."

Her shoulders relaxed and Mel could tell, even from across the room, her expression did, too.

"Oh," she said. "I see what you mean."

"You've got talent for renovation projects," Mel continued, filling in the silence as June painted. "Good ideas. A real eye for design.

If you ever give up performing, we could put you to work in the maintenance department."

"I'm never giving up," June said. Without looking at him, she held up her left hand with her thumb and index finger posed half an inch apart. "I'm this close to getting a part where I can dance and even more."

"What's even more?"

"Sing. Act. Have lines instead of only being in the chorus line. I thought I just wanted to dance when I left here years ago." She paused and a flush spread over her face. Was she thinking about leaving him behind?

June left her words hanging in the musty air between them as she rolled smooth swaths of matte black paint, neatly covering every inch of the stage. After five more minutes of painting in silence, she sat back, roller in hand, and surveyed her work.

"Looks great from where I'm sitting," Mel commented. "And I'm not just saying that because I'm so hungry I'd consider eating out of this condemned kitchen."

June laughed. "Think anyone will care if I pitch this roller in the Dumpster when I paint myself out the side door? It's cheap and I'll never get the black paint off it—at least not tonight and tomorrow it'll be too late."

"Pitch it. Got dozens of those in the warehouse and I sure don't feel like washing it out tonight. I can get the house lights and meet you outside. Give you a ride in my truck."

"I'd love to wash some of this paint off my hands."

"No running water in here yet, not till we get it turned on, which I'll do tomorrow. I promise. I've got some stuff in the truck that'll take most of the paint off."

June sent him a crooked, tired smile. "The man with a solution for everything," she said.

"And I can make fries and serve up hot dogs if Starlight Point gets desperate enough."

She shook her head, smiling. "That was quite a day. Looking back on it now, it was the most fun I'd had in quite a while," June said. "I hope I said thank you."

"You did. Evie, too. Your brother has no manners, of course."

June rolled on one more swath of paint. "Okay," she said, blowing out a long breath, "I'm done. You can kill the lights now if you don't mind."

Mel slid off his chair, weary legs complaining, and headed for the control panel by the bar. He'd forgotten he'd left his truck running out front, but now he was glad. The headlights illuminating part of the trail were his only light when he killed the main switch. In the dark, he felt his way around the bar and headed out the front door. It was a short walk around the side of the saloon to the stage door.

He was surprised to find June still sitting on the ground. He figured she'd be halfway to his truck before he could count to five.

"You okay?" he asked.

"Sure," she said, her voice sounding distant. Maybe she was just tired. Heck, they were all tired. The summer season was always a meat grinder. This year's improvement projects were taking a toll—not that she hadn't brought some of that on herself. He hoped she wouldn't ask about the parade again. He'd pulled the beer truck out of the far corner and looked into it. It was…rustic. And that was a compliment.

She wasn't moving, a slender shadow on the ground just outside the stage door. She extended a hand toward him in the darkness. "Help a girl up?"

"Sure," he said, reaching for her automatically. "You sure you're okay?"

"Uh-huh. My leg is just…asleep. All that kneeling and painting."

"Told you."

He could've sworn she caught her breath as he pulled her to her feet. She leaned against him, her head on his shoulder. He smelled her hair, just a hint of some kind of berry-scented shampoo. Maybe a little paint and dust mixed in, but still sweet and tempting. He cautiously put a hand on her back and massaged in a small circle.

This is not what I expected. June the flight risk was standing still. Practically in his arms. It was more wonderful and frightening than he cared to admit.

"If I weren't so tired, I'd stand here all night and let you do that."

"I'm available."

"Just a little more until my knee—I mean my leg—wakes up. Then I'll be out of your hair and you can go home. Long day today," she said quietly. "Long day tomorrow, long months ahead."

Mel kissed the top of her head so gently she probably didn't notice. Even as close as she was now, June Hamilton had been out of reach his whole life, like a circle drawn an inch too wide all around him.

"I should give you that ride I promised," he said.

June nodded. Mel reluctantly loosened his hold on her and turned them both toward the white path made by his truck's headlights. He kept an arm around her, and she didn't make a move to shake him off.

He opened the passenger door and winced at the creaking sound from his aging truck. When June climbed in and he shut the door, the noise echoed in the deserted park.

"Lonely here tonight," Mel commented.

"Not during the day. I heard the train, the shooting gallery, the Western Streak and the horns on the antique cars all day long."

Mel leaned on the door frame and regarded June through the open window. "Do you ever get lonely in New York?"

He had no idea what made him say it. The cold steel under his fingertips reminded him he was a fool for asking, for hoping for anything where June was concerned.

"Plenty of people and noise there, too," she said lightly.

Mel circled the truck and got in the driver's

seat. "Bet they don't have a shooting gallery where you get twenty-five shots for only twenty-five cents."

"Have you put in some time there with your son?"

Mel laughed, glad to break the tension for the drive. He started down the Western Trail and along the silent midway to the parking lot. "I save up my quarters all winter long."

June drew in a quick breath. "What about Ross? Who's taking care of him tonight?"

Was that genuine concern and alarm in her voice?

"Left him home alone with a phone and a take-out menu. Like I usually do. Made sure he knew where the matches are hidden."

June punched him lightly on the upper arm. He grinned.

"Sleepover at my parents' house. I don't know what I'd do without them. Right now he's probably wearing superhero pajamas and a goofy smile, sound asleep with my mother's cat."

"He's adorable," June said.

They crossed the empty parking lot and took the Old Road to June's mother's house, where June was staying for the summer. Mel pulled into the driveway and put a hand on her arm before she could slide out.

"Thank you," he said.

"You're the one who gave me a ride."

"But you painted that stage floor so I don't have to find someone to do it. And you helped me finish those vending-machine doughnuts. Probably saved my life."

June's smile shone in the faint light from the dashboard. "Good night, Mel."

Mel waited until she went in the house before he backed out and headed home. He couldn't help but wonder…who watched over June when she was alone in the big city?

CHAPTER SEVEN

GLORIA, THE HEAD of the wardrobe department at Starlight Point, rolled a big bin through the back door of the Midway Theater.

"Got costumes for your dress rehearsal today," she said, giving June a reproving look. "Since you keep forgetting to send your performers over to me in Wardrobe, I thought I better come to them."

"Sorry," June said, "we were—"

"Busy. I know. Happens every year. Everyone wants their costumes exactly how and when they want 'em. Think they come out of thin air." Gloria sighed dramatically and wiped her brow. "I'm used to you showbiz types."

For decades, Gloria had made costumes for the live shows, decisions about all the seasonal uniforms, and hemmed and altered more clothes than an army needed. In charge of laundry, fitting, ordering and cajoling, she'd shoved people of all sizes and ages into something befitting their jobs at Starlight Point. Staying on her good side, June knew from experience, had many benefits including emergency repairs and other situations where it was good to know a professional seamstress.

June gave the older woman a long hug. "I love you, Gloria," she said. She laughed and pulled the covering off the bin. "Let's see what you've got."

She drew out six sets of sparkling silver costumes for females and six matching vests for the male performers.

"Ooh," she crooned. "These are amazing. I love this material—I knew it was a winner when I saw it on the bolt."

"You've got a good eye," Gloria said. "All the costumes are fresh and people are going to be dazzled."

A good eye. Mel had said the same thing about her work on the theaters.

"Thanks. And thank you for all the extra work you've done. I know we don't usually start from scratch with every single costume, but I wanted this year to be special."

Gloria nodded, helping June sift through the costumes and hang them on waiting racks backstage. The Broadway revue June had produced required three costume changes, all of them lightning-quick. June's favorite costumes were the ones with feathers and boas, reminiscent of the glamorous big musicals of the middle of the twentieth century.

"The top hats were tough," Gloria said as she lined up tuxedos with tails on the rack. "I had to send back the first ones we ordered because they were cheap-looking. And they shouldn't have been," she huffed, "considering the amount we paid for them."

June had paired elegant red evening gowns with the tuxedos, and she pictured herself wearing one and dancing to the Broadway medley she'd choreographed. It would be so nice to dance in her own show, but this summer was about helping Starlight Point while also helping herself. Resting her knee was her smartest move if she wanted to grab as many years of the spotlight in New York as she could.

She'd get her chance to sparkle on stage in a few short months. If she got the part of her dreams, a lead in *White Christmas*, it would take her through the fall and holiday seasons and showcase her ability to sing and dance. That role would open doors for the rest of her career. And that show had amazing costumes from the World War II era, a period of Broadway musicals she truly loved.

"Seems to me that planning shows is a real talent of yours," Gloria said. "In addition to singing and dancing."

June smiled and warmth spread across her cheeks. Gloria had always been a part of her life, almost like an aunt. A somewhat grouchy aunt who was difficult to please.

"I sat in on a rehearsal yesterday," Gloria continued, "and this is the best we've ever seen at the Point. Of course I've only been doing costumes twenty-five years, so what do I know." She pulled out a red tomato stuffed with pins and draped a measuring tape around her neck. "But I think it's obvious these shows are going to be a tough act to follow for whoever's in charge next year."

June draped a red sequined gown over her arm. The heat drained from her cheeks when she realized the direction Gloria was heading with her praise.

"Just saying it's a shame you won't be around next year," Gloria added, patting June's arm. "But I know you're after the big prize.

You won't win a Tony Award burying your light here at Starlight Point."

Gloria pulled a pair of sewing scissors from her apron pocket and clipped a loose thread from the dress over June's arm. June scooped more costumes and accessories from the waist-high bin, organizing them according to act and dancer. Methodically, she slipped costumes on hangers and lined them up on the bar. She didn't resent Gloria's questions. It was hard to be offended by someone who'd made her first ballet costumes two decades ago and had been a friend and mentor all her life. And Gloria understood…right? June had gone so far, but she wasn't done yet. *Why come within an arm's length of your dream and not grab it*?

"You better use these for dress rehearsal later today," Gloria said. "If there's a problem, we'll be working all night to fix it."

"Sorry to cut it so close," June said. "I took on a lot, and I know I've made more work for you, too."

"I don't even want to hear about your parade costumes for at least a week," Gloria said.

June laughed. "I think I can promise it will be a while. Mel is not enthusiastic about fixing up one of the old beer trucks for a parade float. I'm not sure he'll do it at all."

Gloria cocked her head to the side. "He may not be excited about it, but I think he's working on it anyway. He came in to wardrobe early this morning for a fresh shirt because he ripped the sleeve almost off his other one."

"How did that happen?"

"He said he was crawling under a retired beer truck and hooked his shoulder on something. I wondered why he was wasting his time on one of those old beasts, but now I know."

Performers started coming through the cast entrance, and June called them over to review their costumes. An enthusiastic group by nature, the summer performers oohed and aahed over the costumes as if they were a royal wardrobe. Twelve young men and women ranging from eighteen to twenty-two—they were talented, excited and nervous. *I was one of them not that long ago.* June knew they hoped to use Starlight Point as a stepping-stone to something bigger, perhaps even Broadway. That's exactly what she'd done, and she wanted to help them.

"May have to fatten you up just a little," Gloria said to one of the dancers, patting her

cheek in grandmotherly fashion. "I don't think
I ever made a costume with such a small waist.
No idea how you have the stamina to do five
shows a day."

June glanced at the dancer, wondering what
her reaction would be. Christina was a sweet,
but very quiet college sophomore who hoped
to make it big as a dancer. *But, my goodness,
she is a walking skeleton*. Why hadn't June
noticed before?

Christina glanced nervously around as if she
hoped the other dancers hadn't heard. *Competition*, June thought. There was too much of
it among performers. It was healthy when it
made them strive to be their best, but it had a
dark side, too. June understood too well. She'd
never breathed a word about the weakness and
pain in her knee, not even to her own sister.

"Meet you at the Saloon after lunch," Gloria
said. "We'll do the same thing there. Wait until
you see what we've got for your steampunk
show. Some of the craziest-looking things I've
ever made."

Gloria rolled out the door leaving June and
Megan to run the dancers through the first of
several dress rehearsals. Dancing in tights was

one thing, dancing in a sequined gown with accessories was another.

Two hours later, the backstage dressing area started to look like it was ready for the live show's premiere in only two days. The sets were on stage, with parts of them in the wings for quick changes. Her Broadway-themed show would definitely wow Starlight Point guests. June had high hopes for the steampunk show, too.

And then there was the parade.

A little part of her wanted to admit Mel was right. Doing ten daily shows and a parade was nuts. But she'd dreamed some big dreams before and, so far, she was still climbing the ladder, not backing down.

MEL FELT THE BURDEN of single parenthood most in the two months before opening day and throughout the summer. Being able to grab Ross from the Lake Breeze and ride the carousel during his lunch break helped alleviate some of his guilt over his long summer hours. But he could never make up for the lack of a mother.

"Got one stop to make, buddy," he said as they walked up the midway. Mel's aging silver truck was parked in the marina lot, and it was a nice day for a walk through Starlight Point holding his son's hand. He wished Ross could stay five forever.

He stopped at the theater. Mel hadn't been inside the place in a week. He'd put his electricians on a wiring job here, but he wanted to do a quick final check himself before they started pulling heavy amps with all the new lighting June thought they needed. They should be able to land airplanes with all the lights she ordered.

He and Ross came through the midway doors under the marquee. As part of a surprising compromise, June and Evie had agreed on fresh yellow paint and rows of new lightbulbs instead of a major face-lift. They'd cut ties with the architect and put major changes on ice. Maybe they were lucky June was using all her energy inside the theater on new shows, costumes and choreography.

In fact, she was still there. Playing the piano on stage while two dancers perfected a romantic routine. Young lovers spun and dipped, looking into each other's eyes and smiling as they held their position right at the front of the stage.

"Again," June said, playing and watching the dancers, nodding. *How does she play the piano with both hands while talking to people and watching them dance*? He knew she was talented, of course, but he'd never really thought about what that entailed. When it came to wiring, fixing roller coasters, hydraulic brakes and keeping Starlight Point running, he had skills. He was also a master at applying Band-Aids and juggling fatherhood. But June's light shone so brightly, no wonder she didn't want to be shaded by the family business. Even in the dim light of the theater, she was something special.

"Cool," Ross said. "Can I watch the show?"

"They're just practicing right now, but you can watch for a minute. Sit here," Mel said, shepherding him to a seat right off the main aisle and catching June's eye for a moment.

He didn't need her to watch Ross. His son was used to being in every nook and cranny of Starlight Point and he knew the cardinal rules: don't interrupt and don't touch anything. Ross would sit quietly and wait for him. It should only take five minutes to make sure the box had been tagged by the electrical in-

spector so June would be safe pulling enough
amps in here to light a city.

ON TOP OF BEING dog-tired from all-day dress
rehearsals, June lost the power of concentration as soon as a prickle down the back of her
neck warned her that Mel was coming through
the front door. People had been in and out of
the theater all day, working on the snack bar,
cleaning, training new ushers and technicians.
She was used to ignoring interruptions, but
she'd never developed a knack for ignoring
Mel.

Without taking her eyes off the performers
in front of her, she followed his progress up
the center aisle and heard the soft creak of the
theater seat. She allowed herself a look, and an
unspoken agreement to keep watch over Ross
passed between her and Mel. Mel moved behind her, heading, she imagined, for the maintenance closet and new electrical panels.

She'd vaguely followed the progress of two
other electricians throughout the week. June
had stayed out of their way, wondering when
Mel might come by to check their work. She
knew he would eventually because he treated
projects at the Point like they were his per-

sonal property, never letting anything slide that could cause a problem later.

"Good enough," she told the dancers after she'd run them through the song one more time, partly for Ross's benefit since he appeared to be engrossed in the show. "You'll be ready to dazzle the day after tomorrow." The dancers needed rest, and this show, with or without more fussing from her, was going to be the best one the Point had staged in her lifetime. *She hoped.*

The stage empty, she turned on the bench to face the lone audience member.

"Do you want to come up here?" she asked.

Ross launched from his seat and pulled himself onto the stage, working one short leg up and then the other. He could have used the steps, but he seemed to enjoy the challenge.

"You've been up here before, haven't you?" she asked.

"Yeah. But it's cooler now."

"I hope so. I'm trying. And we did a lot of work to this theater."

Ross wandered over to the piano and slipped onto the bench next to June. Like most kids, he blissfully ignored the laws of personal space. His hair was the same sandy color as his father's, and he had an irresistible grin, but his eyes were darker and more serious than Mel's. He reached a tentative hand onto the keys.

"Go ahead. You can't break it."

Ross used one finger to pick out the melody of "Twinkle, Twinkle, Little Star," only missing and retrying a few notes. He looked to June for approval when he finished.

"Nice. Where'd you learn to do that?" June asked.

Ross shrugged. "Just figured it out. I have a music box that plays it. When it's on, it makes a star pattern on the ceiling of my room."

"That makes you an expert on this song. It sounded so good, you should try it again," June said.

The boy played the melody again, a little more confident this time, stumbling over only one note.

"Let's add some harmony, just for fun. You keep doing that, and I'll play on the lower keys. All you have to do is keep a steady rhythm."

Ross turned a questioning look to her.

"I mean don't speed up or slow down."

"Oh. Okay."

Ross played melody, and June filled in a

robust harmony, improvising and having fun. The music filled the theater, echoing from the empty seats and balcony. She'd played that piano all day, concentrating on making every single thing perfect. But this was different. *It was fun*. No competition, no need to be perfect.

"One more time," June said. "We're a great team."

They ran through the song again with June adding some variations. Ross had a smile a moonbeam wide and had gained enough bravery to use two fingers at a time.

"That was awesome," he said. "Can you teach me to play all by myself?"

June ached to say yes, but she wouldn't be in the area long enough to get through the first few songs in the piano lesson book. He needed a piano teacher who'd stick around.

"Well," she began, "with talent like yours, I think you could pick it up really fast. So you probably need a very good teacher who can keep up with you."

A floorboard creaked behind her. She and Ross turned quickly, almost bumping heads above the piano bench. Mel leaned against a pillar at the edge of the stage, arms crossed, intently watching them.

"Did you hear me playing, Daddy?"

Mel smiled at the boy. "Sure did. You were amazing."

"He has quite an ear," June said. "Where'd he get all that artistic talent?"

She wished she could go back in time five seconds and tell herself to shut up. Remembering too late that Ross's mother was off somewhere trying to build a career as an artist instead of being here seeing her son grow up made her heart feel as if someone was squeezing it. She could only imagine how Mel and Ross felt. How could anyone not want to be around a kid as sweet as Ross?

Mel's expression became unreadable. "Ready to go, son?"

"Can I play a little more? Want to hear the whole thing again?"

His expression softening, Mel nodded. "If your partner doesn't mind."

"Are you kidding? I love this. Takes me back to when I was his age doing exactly the same thing." She leaned closer to Ross. "I used to hang around this theater all the time."

"Did your dad work at Starlight Point, too?"

June laughed. "Yep." She bit her lip and glanced back at Mel. He was smiling, too. "From the top," she said.

CHAPTER EIGHT

JUNE TAPPED HER foot and scrutinized the front
of the Midway Theater. *Finally.* Opening day
for live shows. The past four weeks were a blur
of crowds, rides, popcorn and plenty of long
hours. And today was a huge debut. She was
as nervous as she'd been on opening nights
of the Broadway shows she danced in. Even
though she wasn't performing, her heart was
on stage with those young dancers.

She'd thought of everything. She hoped.

Music, pacing, lighting.

Zippers, hairpieces, smiles.

Everything. Except getting someone to replace the letters on the Midway Theater marquee. When the workers painted the building's
facade a fresh yellow and changed all the lightbulbs, they left the sign with the sliding letters
and numbers untouched. The posters were in
their glass cases. Flyers and ads were printed.
But the heavy old marquee still advertised

last year's show. With half of the black letters missing.

It had to be done, but she needed someone to climb up there. June's knee was better than ever, but climbing was still not her friend. She wasn't risking all her progress by standing on a ladder.

June strolled over to Augusta's midway bakery, its pink awning adorned with tempting graphics of doughnuts, cookies and cakes. Although the front shutter was still rolled down, she knew Gus would be in there with a few seasonal bakers making doughnuts and icing cookies for the sunny Saturday in early June.

Opening the employee door at the back of the bakery, June leaned in and looked around. "You in here, Gus?"

The smell was heaven. Sugar. Grease. More sugar. *Temptation.*

Augusta's voice carried over the growl of the stand mixer. "Over here." Gus wore her pink apron—the uniform of all her employees. Hair pulled back, a Starlight Point hat on her head, she towered over a mixer, peering into it.

"Cookies?" June asked.

"Icing," Gus said. One spoonful at a time, she added water from a small bowl. "Have to get it just the right consistency or it won't flow onto the cookies."

June leaned on the counter and watched. "I don't know a thing about baking."

"I could teach you," Gus offered, never taking her eyes off the icing.

"Why? I'll just eat your cookies. I feel guilty about stealing them, so I don't eat too many."

"Good plan. Your brother doesn't have the same strategy."

"But he has testosterone. So he can eat a lot more useless calories than I can. And he can hide the evidence under those business suits. Dance costumes are not so forgiving."

"Men have it made," Gus agreed, testing the consistency of her icing by dribbling it from a rubber spatula. "And they're good for business."

June watched her for a moment, tempted to swipe her finger through the icing and lick it off, but Gus had rules about that. Serious rules. Family was not excluded from the prohibition on licking the bowl. Ever.

"It's opening day for live shows," June said.

"I know. I wanted to make a special cookie for you, but it's hard to come up with the right shape. The star theme seemed too easy, guitars and music notes never really look like what they're supposed to be, so I gave up on those. I did consider making a cookie shaped like your parade float."

"But?"

Gus drew her eyebrows together and made a face like she'd eaten a lemon. "I didn't see the float until last night, so there wasn't enough time. And…it's not really inspiring as a food shape."

"You mean it's ugly."

"I think its beauty would be lost in translation to cookie form."

"You're just being nice. You think it's ugly."

"No," Gus said. "I think it looks like an old truck. You haven't worked your magic on it yet, but don't worry. If you put enough dancers around it and turn up the music, no one's going to care. Besides," she added matter-of-factly, "people love parades. I hope they line up right in front of my shop and devour cupcakes while they wait."

Gus divided the icing into several smaller glass bowls and added color paste to most of them. She deftly blended blue, red and green, leaving the largest bowl white.

"I can't wait to see your shows." She looked

up from her icing and grinned. "You've been knocking yourself out. Feel like you're ready?"

June nodded. "I think both shows will be amazing. The musicians and performers are awesome. I could use a little more training time with the ushers and the servers in the Saloon, but they'll pick it up soon. I hope."

Gus laughed. "I had absolutely no idea what I was getting into last season. Didn't know if I'd need a dozen cookies or a thousand on opening day. But we figured it out." She handed June a freshly iced carousel horse. "You'll be fine."

June bit the head off the horse and savored the hint of lemon and vanilla in the icing. "You wouldn't happen to have a ladder, would you? A tall one?"

Gus shook her head. "Nope. I hardly have room to store my supplies. I was hoping for a bigger shop this year, but here I am. I can call maintenance if you like. Someone would bring you a ladder. Especially that cute one who appears to take an interest in theater. What's his name? Marv, Max—oh, that's right—Mel."

June was glad her mouth was full so she didn't have to make a quick response. Gus thought Mel liked her? Who else thought that? *Did he?*

Maybe someone, probably Evie or Jack, had told Gus about the very brief summer romance seven long years ago. When they were practically *children*. Not the adults they were now with obligations making any possibility of a relationship unrealistic.

Gus was a romantic, probably the result of making wedding cakes every weekend. She was imagining things. *Wasn't she?*

"Very funny," June said casually after she swallowed her mouthful of cookie. "I've fallen in love with every member of the maintenance staff here, one at a time, whoever was working on my theaters at the moment."

"Can't believe a guy like that is still on the market," Gus said. "You should snap him up before the summer workers notice him in his navy blues sporting a tan."

He already has a tan. And he was more handsome at twenty-seven than he'd been at twenty. He also had a son who needed his attention. And she had a show waiting for her in New York.

"I could distract Jack for you in case he'd

have some objection about his best friend dating his sister. He can be bought. Easily."

Polishing off her cookie, June shoved away from the counter. "No, thanks. I'm pretty busy, and I'm not planning to leave my heart at Starlight Point when I'm back on Broadway in a few months. Right now, I've only got one hour before the park opens."

"Only an hour?" Gus brushed her hands off on her apron. "I better get moving. You can't believe what it's like in here when those gates open. People work up a sugar craving on the drive and look at my doughnuts with crazy eyes. Hope no one ever opens a doughnut shop right on the other side of the bridge. That would kill me."

A beeper over a big fryer of doughnuts went off and Gus raced to it.

June grinned. "Good luck."

MEL HEARD THE request come over the radio. Somebody needed a ladder in front of the Midway Theater. He'd wondered when June would get around to changing the letters on the marquee. Today was her big opening day and she was probably as nervous as a marshmallow at a cookout. He'd planned to avoid her today.

Ross had talked about her all the way home
yesterday—the pretty lady who bought him ice
cream and played the piano with him.

She was playing Mel, too. But that was a
mistake he'd made before. He'd survived it,
but he didn't want Ross getting attached to
someone who would exit as soon as her song
was over.

"Can you take the ladder, Boss?" Galway
said. "My truck's loaded with traffic cones
'cause I'm helping the parking crew while their
truck is in the shop. Gotta go dump them off
by the tollbooths or it'll be chaos when cars
start jockeying for lanes."

Mel glanced at the ladder leaning against
the wall and his obviously empty truck right
in front of it. *Crap.* He had no excuse.

"Thought you might be headed up there
anyway to check on things," Galway added.
"You've put a lot of work into the theaters this
year."

"I put a lot of work into everything," Mel
said.

"I know. Just pointing out that both theaters
had your attention." Galway grinned at him
and climbed into his truck.

Can't a guy do his job without people read-

ing into it? Maybe he was just being sensitive after listening to Ross review the piano lesson eight times before bed.

Mel waited for Galway to pull away, and then he backed his truck out of the maintenance area. If he was lucky, he'd find one of the summer stagehands with a cardboard box full of black letters and orders to put up the sign advertising the new show. He could drop off the ladder and run.

But he didn't tend to be a lucky man.

As he drove up to the theater and found June standing out front, shading her eyes, his conjecture was confirmed. She flashed him a smile as he got out of his truck that suggested he was exactly who she wanted to see. Of course he was. He had her ladder sticking out the back of his truck.

"That was fast," she said. "And you sent your best man."

He grinned. "Only one available."

"I only need one."

Mel tried to think of something cool and calm. Like the frozen lake in the winter. Or the cold steel of his truck as he got out and shoved the door shut. It didn't help.

"I assume you want this ladder right here?" he asked.

June smiled and nodded. "I do."

He balanced the ladder on one shoulder and set it in front of the marquee, carefully resting it against the sign without damaging it. He checked the angle and scooted the feet out just a little more, bracing it carefully on the concrete.

"Want me to come back and pick it up in a bit? I'm checking on something at the front gate before the park opens, so I'll be in the neighborhood."

June glanced up at the marquee, her expression clouded. "I know just what I want it to say. Got the letters all ready."

"So it shouldn't take you long."

"I thought maybe..." She paused and chewed her lower lip.

"Maybe I could check your spelling?" Mel asked.

"It's pretty high up, and I know you're not afraid of heights."

"Maybe I'm terrified on top of the Sea Devil and I'm just acting brave so I don't get canned or transferred to the popcorn wagon," Mel said. "Besides, marquee signs aren't really in my area of expertise."

"Anyone can slide the letters into the rows. And it would be helpful to have someone on the ground to tell if it looks right. Centered. Stuff like that."

"I'll be right here," Mel said. "I can tell if something is square."

"I think I should be the judge. Besides, you've got on better ladder-climbing shoes," she said, gesturing toward his work boots.

Mel glanced at June's sneakers. Her argument didn't hold a lot of water, but he was wasting time. His truck had to be off the midway in less than a half hour and he still had a string of lights at the gate to troubleshoot.

"Fine," he said. He took the small box of letters she held out and started to climb. "Just tell me what you want this thing to say."

He knew he sounded grouchy, but he was struggling. If he just got this job over with, he could get on with the complicated business of keeping June at arm's length while wishing he didn't want to soak her up like sunshine.

"The top line says 'Fall in love with the Stars,'" June said.

"Okay," Mel said, looking down at her with

a cynical expression. "I thought this was a Broadway review. Dance songs. Stuff like that."

"All songs are love songs."

All songs are love songs. Ridiculous. Mel searched his brain trying to refute her assertion and steer the conversation in a different direction.

"Not 'The Star-Spangled Banner,'" he said.

"All popular songs you can dance to are about love," June said.

He shook his head. He'd have to think about that later.

Mel braced his knees on the insides of the ladder so he could free up his hands to draw letters from the shallow box. "Fall in love with the Stars," he grumbled, digging for letters.

"I'm serious," June said. "Then the line below it says 'A Sparkling Broadway Revue.'"

"Don't tell me there's a third line."

"Just show times. Eleven, one, three, five and seven."

"Long day for performers."

"For everyone around here."

"Next year, we should put up an electronic sign instead of these old slots and letters. Then you can type up whatever you want. Even change it every day."

He made the mistake of looking down. June's expression was pure excitement. Maybe he shouldn't have brought up the idea of a digital sign. He knew from experience she liked things that were bright and things she could change.

"Is it too late to get one this year?"

"Yes."

"But—"

"No way. It would involve wiring, tearing off the face of the marquee you just had painted and more time than I have. There's no way it's getting done with the season already started."

He didn't want to look down and see her disappointment. Why did he wish he could stay up all night running cable to a new digital sign just to see her face when she saw it? June was going to turn him into a lunatic.

"Can you space the letters out a little more?" she asked.

Obligingly, Mel slid the letters along the track leaving even spacing between them. He finished the first and second row and paused, leaning away so June could see it without obstruction.

"Look okay?"

"Fantastic," she said. Maybe it was the bright sun slanting into his eyes, but it seemed to Mel that June was looking at him, not the sign. He was being paranoid.

"I'll just put up the showtimes and I'm done," he said.

Only a few minutes later, he backed down the ladder and handed June the empty box.

"Thanks," she said.

"Easy work. You already had the letters sorted."

June dipped closer and gave him a quick kiss on the cheek. Even though it was a sisterly kiss, his heart turned over like an electric motor. Until he remembered that June was just waiting to flit off like a moth looking for a brighter light.

The metal window at Augusta's bakery rolled up, clanking loudly in the morning stillness. Mel and June jerked at the sound and saw Augusta leaning on her front counter smiling at them.

"Gates open in fifteen minutes, but I've got fresh doughnuts if you want one," she said.

"Nuts," Mel said. "I gotta get my truck off the midway." He lowered the ladder, shouldered it and slid it into the back of his truck all in less than a minute. He'd have to slide out a side gate and drive his truck around front if he still wanted to see about those lights.

He opened the door on his truck, taking one last look at June. She stood alone on the midway, far enough from the theater to see the marquee. And then he remembered.

"Good luck with your big opening day," he said, leaning through the open window of the driver's door.

"Good luck with your faulty lights," she replied, stepping closer.

"Last call for a free doughnut," Gus shouted.

Mel flicked a look toward the front gates where people were already lining up on the other side of the turnstiles. He ran across the midway, grabbed the doughnut from Augusta's outstretched hand and leaned in for a quick kiss on her cheek.

"Don't tell Jack about that."

"The kiss or the doughnut?" Gus asked.

"Either one."

"He'd be more upset about the doughnut."

"I doubt it," Mel said. He dashed across

the midway and dove into his truck. Driving slowly with one hand, he watched June in his rearview mirror as she crossed the midway and stepped under the bakery's pink awning. Maybe he didn't want to know what she and Gus were talking about as he drove away.

CHAPTER NINE

VIRGINIA HAMILTON, WITH her dog, Betty, on her lap, sat across from Mel. The maintenance area was relatively quiet on a Wednesday afternoon halfway through June. The big jobs were done, and Mel's crews were out dealing with details, fine-tuning and the daily problems that arose in an amusement park.

"I hope you don't think it's too early to start on the STRIPE plan for this summer," she said.

As far as Mel was concerned, he'd like to sink the whole STRIPE project to the bottom of the lake. But he'd volunteered for this job—trying to do June a favor and save her the hellish task of teaching summer employees to play the piano.

"Might as well get started," he said, controlling his tone so he wouldn't take out his frustrations on Virginia. Her heart was in the right place—wanting her employees to get more out of Starlight Point than just a paycheck—but running the STRIPE on top of the maintenance department was like asking a professional athlete to balance a book on his head as he rounded the bases or went for a hook shot.

"I know you're going to need plenty of help," Virginia said, "and I'm already gathering up volunteers. You can use the ballroom and we'll set up a big screen and lots of tables."

"Where are these volunteers coming from?"

"Maintenance staff, year-round and seasonal. Plus I got some students and professors from the community college—mostly electrical or engineering majors."

"They volunteered?"

"I offered a season pass to anyone who helps with at least five class sessions during STRIPE week."

"Good deal," Mel said. "And good thinking."

"I'm not just a pretty face," Virginia said.

Mel smiled. He'd grown up an informal extra son in the Hamilton household. When he and Jack wanted to have fun, they hung out at Jack's house, where kayaks and a motorboat were always available. When they wanted to eat, they went to Mel's house, where the food was delicious. Now that Mel had a son, Virginia considered herself an honorary grandma and invited Ross over to play on the beach right in front of her house. With June staying at the Hamilton house on the Old Road this summer, Mel and Ross might be wiser to steer clear.

"I reserved the ballroom for the last week of June," Virginia continued. "We can do an early morning and an evening class. That way we get all the summer workers before things get too busy around here."

Before things get too busy. While it was true that July and August had greater numbers of guests, it was *always* busy.

Mel nodded, resigning himself to even more insanity than the usual one-hundred-day operating season brought. "You should know I'm planning to keep it simple. Messing with electricity isn't like doing ballroom dancing and learning conversational French. A little knowledge can actually be a dangerous thing."

Virginia reached across the desk and patted Mel's hand. "I'm counting on you to know what to do."

"Basics. Like hot wires, neutrals and grounds. Breakers and fuses. Safety in general. Maybe make up a board so they can play with a direct and alternating current."

"Sounds wonderful," she said, methodically stroking Betty's fur while the dog slept through their meeting.

"Just enough to give everyone some clue about electricity, not so much that people try to steal my job or rewire their dorm rooms for tanning beds and big speakers."

Virginia laughed. "They wouldn't do that, would they?"

"Probably not. Just the same, I'll warn them not to even think of touching the wiring in those old dorms. We don't need an electrical fire."

"Thank you, Mel. Go ahead and order any supplies you need and I'll set up the class schedule."

He nodded, shoving back in his desk chair. "Hope Jack will be there. As I recall, he attended almost every one of Augusta's cake classes last summer. I never knew he was so dedicated to the STRIPE program."

Virginia laughed. "I think we all know why he was there."

"Cookies?"

"Ha. I'll test that theory by offering him

cookies if he'll help." She placed Betty in the wagon and pulled her toward the door. "But you're not as pretty as Gus."

He certainly wasn't. And he was going to look like a haggard old man by the end of this summer.

He left the office in the corner of the maintenance building and stopped. *What is that noise?* Mel headed toward the racket coming from the back corner. He could guess what it was. There was only one project in that part of the shop right now. *Great.*

JUNE AND TWO men stood, hands on hips, looking at the former beer truck parked in the corner of the maintenance garage. The first theater show didn't start until eleven, so June had grabbed two of her technicians and brought them to the garage to see what magic they might be able to work on the parade vehicle.

They'd got a huge surprise. June had no idea the truck had been moved, cleaned and painted in the past few days. Metallic silver paint covered every inch of the box truck except for the windows and tires. Exactly what she wanted.

Someone, and she could easily guess who, had taken an interest in the project.

"Sorry it's so ugly." *Speak of the devil.* She swung around and smiled at Mel, who threaded his way past parked vehicles, rolling tool chests and half-finished projects. "But it sure will be noticeable on the parade route."

"It's just what I wanted," she said. "I'm amazed by how much you've done. Thank you."

"I can't take credit for all of it. The garage guys put air in the tires, changed the oil and put in a new battery. It won't break any speed records, but it'll run down the midway all right."

"I love how shiny it is." She really did. She wanted it to sparkle and attract attention. *When the sun hits that paint, people will have to stop and look.*

"It looks like a spaceship," Mel said.

"Right." She nodded. "Starlight Point...you know, a stars and planets theme for the parade." She smiled. "My parade is 'out of this world,' and it will be when you see the whole thing put together."

"How can you run an afternoon parade when

your performers are all…uh…performing in the theaters?" Mel asked.

"I'm not running the three or five o'clock shows in the Wonderful West. According to numbers from last year, those were tiny audiences. I plan to run an eleven and one and then a seven in the evening. I hope it works."

"That still makes a long day for your dancers."

"But there are breaks in between. On Broadway, I did one show a night, but it was a three-hour show. They do twenty-five minute shows spaced two hours apart. Don't worry, I have it figured out."

He laughed. "I never doubted that. Where are you getting the planets and the stars to decorate the old wagon?"

"I ordered them from the props company I used for the theater shows."

"Theater props on a vehicle?" Mel asked. "They have to cover up a lot of ugly."

"Just wait," June said. "Now that it's running and painted, the fun part begins. That's where these guys come in." She gestured to her helpers, who were dressed in the all-black uniforms of stagehands and theater techs.

"You won't recognize this truck when they're through with it."

"Good," Mel said, a crooked grin lightening his expression. "Then I can forget all about it."

June stepped closer to Mel and touched his arm. "I really appreciate it. I know you're busy and the parade doesn't seem like an important project."

He shrugged. "I wouldn't look at the paint job too closely. I had them spray right over the rust. I'm hoping the paint will stick long enough to get us through the summer and then we can do something more permanent for next year. Assuming you want—"

Mel stopped. And she knew what he was thinking. All the work she was doing on the theaters, her crazy idea for the parade. Was it just for this year or would it outlast her brief tenure at Starlight Point? Evie had asked her the same thing last night as they were watching an old movie. Before they'd both gone off to their childhood rooms, Evie had posed the question for which the answer *used* to be obvious.

What did she want? Of course she wanted to be dancing and singing on the big stage instead of following the parade route through Starlight

Point. What person in her right mind wouldn't choose Broadway over the Midway Theater? June turned toward the parade truck and pretended to be very interested in the bumper, the tires, the way the back doors almost matched when they shut.

The question hung between them like exhaust fumes.

"The silver paint hides a lot of flaws," Mel said quietly, his voice carrying only to June. "Shiny stuff always does."

Ouch.

Loud thumping emanated from inside the truck and one of the tech guys, Aaron, leaned out the side window, which was once used for dispensing cold beers.

"You know what we need?" Aaron asked.

A distraction. Thank you.

"What?" June asked.

"Flashing lights. Strobes that'll show up in the daytime. I want to see this machine from the top of the Sea Devil."

"How hard would it be to add those?" June asked, her attention flicking from the tech guy to Mel. She felt guilty asking Mel to do more work, but strobe lights were hard to pass up.

"No idea," Aaron said. "I do sound and

speakers. What do you think?" he said, addressing Mel.

Mel shrugged. "Could be done."

"Great," the man said, disappearing back into the truck. June could hear the two tech guys talking to each other from inside, but their words were muffled. She hoped her conversation with Mel wasn't audible to them.

"With some help," Mel said.

"What do you mean?" June asked, her tone neutral.

"You could be my first STRIPE student."

June groaned. "I almost forgot you got roped into that." *And rescued me from a messy argument with my mother. An argument I could never win.*

"To be fair, I roped myself into it. I was just meeting with your mother about the plans."

June pressed her lips together. Her lungs constricted when she thought about her mother's assertion that she wasn't doing her share at Starlight Point. When June had confided her thoughts to Evie, her sister had shrugged and suggested Virginia just wanted her daughter to be around more. Was that her mother's reason? Both her parents had encouraged her to follow her dream of a Broadway career. If her father were still here, he'd tell her to keep going. She knew it.

"Something wrong?" Mel asked.

June smiled, summoning her acting ability. "I was just thinking how you saved me the job of teaching hundreds of people to play 'Happy Birthday.'"

"Looks like you owe me."

Mel leaned against the truck, crossed his arms and put one foot over the other.

"Well?" June asked.

"I'm thinking about amps." He pulled a notepad and a pen from the pocket of his blue work shirt. "We need to put in an extra battery. Maybe a generator," he said, writing on the pad. "With all the lights and speakers you're adding, we don't want to risk killing the truck out on the midway." He grinned. "Your dancers would look ridiculous pushing the truck all the way back here."

She laughed. "They would. I didn't hire them for their muscle. So, how can I help?"

"How much time do you have?"

June pulled her cell phone from her pocket and lit the screen. There was never enough time when she was running five shows a day in one theater and three in the other. *Maybe this parade was a stupid idea and Mel was right.*

"About an hour," she said. "And then I need these guys to run the tech for the first shows of the day."

"Not enough time to do anything right now, and I may need to order parts anyway."

"Can we make a date to meet here later?" June wished she hadn't used the word *date*. *Appointment* would have been a better choice. *Arrangement. Assignation. Darn the English language...*

Mel smiled at her. Her cheeks were so warm she knew they were pink. Even in the ancient fluorescent lights of the shop, Mel would notice.

"We can make an appointment for that," he said.

He'd stolen the word she wished she'd used. *Sigh.*

"You could tell me where to put the lights and help pull the wires," he continued. "It's a pain, trying to get through the frame, but we'll try to work on the inside of the truck since it looks awful anyway. No guarantees you won't get your hands dirty."

"I can handle that." She shoved her cell

phone in her pocket. "On the condition that you'll sign off on my STRIPE completion so my mother will think I'm a team player."

"Doesn't she already think that?"

June shook her head. "I'm not sure." *And maybe she was right.*

"I'll say you're my best student if you come to the classes and share a practical example of why learning some wiring can be useful," Mel said.

June laughed. "You mean in case any of them ever have to wire strobe lights on an old beer truck to drive in a parade?"

"Precisely." Mel blew out a long breath. "But you'll have to make sure you learn something. I have no idea what kind of a teacher I'll be. I'm used to just doing stuff myself."

"I have the same problem. That's why I didn't want to teach piano lessons. Or one of the reasons anyway. I can play anything you want, but trying to show someone from the beginning is different. I can't remember a time when I didn't know what a D scale was."

"But you did a great job with Ross. He talked about it all the way home."

He did? Ross was so sweet, he almost made her wish she had a child just like him.

"That's different," she said. *Very different.* "He's enthusiastic and a willing participant. Besides, you must be a good instructor. How else would our summer maintenance workers learn how to do their jobs?"

"That's easy," Mel said, grinning and raising one eyebrow. "Got a couple of retired teachers on my staff. I put them on the job of training new guys every year. They have the patience of saints and understand how to teach. I don't."

"So, on top of being a top-notch maintenance man, you're a good delegator, too."

"And I'm best friends with the boss. Helps me keep my job," Mel said.

"Jack's no more your boss than I am," June said, smiling and stepping closer.

"Maybe I wasn't talking about him."

"Do you really consider me your boss?" she asked.

Mel shook his head. "I was talking about your sister. Evie has developed her penchant for accounting into a full-scale assault on all fronts. I think she's getting ready to take over the whole place." He winked at June. "Wouldn't want to tangle with her."

June curled her fingers and punched him lightly on the shoulder.

"Then you better get to work," she said. "We're all on the clock."

CHAPTER TEN

THE SHOWS HAD been open for a week, and June was convinced they were a success. Ushers counted the number of audience members at each show and, compared with last year's information, attendance was up.

New costumes, music, theme and choreography were part of the draw—the part June felt justified taking credit for. But she had to hand it to this summer's group of performers. They could sing, dance and smile with some of the best she'd worked with on Broadway. If they were using this as a proving ground on their way to something bigger—and they were, of course—they had great careers ahead of them.

June attended shows in each theater every day, pretending she didn't know the whole show inside and out, imagining what it must be like to see it for the first time. From front rows, back rows, side rows with pillars partially obscuring the stage, she tried to see each show from a theater patron's perspective.

Today, she was watching from backstage at the Starlight Saloon. She'd dashed over from a meeting with her brother and sister and was too late to grab one of the tables. As she leaned against a wall she'd painted black herself, June crossed her arms and watched the girls smile and dance a circle around the guys in the show. A country and Western–theme show with gadgets and gears giving it a trendy steampunk feel, this show had several solo singing performances.

One of the girls, Christina, had a perfect voice for the venue. Patrons set down their drinks and listened. It was hard to believe someone so thin could produce that kind of volume.

Usually.

But something was off today. June pushed off the wall and focused on the performers on stage. Christina sang the familiar country tune, but without any gusto. She skipped the second verse. Even though her smile never faded, she waved to the audience and left the stage.

June briefly noticed the other dancers

scrambling to ad-lib in her absence, but it was soon the last thing on her mind. Christina clutched her chest and staggered to her knees as soon as the side curtain hid her from the audience.

"What's wrong?" June whispered urgently, hurrying to her side and kneeling next to her.

"Heart. Racing. Can't breathe."

June laced an arm under Christina's shoulders and raised her to her feet.

The girl weighed nothing.

June persuaded her into the green room behind the stage and flipped on the light. Loud music from the show was thumping through the wall, but June's heart was thudding in her ears. She lowered Christina onto the couch and took a good look at her. She was ghost-white, a clammy sheen of sweat covering her skin. She still clutched her chest and struggled to breathe.

Hands shaking, June called the central dispatch at the Point and made an urgent request for the fire office scooter. They were close by, an access gate not far from the Saloon led right to the fire office and maintenance building.

June propped open the back door so the firefighters could easily find them and returned to Christina.

"What can I do?" June said, kneeling in front of the girl, willing her to breathe.

Christina shook her head.

"Do you have a heart condition? Has this ever happened to you before?"

The girl shook her head, still clutching her chest, her breathing worsening.

"Do you need medicine? Can I look in your bag for it?"

June would have raced up the stairs on any roller coaster in the park at that moment if only Christina would keep breathing until the fire-fighters got there. CPR. She'd taken a course several years ago to refresh her memory from the lifeguard training she did when she was fifteen. She could do it.

If she absolutely had to.

"Christina, tell me what happened. Did something happen?"

She shook her head, unable to speak be-tween gasps. Her tiny frame shuddered with the effort. June wrapped her fingers around the girl's wrist, trying to find and follow a pulse. There was no flesh on her skinny arms.

Reality slapped June in the face. *Why hadn't she seen it?* The bane of professional dancers.

"Have you had anything to eat today?" June asked.

Christina's head snapped up for a second and then she returned to watching the floor as she struggled to breathe.

June heard movement behind her and the buzz of a radio. *Thank goodness.*

"What do we have?" a firefighter asked. June knew him, an older man who'd worked summers at the Point for years. She glanced at his name tag. Of course. Andrew. She knew that. But she was so panicked she hardly knew her own name right now.

Andrew gently moved June aside and took her place right in front of Christina, where he could evaluate her.

"Medical history?" he asked June.

"No idea. None I know of, but I don't know."

He felt the victim's pulse and watched her struggle to breathe for only five seconds.

"We've got to move. Now." He scooped up the frail girl and walked out the door as if he carried a doll. June followed, numb with shock. Andrew placed the girl on the cot and his partner got in the driver's seat of the scooter.

"Get in," Andrew said, nodding at June and indicating the front passenger seat.

June jumped in the scooter and they took off. The younger firefighter said something over his radio. When they approached the gate that led to the fire office and maintenance area, Mel was there holding the gate open. June's cheeks were cold and she realized it was the combination of tears and the breeze created by the fast-moving open scooter.

The scooter pulled up right behind the ambulance. It was already running. Mel probably started it, too. The firefighters loaded Christina in the ambulance while June stood nearby, devastated by watching the girl try to breathe. They both got in the back with her.

Mel raced up on foot. Andrew leaned out the open back door and eyed Mel. "Can you drive? We could use two people in the back on this one, and the other squad's already on a call at the marina."

"Yes," Mel said. He headed for the driver's seat.

"You come, too, ride up front," Andrew said to June. "Let's move."

June climbed in the front seat and Mel put

the ambulance in gear and drove swiftly out of the lot.

"Don't run the siren on the outer road," Andrew said. He stuck his head in the pass-through from the cab area of the ambulance to the back. "You can hit it as soon as we get to the parking lot."

"Andrew," June said, catching his sleeve. "I think she has an eating disorder. Maybe anorexia or bulimia. I've seen it before with dancers. Does that help you understand what's going on with her?"

"I know what's going on with her. Her heart's way out of rhythm and we'll be lucky if we're not using the defibrillator before we get to the hospital."

Mel's fingers ran over the switches on the dashboard as he tried to watch the road. They were all labeled with their purpose.

"I'll do it," she said. "I see the one labeled siren and overhead lights. I can run them."

"Thanks," Mel said grimly, carefully navigating the curves around the amusement park. The blue lake sparkled on their right as they rounded the peninsula, but there was nothing to be cheerful about.

"I've driven this vehicle before, for maintenance and such, but never for something like this."

"Are you…licensed or anything for driving an ambulance?" June asked. Her voice shook and she let the tears roll freely down her cheeks.

"No. But I sure as hell wasn't going to refuse."

June's hands still trembled, but she leaned forward and found the siren switch as soon as Mel reached the front parking. Her cell phone rang and Evie's picture popped up.

"It's Evie," she said. "I'll call her back in a little while."

Mel nodded, focusing on driving as they passed the tollbooths and started across the Point Bridge. It would only be ten minutes, tops, until they got to Bayside Hospital.

"I should have realized weeks ago that something wasn't right," June said. Over the siren, she couldn't hear what was happening in the back of the ambulance, and she was afraid to look.

"What do you mean?"

"I'm afraid Christina has an eating disorder. You can't believe how much of that there is in the dancing world." She took a deep breath, trying to control her sobs before they broke free. "It's so competitive."

Mel took one hand off the wheel and closed it over June's hand. "Did she confide in you or ask for help?"

"No. I can ask the other dancers if they had any idea, but my guess is she was hiding it. That happens too much."

"Don't blame yourself. You were there when she needed you most. You may have saved her life."

"I hope so."

Barely taking his eyes off the road, Mel raked her with a quick glance. "You'd never do that, would you? Hurt yourself to compete in New York?"

"Of course not," June said. She smoothed her skirt over her knee with a guilty sinking feeling. *It isn't the same thing. Right?* She had to keep her thoughts on Christina and what they could do to save her right now.

June watched the traffic ahead and blew the air horn as they approached an intersection.

"You're pretty good at that," Mel commented.

"Desperation," June said. "I'm glad you're

at the wheel. I couldn't drive right now if my life depended on it."

"Yes, you could. You're strong enough to survive the dog-eat-dog world of Broadway."

If he only knew how close she'd come to causing permanent damage to her knee.

June swallowed. "Two years ago, a dancer who was in the same production as me died suddenly. They figured out later she'd been hiding an eating disorder and had been slowly damaging her heart for years."

"Did you know her very well?"

"No, but she roomed in the same building with a lot of the company."

"I'm sorry," Mel said. "I'd think her friends or roommates might have noticed."

"I wish they had." June thought of her three closest friends in New York. Would she notice if Cassie, Macy or Ian had a serious problem? *I'm never letting this happen to someone again if I can help it.*

Mel steered into the emergency entrance of the hospital and parked. He unhooked her seat belt and then his. They both heard the back doors of the ambulance open. "I'll be right by your side," Mel said.

A crew from the emergency room was waiting and they worked with the firefighters to whisk Christina inside. June followed, glad to have Mel's arm around her.

MEL AND JUNE waited in hard plastic chairs outside the emergency room. The Starlight Point firefighters had left as soon as they could, needing to get themselves and the ambulance back in service.

"You should call Evie back now," Mel suggested. "She'll wonder what happened, and we're eventually going to need a ride back to the Point."

"I'll step outside," June said.

"Want me to come with you?"

She shook her head. "I'll be okay."

June didn't look okay to him. Tear-stained cheeks, shaking hands, eyes that looked like they'd seen a ghost. He'd find a machine and get two cups of coffee while she made her phone call. It was all he could do.

Lucky for him, he had several dollar bills in his wallet and the coffee machine was close by. He was waiting for June, hot coffee singeing both his hands, when she returned.

"Evie's on the way," she said. "She heard

what happened with Christina and wanted to know how she is. I wish I knew."

"Maybe we'll hear something soon."

They were halfway through their coffee, sipping in silence, when a nurse called for the family of Christina Bertram.

"She's stable right now," the nurse explained when June and Mel had followed her into the hallway of the emergency room. Gloomy fluorescent lights illuminated curtained rooms in long, solemn rows. "The doctor wants to talk to a representative from her family."

"I'm not family," June said, "but I'm her employer and I work with her."

"Can you get her family contact information?"

"Yes, my sister is bringing it. She'll be here soon." June touched the nurse's arm. "Will she be okay?"

Please let her be okay, Mel thought. Ever since he had a child of his own, his heart had found a whole new dimension. He looked at everyone and remembered they were somebody's child, and that somebody loved them desperately. He wondered if Christina's parents knew about their daughter's medical condition. They had to. They would now.

The nurse glanced from June to Mel and back. "I can't say much, but I can tell you she's going to need a lot of treatment."

Evie arrived soon after Mel and June returned to their plastic chairs. She hugged June so tightly a bystander would have thought it was June who'd just escaped death.

"I'm so sorry about Christina," Evie said. "Do you know if she's going to be okay?"

June told her sister everything they knew, which was very little. Evie gave the hospital staff the emergency contact information and offered to stay until Christina's parents got there. She had already called them before she left the Point, and they would be there in less than two hours. The nurse said it wasn't necessary for them to stay as Christina would be resting anyway.

"Can I see her before we go?" June asked.

Mel thought June was braver than he was. He just wanted to go hug his son and take him to lunch. Let his five-year-old smiles erase the pain he'd witnessed.

"Just for a minute," the nurse said, "but she's sleeping. You can take a peek."

"Want me to go with you?" Mel offered.

"No, that's okay," June said. She followed

the nurse back through the maze of curtained rooms.

Evie sighed. "What a lousy day."

"Yep."

"I heard you drove the ambulance. First time?"

"First time with a patient in the back and your sister running the siren. And I hope it's the last time. Everything okay at the Point? I left in a hurry and didn't grab my phone."

Evie shrugged. "The motorcycles in Kiddieland are down. One of your guys is over there trying to figure out why. And a man fell on his boat in the marina and broke his leg. That's where the other ambulance was."

"We should get back there before all you-know-what breaks loose."

"As soon as June's ready."

When the three of them went out to the parking lot a few minutes later, Jack's aging SUV in at least two shades of brown was in the visitor's lot. "Sorry," Evie said. "It was handy and I was in a hurry."

"I've put in a lot of miles in this," Mel said. He climbed in the backseat and June sat up front with her sister.

"She looked a little better," June said. "I

guess they injected her with something that straightened out her heart rhythm. She was hooked up to all kinds of machines and they were getting her ready to move to cardiac intensive care, but she was alive and breathing."

Mel could hear tears in June's voice.

Evie's cell phone rang. She handed it to her sister. "Will you answer that? I hate trying to talk and drive at the same time."

June glanced at the caller ID. "It's somewhere at the Point, I just don't recognize the number."

"Hello," she said, "Evie Hamilton's phone."

She listened in silence for a moment and then said, "Mel Preston is with me right now. I'll hand you off to him."

June turned around. "It's the hotel day care."

Mel's heart went straight to his feet. He grabbed the phone from June, noting her look of genuine concern but too worried to process it.

"Mel Preston. Is my son okay?"

"Yes. He's fine," the woman said. Mel knew her voice. It was his third grade teacher, Mrs. Nelson, who had retired a few years ago. She was in charge of the day care now, and she had a smile on her face every day.

But she sounded tense right now.

"What's going on?" Mel asked.

"There's a woman here," Mrs. Nelson said. "She says she's Ross's mother and wants to pick him up to go out to lunch."

"No," Mel thundered. "Do not release him to her." On a normal day, he'd regulate his voice. Ask questions. Consider his ex-wife's position. This was not a normal day and his nerves were like wrinkled aluminum foil. It would be nearly impossible to smooth them.

"She produced photo identification, says her name is Sandi Dorn," Mrs. Nelson continued, "and Ross says she's his mother."

Of course she went back to her maiden name. She'd never hidden the fact that she considered her marriage to Mel a mistake. And having a child an inconvenience. *Why was she suddenly back trying to play mother?*

"She is his mother. But she gave up custodial rights and left town two years ago. Ross and I haven't seen her since. He probably only recognizes her because he has a picture of her at home."

"Do you want me to call security and have her removed?"

Mel sighed. Rubbed his eyes. Evie and June

had heard every word he said and probably every word Mrs. Nelson said. She was getting older and tended to shout over the phone.

"I'll be there in fifteen minutes. Tell Sandi to cool her jets and do not let Ross out of your sight."

Silence on the other end.

"Please," Mel added.

"All right," Mrs. Nelson said, "I'll have them sit down and play a board game. I wouldn't mind a round of Hungry Hippos myself."

"Thank you, Mrs. Nelson."

"See you soon, young man."

CHAPTER ELEVEN

MEL ENTERED THE side gate, offering his employee ID to a security guard who laughed and waved him through. Even though Mel wore khaki shorts, sneakers and a bright blue T-shirt advertising last year's new ride—the Sea Devil—the aged security officer recognized him immediately and handed a sucker to Ross as he opened the gate.

"You picked a good day to play," the old guy said. "Sun's hot already and I hear it's going to hit eighty by afternoon."

"Lucky me," Mel said, swinging Ross's hand. "I mean us."

"Scrambler first," Ross said. "Then the helicopters. Maybe you can ride, too, this time."

The security guard sent Mel a sympathetic glance. "Hope your breakfast's settled. You're in for it today."

Mel grinned. "Wouldn't trade it."

And that was true. His ex-wife, Sandi, had

finally gone home after staying in a hotel in town for five long days. Although she had signed away her parental rights in their divorce agreement, she'd come to town hoping to make amends and see Ross. After the initial shock of her showing up unexpectedly and the panic Mel felt at her trying to take Ross from day care, his feelings cooled. Sandi was only there because she felt guilty and because she was between boyfriends. One artist had dumped her and she hadn't moved in with the next one yet.

Mel tried to shrug it off. After a few days of attempting to play mom, Sandi was obviously bored. She left town, vaguely promising Ross she'd come back and see him sometime. She made Mel no such promises and didn't ask for a change in custody rights. If he was lucky, he wouldn't see her for another two years.

"Come on, Dad," Ross said, tugging Mel's hand.

"Take it easy on your old man," the security guard said, winking at Ross. "Don't let him stop and fix anything today. You make sure he has some fun, okay?"

Ross nodded seriously. "I will. Daddy needs a day off."

"Got that right."

Mel and Ross passed a cotton candy stand and the bumper cars. Ross slowed down and considered each of them.

"Later," Mel said. "We've got all day, remember?"

They lined up for the Scrambler, the morning sun slanting in their eyes as they watched the summer employee in her ponytail and blue uniform load and unload all twenty cars twice. When it was finally their turn, they squeezed into a red car and Mel dutifully slid the pin into the door latch and fastened their seat belt.

"Ready?" he asked.

"Uh-huh. But you should let me sit on the outside. It's fun getting smashed."

"Next time."

The ride started, its simple hilarity irresistible as they careened toward the outside perimeter, then back and forward again. Ross laughed crazily as he slid around, crushing his dad and struggling for a handhold. Mel tried to find a focal point so he wouldn't lose his breakfast. Coasters he could handle; spinning rides were his kryptonite.

This was summer—and life—for Mel and anyone else in this business. Waiting, waiting, a brief flash of finite excitement and ecstasy, then a gradual slowing down and getting off the ride until the next time.

It always went too fast, but Mel wouldn't exchange it for any other life. He never managed to tune out the midway music, the hot-dog smell, the crush of people and screams from the coasters. It didn't get old. Because every day new people were sharing it with people they loved and having fun. Making a summer memory. He was lucky this was his life and, he thought, holding the door open for Ross, he got to have those fun summer memories, too. With Ross.

"Again?" Ross asked.

Mel considered it, regretting the big breakfast they'd put down this morning. "How about something different? Maybe come back to this later."

"Helicopters."

"You're a beast," Mel said.

Ross laughed and roared like a lion, catching the attention of a girl rolling a popcorn wagon on the midway. The college-aged girl smiled and tossed her hair at Mel, not recognizing him as the head of maintenance. She was cute and only about six or seven years younger than he was, but he didn't dabble with summer employees. As a rule. He'd made that mistake once.

"She seems nice," Ross said. "We could get some popcorn and make her happy."

"A little too early for that. I believe I have to catch a flight first."

"Let's try to get a red helicopter. We had a red car on the Scrambler. We could do all red stuff today."

Mel ran through the list of Kiddieland rides. There were red motorcycles on the track, red bumper cars, red race cars, red horses on the carousel and red Skyway cars stretched on cables over the midway. He might have to pull in a favor with the ride operator, but it could be managed. He wondered if they'd have to try all the blue or yellow ones next time. It could be worse. If he had a daughter, they'd be doing all the pink things, and they were harder to come by in amusement park rides.

The trademark beeping, flashing and honking of the kiddie rides was probably responsible for the numbers of painkillers First Aid doled out to beleaguered parents. Coupled with crowds, strollers and kids, it could be chaos. It was early, though, and Mel and Ross were the only ones lined up for the helicopters.

"Cool," Ross said. "We could each get our own."

Mel looked doubtfully at the ride, wondering where his long legs would go and if he could get away with watching from the ground. Having personally supervised the winter maintenance and spring installation of those choppers, he had no fears about Ross's safety. Especially with the new safety belts.

"Think I'm too tall?" Mel asked.

Ross glanced at his dad as they clunked through the silver turnstile. "You're not afraid to fly, are you?"

"No way. I think I'll race you. See who can fly faster and higher."

Ross frowned, looking at the ride and back to his dad. "They're on a pole," he said. "You're not really flying them, but it's fun to pretend."

"You can still pull the lever back and fly higher than the other ones," Mel said.

"Really?" Ross's face brightened.

"Trust me," Mel said, leaning down and making a mock-serious face. He lowered his voice. "I work here."

Ross giggled, happily following the ride operator to a red helicopter and making sure his dad got in the only other red one on the opposite side of the circular track. Mel settled in, secured the lap belt and prepared to hold the lever back to fly high. If he folded one leg under him and propped the other knee against the door frame, he could manage. But he was glad it was a short flight because it was going to be a long—but fun—day.

Two hours later, after exhausting Kiddieland, the cable cars, a minicoaster near the hotel entrance and two round-trip excursions on the train, Mel was ready for an air-conditioned lunch. A cold beer would also be nice, but Ross was soda-pop company. It was fun seeing the park from the angle of a day visitor. But he had to pretend he wasn't in charge of every yard of concrete, inch of wire, gallon of paint and piece of wood here.

He tried not to notice some flaky, dingy paint over the sign for the water ride. He tried not to look down, searching for raised or cracked concrete and trip hazards. He looked away, but made a mental note, when he found a loose rail in the queue lines for the mini motor speedway.

He was here to have fun, but it was hard to hang up his maintenance hat. Starlight Point was as important to him as if he owned it. Maybe it owned a piece of him.

Settling for a round metal table under a shady umbrella instead of one of the climate-controlled restaurants, Mel and Ross dug into hot dogs and fries as they watched the army of visitors with strollers, wagons and beginning sunburns go by. Ross showed no signs of slowing down and there were plenty of rides left. Long days at the Point were nothing new, but for some reason Mel's feet were already killing him.

Their table wasn't far from the entrance to the Midway Theater. The one o'clock show must have just ended, Mel realized, when a throng of people coursed out the front doors and headed for the food stands flanking the midway. One glance at their faces and it was obvious. They liked the show. A lot.

"There's the lady who plays the piano, Miss June," Ross said, mouth full of fries and pointing toward a small group in front of the theater.

Mel followed his son's gesture and watched June and an usher marking down notes on clipboards while talking with people who had apparently just come from the show.

"Exit surveys," Mel said aloud.

"What's that?"

"They ask people if they liked the show and write down what they say."

"Like if the music is good? And the dancers?" Ross asked.

Mel nodded. "And costumes, lights, stuff like that."

"I'd tell them to put in better seats," Ross said.

Mel smeared ketchup on his hot dog and took a bite. He watched June, her navy blue skirt swirling around her knees as she moved among guests. Her long light brown hair fell over her shoulders. He imagined her sweeping it into a ponytail, letting the heat escape her neck. It was hot, even under the giant umbrella shading their table.

He took a long drink of ice-cold cola and tried to think about something practical. Like maintenance.

"What's wrong with the seats?" he asked his son.

"They creak. With a bunch of people sitting

in them, they probably creak so loud you can't even hear the show," Ross pronounced.

"I'll have to ask Miss June about that. Anything else?"

"If you don't weigh enough, they fold you up like a taco," Ross said, dumping his fries out on his paper hot-dog plate. "Kids hate that."

"Good suggestions," Mel said, pouring a neat puddle of ketchup on his son's plate before Ross could try the industrial-sized ketchup dispenser on the table and end up wearing it. Being a single dad, he'd learned a lot about laundry, but ketchup stains were out of his range of talent.

"I'll tell her," Ross said, waving enthusiastically until the movement caught June's eye.

She handed her clipboard to the neatly dressed usher and headed toward their table.

FRESH, LIVELY, FUN. The three words she repeated to her dancers and crew every day. That's what people were looking for in a day at the Point and a live show. The word *escape* always played in her mind, too. People wanted a day away. They didn't want to think about their dog's shedding, their aunt's bad habit of dropping in, their kid's nightly struggle with math homework. She didn't try to convey the idea to her summer crew, though. Mostly young, carefree and doing exactly what they wanted—working in a quality live show—they weren't likely to be inspired by an audience member's need to escape life for a day.

They were having fun on stage, and their energy spread through the audience like juicy gossip. The exit surveys glowed with praise, the sun was shining and a cute little boy was waving at her like he knew her.

The bright sun, especially after the darkness of the theater, was blinding. She squinted to see the boy and the man with him, deep in shadow under the umbrella. It didn't take long to identify the set of his shoulders, tousled hair and obvious height as the man stood.

Although she and Mel had not officially crossed paths in the long week since Christina's nearly fatal heart condition, June knew Mel was thinking of her. Each day, the sound technicians went to work on the parade truck, but the work was already done when they got there. It was wired, lit and loud. Ready for its inaugural run today. She knew she had Mel to thank, even if he hadn't appeared enthusiastic, and this was her opportunity.

She handed off her clipboard and started walking, hardly thinking about her sore feet. Seeing Mel in a T-shirt and shorts having lunch with his son jolted her. No uniform, no tool belt, no professional armor. Not that his armor had much effect on her anyway. Their positions at Starlight Point brought them together over and over, but she wondered what would happen if they were just a man and a woman. No complicated past. No complicated future where he was married to Starlight Point and she was devoted to her dream of Broadway.

"Sorry to drag you over here," Mel said as she approached the table.

"That was some serious waving," June said to Ross. "I was afraid it was a distress signal of some kind, like you were out of mustard or fries." She smiled. "Or both."

"Actually, Ross had some important feedback for you," Mel said. "Why don't I buy you some lunch and he can tell you all about it."

June checked the time on her cell phone. "I have an hour before the parade lines up. Wish I had the whole day off like you two, but I sure wouldn't turn down lunch. Especially if it comes with important advice."

"Want me to grab you a menu?" Mel asked, shooting her a smile as he used a napkin to wipe off a seat for her. While the picnic tables started off every day spotless, countless diners tended to leave their mark.

"Thanks," June said. "I've sat in sticky stuff before, but this is a new skirt."

"It's nice," Mel said. "Dog and fries?"

"Why not? I'll walk it off in the parade."

"Be right back."

June studied Ross while his father strode over to the food window. Even with ketchup smeared around his lips, the kid was cute. More than cute. No doubt he would have his father's good looks when he grew up.

Looking at Ross with his adorable smile and sunny attitude, June wondered how anyone—especially his mother—could resist him. Someday, he'd be stealing hearts as he worked a summer job at the Point. If he was like his dad, he'd be around here for a long time. Something tugged at June's heart and she wondered for a moment what it would be like to watch Ross grow up.

"What's the parade like?" he asked, suddenly looking up from his fries.

"Loud and shiny."

"Sounds good. Does it have those big floats like the parades on TV? And giant balloons?"

"Just one actual float, and it's more of a fixed-up old truck painted shiny."

"Oh," he said, looking deflated.

"But there's a band."

"A rock band?"

June laughed. "Nope. A high school band. Different one every day."

Ross nodded, sipping his drink.

"And dancers. With colorful costumes," June added.

"Can they dance and walk at the same time?"

"Uh-huh. They sort of move along with the shiny truck and dance at the same time. The band goes first."

"Sounds awesome."

An idea flashed into June's mind and she almost said it aloud, but Mel returned with a plastic tray laden with an enormous hot dog and a cardboard container of fries. He carried a soft drink in his other hand and set it all down in front of June.

"Thanks," she said. "But I'll never eat all this."

"Got the employee discount," he replied, winking. "And Ross will finish whatever you don't eat. Five-year-olds are garbage disposals."

"Almost six," Ross protested. "I want to get a job here at Starlight Point. I'm good at lots of things."

June smiled at Mel and he raised both eyebrows.

"What kind of job are you thinking about?" she said. "I know the owners and might be able to help you out."

Ross looked serious, holding one hand out flat and ticking off the fingers with his other hand. "I like cars, and I know a lot about 'em. I also like trains and I know lots of stuff about trains, too," he said, two fingers down. "I know where everything is because I spent my whole life pretty much here. I could be a tour guide or something. I could also work for Aunt Augusta and sell cookies. I'd be real good at selling cookies. And I can fix stuff. Dad lets me help," he added, using up all his fingers and looking satisfied.

"That's quite a list," June said. "Will you help me right now by returning this tray and asking the lady at the window for some more napkins?"

Ross took off, obviously anxious to be useful.

June laid her hand over Mel's and leaned close across the table. "Thank you for getting my parade truck ready."

He shrugged. "I didn't do much."

"Yes, you did. My tech guys told on you."

"I had help." He didn't pull his hand from under June's and they sat under the umbrella, connected. "Have you heard how the girl is doing?"

June nodded. "Released from intensive care, and now she'll go home and enter a treatment program. She didn't want to. She doesn't want to give up the stage." June swallowed. "But it will kill her if she lets it." She shook her head.

Mel glanced over at Ross, who was chatting with the lady at the counter as she reloaded the napkin dispenser.

"Did things turn out okay with your ex-wife's visit?" June asked. She took her hand off Mel's and tried for complete neutrality in her voice.

Mel kept his eyes on his son and avoided looking at June. "She attempted to play mom for a few days, got tired of it and left."

"Sorry."

"Not your fault." Mel attempted a smile.

Ross had a fistful of napkins and was about to return to their table.

"I didn't want to say anything without asking you first," June said quickly, "but what do you think of Ross riding along in the parade?"

"Today?"

"Any day. He's adorable. He could ride in the cab and toss out candy to kids."

"I don't know," Mel said.

"Why not? He'd be a great mascot. He's here every day anyway. We could pull him out of the hotel day care for an hour every afternoon. It would be fun," June insisted.

"Slow down a minute." Mel pulled his hand away and took a drink.

"What could it hurt? I could ask Gloria to whip up a cool costume for him. He'd love it."

"He's *my* son," Mel said, his voice dropping low. "I'll decide what he loves and whether he gets pulled from day care."

Ross slid onto the seat next to his dad and overheard his last word. "The day care is nice. They give us cookies and we play games. In the summer, we get to go on field trips and ride rides."

"See?" Mel said.

"It gets a little boring after lunch sometimes,

though. But it helps when Grandma Virginia comes over with her dog and tells us stories. She's funny."

June snorted and got soda up her nose. "Sorry," she said, coughing.

"The dog usually sleeps in a wagon. I think she's older than Grandma Virginia."

June handed her nearly full French fry container to Ross. "You can split these with your dad. I have to go line up the parade." She sent a meaningful glance to Mel. "Right outside the gate behind the depot in the Wonderful West."

"I know where it is," Mel said. "Good luck."

"See you around, Ross. Make sure your dad takes you on the Swirler," she said, grinning. She walked away but heard Ross say, "I thought you hated the Swirler, Dad."

She didn't risk a glance back because she knew Mel wouldn't look pleased. Not many people knew that the big, tough head of maintenance—the man who'd walk the tracks on the tallest coaster—hated spinny rides. In fact, they brought Mel to his knees, begging for mercy and a puke bucket.

CHAPTER TWELVE

WHY WAS HE saying yes to an idea that made every possessive gene in his body break out into a cold sweat? Handing Ross over to wave and smile at thousands of people in the daily parade was like sending him off to college. Okay, maybe Mel was panicking out of proportion. But Ross was all he had and he was all his. For at least another decade.

Still, the kid was excited about having a "summer job," and Mel knew no one at the Point would let any harm come to Ross— they'd be afraid Mel would pull out a power tool and exact an excruciating revenge.

He had to let go once in a while. Today was just a little test.

Clutching his son's hand, he walked Ross to the employee gate behind the train depot in the Wonderful West. June had mapped out a course winding from the West, up the Sea Devil midway as it was now called, up one side of the front midway, a tight turn at the front gates, and then back the other side of the midway and through the Wonderful West to the depot gate. The entire course was almost two miles.

Mel had walked this course a thousand times, driven it in a pickup or ridden in a maintenance cart. Never had he been part of a moving spectacle like a parade, complete with a high school band and light-footed dancers. Today, he would be a stalker moving alongside the parade, keeping his eye on his son.

"Sure you want to do this?" he asked as he used a key from a large ring to unlock the gate. Even on his day off, he had keys to almost everything in the park. Just in case.

"Uh-huh. It'll be fun. I get to ride in the front seat and throw candy. It's an important job."

Mel nodded seriously. "You're right about that."

He spied June talking to a small group of performers standing behind the silver parade truck. He imagined her giving them last-minute orders. She still wore the trim navy blue skirt and white blouse she had on at lunch, but she'd added a sparkly silver vest.

He hoped she was wearing comfortable shoes. Starlight Point was a beast on the feet.

She turned quickly, seeing the gate swing open or sensing their movement. A wide smile crossed her face when she saw Ross and she motioned for him to come over. Mel had to jog a little to keep up.

"This is the young man I was telling you about," June said, presenting him to the dancers. "Ross Preston. Lucky for us, he's available nearly every day, so he's going to be our official mascot and candy tosser."

The summer performers all smiled at Ross and welcomed him while June swung open the back door of the truck and rummaged for something. She reappeared, grinning at Mel, as she presented Ross with a sparkly silver baseball hat.

Mel grimaced at the sequins. He wanted to say something about sparkly stuff being for girls, but he held his tongue in deference to the other male performers who flashed and glimmered in the sun like silverfish.

"Cool," Ross said.

"Very shiny," Mel said, addressing June.

"I knew you'd like it," June replied, shooting him a challenging look. She knew he wouldn't wreck this for his son no matter how much he hated the shiny hat. And the shiny beer truck.

"You're getting a little sunburned," June said. "Maybe I should get you one of these. Really deflects the sun."

"No, thanks, I'll just stick to the shady side of the parade route."

"Good luck with that. It's going to be a long walk."

"I can hardly feel my feet anyway."

Mel had no idea where the idea came from—well, maybe he did. Maybe this thought had been in his head for as long as he'd been trying to get June out of his head.

"Are you busy later?"

"Later?"

"This evening," Mel said. "Ross is still going strong—especially if you let him ride in the truck and have candy. He won't want to give up on our day of fun until the lights go out on the midway."

"And?"

"And I'll almost be desperate enough to pull a main breaker and shut down the park about eight o'clock tonight. I'm going to need reinforcements."

"Come on," June said, tapping Mel playfully on his chest. "You're used to long days here. Don't tell me you can't handle spending twelve hours hitting the rides with the cutest boy in the state."

"Working twelve-hour days is easier."

"How?"

"I can put my feet up on my desk while nobody's looking."

June raised an eyebrow. "Really?"

"We also get free massages at lunchtime since maintenance is the heart and soul of this place."

"No kidding?"

"Bet you didn't know about that part. I'm pretty sure it was Evie's idea."

"Right. That sounds just like my practical accountant sister whose favorite question is 'How much is that going to cost?'"

"And when I'm working, I have my own cart," Mel continued. "And a truck. My feet—"

"Give me a break. You're wearing sneakers, so you don't get to whine. Look at these," she said, pointing at her shoes.

Mel took the opportunity for a long look. He started where her skirt ended just above her knees and let his eyes linger on her shapely calves, trim ankles and feet he'd like to massage the miles out of.

"They're dancing shoes," June supplied.

"I imagine."

Ross barreled over, looking at the ground between his dad and June. "Is there a cool bug or something? Spider?"

"Nope," Mel said. "Just feet." Ross sighed and returned to the back of the truck where the performers were gathered. He put on his hat and joined the circle, looking like he took his new job very seriously.

"So, you were attempting to ask me something?" June asked.

"Want to play with us this evening? Ride some rides?"

"Will you stop complaining about your feet?"

"Probably not. But I'll move on to my head or my ears or something."

"If you didn't scream so loud on the kiddie coasters, you'd be okay," June said.

"Maybe you should hold my hand."

"Not in front of Ross. I'd hate for him to think his dad's a fraidy-cat when it comes to rides."

"Only the spinny ones," Mel said.

"I could take mercy on you and send you out for ice cream while I ride those with Ross. It'll be our little secret."

June stood very close, the sun lighting her cheeks and making her hair shine in waves over her neck and shoulders. Heat seared Mel, and it wasn't just the white-hot concrete they stood on. He was probably inviting trouble by asking June to spend the evening with him and Ross.

But there was almost nothing he could touch or think about at the Point that didn't have a little piece of June attached. Even if—*when*—she left for good at the end of the season, she would leave an indelible mark everywhere. Especially on him.

The visit from his ex-wife should have reminded him how foolish it was to open your heart to someone who had no intention of sticking around.

He was being a fool.

But if he only had a little longer with June, then he had a right to enjoy it. Maybe it wasn't fair to drag Ross into it, but the little guy would also be a safety barrier between them. And Mel needed it more than he was willing to admit.

JUNE DROVE HOME in the late afternoon and changed her clothes. Nondescript shorts with a secure pocket for money, T-shirt, sneakers. Nothing extra they'd have to store in the bins on the coaster platforms. She and her siblings often had play nights in the park when they were younger, when they wore nothing to identify them as the owners' kids. Now owners themselves, they still had good reason to go undercover.

When they were teenagers, June, Evie and Jack would try to break their own records for the number of rides in one evening. They'd racked up countless trips on the coasters, Skyway cars and carousel. They'd been thrown off the kiddie rides by summer employees who didn't recognize them as the Hamilton trio. They'd spent an excruciating summer evening trying to see how many round-trip excursions they could tally on the steam train.

"You look happy," Mel said, coming up on June's blind spot as she watched a young couple trying to decipher the park map while fighting a small breeze off the lake. They'd probably end up in a fight in another five seconds and June had been considering helping them out when Mel and Ross arrived.

"I was thinking," June said, "about all the fun I had with my brother and sister on summer nights like this one."

Mel slid onto the bench next to June. He was so close their thighs touched. June wrestled with wanting to scoot away and wanting to savor the feel of his skin on hers.

Moving away quickly became impossible because Ross parked himself on her other side, disregarding personal space and smelling like a combination of sunscreen and cotton candy.

"Give her some space," Mel said.

"Sorry," Ross said, putting some space between him and June.

June put an arm around Ross's shoulders and pulled him back. "You can sit right next to me," she said. "Everyone on my team agrees you were a fantastic grand marshal of the parade today. We couldn't have done it without you."

Ross beamed. "Do you really think so?"

June smiled. "I sure do."

The midway lights were coming on, but the stars wouldn't be visible overhead for hours. June wondered if she'd still be riding rides with Mel and Ross or if they'd all be tucked in their beds by the time the Big Dipper hung over the giant wheel.

Sunlight still bathed the three of them as they stayed on the bench a moment longer. Pink and orange glanced off June's folded hands and bare knees. A hot day promised a warm evening. She sat between two people—one who'd had a sliver of her heart for almost as long as she remembered. And one who slipped under her skin a little more every minute.

Mel covered her hand with his and pulled it onto his leg.

"Thanks for meeting up with us tonight."

In answer, June curled her fingers into the edge of his cargo shorts, feeling the hard muscles underneath.

"I better help them out," Ross said, jumping up and walking over to the young couple now arguing over the outspread map.

"He knows his way around here," Mel said. "And is desperate to be helpful."

"Like you." June turned to Mel, his arm on the back of the bench creating a haven for her. "He's a lot like you, isn't he?"

Mel smiled. "Assuming you mean that nicely—yes."

"Of course. Ross is adorable."

"Just like me."

A passing summer employee with a short broom and dustpan paused and gave June a look that suggested *she* found Mel adorable, too. Sigh. *In a perfect world*.

Sitting on a bench washed in sunset glow, with a man who melted her inside and out made her wonder. Just for a moment. *What if?* What if she didn't leave Starlight Point? What if evenings like this were there for the taking all summer? What would she lose—and gain—if she stopped chasing a dream and focused on the stars that were a little closer to her horizon?

The small coaster running parallel to the beach whooshed behind her, screams and rattling shattering her thoughts of a perfect life with Mel. Married to Starlight Point, a prisoner of Starlight Point. Just like the rest of her family. They were willing prisoners, in love with their jailer, but that was no life for her.

Ross plopped down beside her, looking very serious. "I told them exactly where to go," he said.

Mel's smothered laughter shook the bench while June tried for an appropriate expression.

She didn't know much about kids, but Ross was obviously unaware of his own joke.

"I'm sure you made their day," she said.

"Ready to start riding stuff?" Ross asked. "Dad says you're not afraid of anything."

June flicked a glance at Mel and returned her attention to Ross. "Everyone is afraid of something," she said. "Especially your dad. He's afraid of rides that go in very fast circles. Which is why we're taking mercy on him and starting with the Space Drop."

"Cool. I'm only afraid on that one for a minute when you're hanging at the top. Once it drops you, it's fun."

"The waiting is always the hardest part," June said.

"How about dinner first?" Mel asked. He rubbed his belly. "Dying here."

"No way," June said. "The first rule of serious ride-riding is no heavy food. No burgers, no fries. Especially no ice cream." She pursed her lips and gave Ross a deadpan face. "Ice cream is always a mistake. Trust me."

Mel groaned.

"Maybe we'll get a hot pretzel. It can settle while we're in line for the Swirler," June said.

"Hurler," Mel complained. "How about I get the pretzels while you two ride."

"Chicken," June said.

"I thought you said no heavy food."

"She means you, Dad," Ross said.

While Mel waited in a long line for hot pretzels, June and Ross rode the Swirler. Twice. It was obvious after the first round that Ross was a lot like his father.

But Ross wasn't a carbon copy of Mel. She wasn't exactly like her parents, either. From her mother, she'd gotten a sense of whimsy and imagination. She didn't picture herself coming up with crazy STRIPE plans or hauling an old dog around in a wagon, but choreographing and costuming shows definitely tapped into a sense of imaginative artistry. From her father, she'd gotten stubbornness and ambition. A driving sense of what she wanted in life that didn't always include sharing her plans with other people. Especially when she was afraid they wouldn't understand them. Her father's reluctance to share his business practices and keep his dream alive at all costs had finally cost him everything.

Her siblings handled things differently. Evie added up columns and took control by estab-

lishing order. Jack relied on charm, relation-
ships and cookies. They made a great pair,
running Starlight Point with the same devotion
as their parents, but with a more inclusive and
organized plan. Maybe June with her "flaky"
streak, as Jack liked to call it, was superfluous.
Not needed. Perhaps that was a relief, and she
could keep going on the Broadway highway
until she finally got where she wanted to be.

It was a lot to think about as she ushered
Ross off the ride, wondering what qualities he
would eventually end up with from his father
and mother. Seeing Mel standing at the ride
exit, three pretzels balanced in his large hands,
made it obvious where Ross's good qualities
would come from. As for his mother, apparently she had a "flaky" streak, too.

Where do I fit in?

"Which one is for me?" she asked.

"Lady's choice," Mel said. "There are three
different kinds. I like them all, and Ross is a
human garbage disposal. We'll take whatever
you leave us."

June carefully selected the salted pretzel,
knowing Mel liked sweet things, Ross liked
mustard, and feeling the weight of the little decision like a small star in a galaxy of millions.

THREE HOURS LATER, June concluded that playing in the park took a greater toll now than it had at thirteen. She felt an inch-thick layer of sweat and grime on her skin, and her feet were swollen blocks inside her sneakers.

Those problems she could admit to Mel, knowing he shared them. The heavy ache punctuated by sharp streaks in her knee was not something she cared to admit even to herself.

They walked the Western Trail, heading slowly toward the junction where the marina exit gate would veer off. Mel carried Ross with one arm and the boy's head had dropped lower and lower, giving away the fact that he'd fallen asleep somewhere near the frontier fort.

"Want me to carry you, too?" Mel asked. "Still got one shoulder available and you're not heavy."

"Tell that to my feet."

"Noticed you limping a little."

"No, I wasn't," June said quickly.

Mel laughed. "Okay, you've been dancing since we got off the train at the Wonderful West platform."

"What made us think getting off the train would be a good idea?" June asked.

"My fault. I remember saying something asinine about tiring Ross out so he'll sleep tonight."

"Who knew you were such a genius?" June said, grateful that Mel carried a heavy burden so he wouldn't notice her slow, small steps. The past month had allowed her to forget about her knee for the first time in almost a year. Exercises and stretching, lots of walking and limiting her dancing to almost zero had refreshed her body. Her immense physical well-being, despite long days, overshadowed her worry about the brief window of opportunity on the big stage.

However, on a night like this, when her body refused to play along, she wondered if that window had already closed.

"How are you getting back?" Mel asked.

June's head snapped up. Had he guessed her thoughts?

"Home," Mel said. "Did you walk like you usually do?"

She nodded. "Habit. Not much sense driving across the parking lot to the Old Road."

Mel shifted the weight of his sleeping son to the other shoulder. "Come with me to the marina lot and I'll drive you home. Save you a lot of walking."

"Don't worry about it."

"I'm serious. My feet would never make it that far. And I owe you for riding the spinny rides with Ross."

June laughed. "You do owe me, but you have to get Ross home. And if you don't merge onto the Point road in the next twenty minutes, you'll get caught in the closing traffic and sit for an hour."

They came to a bench near the railroad crossing and a nacho stand. "I'm parking myself here with a cold drink. When security sweeps the trail in half an hour, I'll bum a ride."

Mel paused and looked hesitant. His T-shirt was creased, hair awry, five o'clock shadow visible even in the dim lighting on the trail. It was time for him to go home.

June plopped down on the bench. "I'm not moving another inch and you're flirting with a traffic jam every minute you hang around."

Mel shifted Ross a little higher and eyed the bench enviously.

"Rather flirt with you."

"Rain check."

"That's what I was thinking." He paused, screams from the roller coasters breaking the silence. "Tomorrow night. A date?"

June swung both legs onto the bench, buying herself a moment before she answered.

"Dinner and adult conversation. No spinny rides or queue lines," he added, sweetening the deal. "And not at the Point. We'll go somewhere. Wherever you want."

Saying yes was tempting, but it was risky. Crossing a line.

"Are you sure this is a good idea?" she asked. "We've…uh…been down that road."

Mel nodded. "I remember."

"And nothing has changed."

"If by nothing you mean you're still leaving—again—at the end of the summer, I know," he said. "I'm just feeling brave today. My only son left the nest and got a job for a few hours and I survived it."

"If we go out to dinner," June said cautiously, "what about Ross?"

"I'll arrange a sleepover with Grandma."

"What if we're still too tired to move by tomorrow night?"

"Say yes, June. We've known each other for twenty years and eaten a lot of meals together. I want to say thank you for giving my son a fun day."

June lay full out on the bench. It was cold and hard but still a slice of heaven.

"Yes. Now go away and let me die."

Carefully supporting his sleeping son, Mel leaned way down and kissed June on the forehead. She closed her eyes, letting the heat from his lips breathe energy through her. More than energy, adrenaline spiked all the way to her toes.

"Good night," she said.

"I'm calling security and reporting a vagrant on a bench by the Nacho Rocket Shop."

"Mention my name and you'll get good service," June said sleepily.

"Tomorrow night," Mel replied, walking away on unsteady legs.

CHAPTER THIRTEEN

"WHERE'S MOM TONIGHT?" June asked, finding Evie having a salad on the patio overlooking the lake. Betty was sprawled on a chair next to Evie, soaking up the late afternoon sun.

"Downtown. Having dinner with her friends from the historic-preservation society. Then they're having a meeting about their summer fund-raising gala."

"Afraid to ask."

"You should be. I'm pretty sure the gala is going to be held *here*." Evie gestured toward the back lawn. "Big tent. Lots of booze. Overdressed people. Overpriced tickets. All for the sake of preserving local history."

"Sounds either insane or really fun," June said.

"They'd planned it for last year—at least they started to—but when Dad died, they scrapped the plans. Temporarily. Looks like it's on for this August."

June stood by the table and ruffled Betty's fur.

"You look nice," Evie said. "Too nice for any place in Bayside."

"Thanks. I think we're headed over to Port Warren."

"Sounds serious. Have you finally noticed what's right in front of your face?" Evie asked.

"It's just dinner between old friends."

"Uh-huh."

A truck pulled into the driveway with a low rumble.

"See you tomorrow," Evie said.

"Very funny."

Evie smiled. "I'm just saying if you don't come home tonight, I won't file a missing-persons report. Unless Mel fails to show up for work tomorrow. Then I'm going to be mad you eloped without telling me first. I want to use my bridesmaid's dress from Gus and Jack's wedding at least one more time so I can justify the cost."

Both sisters glanced up when Mel stepped around the house on the curving sidewalk. They were used to seeing him there, goofing off with their brother and hanging around since they were kids.

But tonight he looked very different. He

wore trim black trousers, a crisp striped oxford, blue tie and dress shoes. Clean-shaven, he'd even gotten a fresh haircut. Devastatingly handsome no matter what he wore, tonight he was six foot three of danger.

"He looks like he means business," Evie whispered. "I'm getting that bridesmaid's dress dry-cleaned and ready."

Mel walked over and paused at the edge of the flagstone patio, his glance stopping politely on Evie and then focusing on her sister. June wore a red sleeveless knee-length dress and low-heeled sandals with a strap around the ankle. She hoped she looked good enough for a man to take a second look. Mel was going back for thirds already.

Evie cleared her throat. "June just invited me to come along," she said. "I'll grab my purse and Betty's travel bag."

Mel broke his concentration and turned a puzzled look on Evie.

"Just kidding. You kids have fun. Betty and I have the house all to ourselves tonight. I think we'll get drunk and do our nails."

June gave her sister a quick shoulder-hug.

"Ready when you are," she said to Mel, hoping to hit a light tone.

Mel waved to Evie with one hand and put the other arm around June's waist.

"You are too beautiful to ride in my eight-year-old truck with a dent as big as my leg. If you give me a minute, I'll steal something nice out of the Starlight Point parking lot."

"It's not stealing if we return it before the park closes," June suggested.

"I hate operating with time constraints." Mel opened the passenger-side door. "How did you get back to your house last night?"

"Evie picked me up in the first-aid scooter. I didn't even know she could drive that thing. Apparently someone called and told her I was near death on a bench outside the nacho stand."

Mel smiled and closed her door. He walked around the front and slid in behind the wheel. Even in a truck, he looked too tall for his surroundings. Dressed as he was, he should be sliding behind the wheel of a flashy sports car.

"Might be a Porsche in that lot somewhere. Still willing to risk wrecking my friendship with all the local cops if you'd prefer a ride that's less…industrial."

"I like your truck. It's you."

"Good thing since it's all I have."

"It's all you need," June said.

Mel backed onto the Old Road, no traffic in sight. The only people who traveled on this narrow strip of asphalt were the few families who lived there—two Hamilton houses and a handful of others. It was a magical place to live, sandwiched between an amusement park and a beautiful lake. The disadvantage— if one could consider it that—was the quiet but steady buzz of summer resort sounds all season long. Trying to cut across the Starlight Point parking lot and get onto the Point Bridge could always be a matter of delicate timing in the summer, although the Old Road did eventually meander into Bayside.

No cars were leaving the Point in the late afternoon of a perfect summer day. June watched Mel's hands on the steering wheel—strong, capable hands that fixed things and kept her family's business going.

"No traffic tonight," Mel remarked. "Everyone is staying until closing I bet. Too bad we only have fireworks once a year on the Fourth of July."

Was Mel making polite conversation to cover—what, nerves? Or maybe they didn't know what to say to each other on an actual date. But then, what he'd said struck her. Fireworks every night. She pictured the massive crowds that stayed until the gates closed every year on the Fourth of July. Was it the holiday or the fireworks? What would persuade people to ride, eat and shop until they turned out the lights? Fireworks, maybe, but there were other ways. This could be genius—upping daily revenue by 5 percent? Even 10 percent?

"You're quiet," Mel said. "What's got your wheels turning? Or shouldn't I ask?"

"Fireworks. Every night. It would give people a reason to stay until closing."

"They pretty much do, don't they?"

"Not all of them. You can watch the front turnstiles and see how many people pour out of there between eight and ten o'clock. The gate tallies would tell us for sure."

"Maybe people have little kids and long drives home. Have to work the next day. Their feet are bloody stumps. Stuff like that. All kinds of reasons people get on the road."

"I guess. But it's still a cool idea."

Mel laughed. "Like to see Evie's face when you suggest exploding a couple of thousand bucks every night. She'd probably pull up her spreadsheet and stare you down over her reading glasses."

"I know it's way out of our price range. This year. But it's worth at least considering. The idea of it. Maybe we could do a nighttime show of some kind."

"Let's hear it," Mel said, crossing the small hill on the Point Bridge. "We've got at least twenty minutes before we get over to Port Warren."

June giggled. "Thanks for thinking I've got twenty minutes' worth of new ideas. But we shouldn't talk business tonight."

"All right," Mel agreed.

June silently watched Bayside go by as Mel got on the bypass and skirted the small city. They'd be crossing a large bridge over the bay as they neared Port Warren. June had always loved the massive bridge, remembering childhood trips in the backseat of her parents' car. In the daytime, fishing and pleasure boats dotted the blue water far below the bridge. Stars hung low on summer nights, visible because the bridge was several miles from the bright lights of the Point or any of the small cities in the region.

"We could build a stage in front of the Crazycat. Have lights and a dance show.

Maybe involve the crowd with a dance competition," she said.

"Not great for the sore-footed, but teenagers would stick around. Building a stage and setting up lights isn't free, but it's also not ten grand a night like good fireworks would be."

"Is it doable?"

"You could talk me into it. But you'll have to be creative."

DRINKS ON THE table and dinner orders placed, Mel and June faced each other across a gleaming white tablecloth at the Port House Inn. Not really an inn in terms of having overnight accommodations, the restaurant had kept the name from a time when the lighthouse and coal docks had made it a safe and profitable port. Generally too fancy for Mel's taste, he figured the sight of June in that red dress was going to be worth the bill. Now that the inn catered mostly to the boating and yacht club crowd, his tie and her fancy shoes fit right in.

"I've only been here once," June said. "I think it was some special occasion like my mom's birthday or Mother's Day." She half shrugged. "It was ten or fifteen years ago. But I still remember the strawberry cheesecake."

Mel smiled. "Must have made quite an impression. You should have something else for dessert tonight."

"Why?"

"Because if you're going to remember something that happens tonight for the next decade and a half, I want it to be better than strawberry cheesecake."

"Hard to compete with that," June said.

"I'll work at it."

He cut a slice of bread from the small loaf delivered on its own little cutting board. Serving June first, he lopped off another slice and devoured it in two bites.

"Sorry. Starving. Worked through lunch so I could knock off early and get Ross and his luggage to my parents'. Thought I was going to be late when we realized his favorite pajamas were in the washer."

"What did you do?"

"Put 'em in the dryer by themselves on high while I packed the other stuff. Amazing how fast polyester will dry like that."

"You're a superhero," June said.

"Nope. But when you have a kid you realize your life doesn't belong to you anymore.

And you're usually one lost backpack or one loose tooth away from disaster."

"I don't know how you manage it all alone."

"I'm not alone. I'm luckier than a lot of single parents. I have free day care at work and my parents do everything they can to make up for..."

He poured them both a glass of wine, not bothering to finish his last sentence.

"Does Ross ask about his mother?" June said.

"He used to. Used to ask when she was coming, why she didn't live with us. Stuff like that. He doesn't ask much anymore."

"Poor Ross."

Mel ate another piece of bread and sipped his drink.

"I haven't been on a date in years," Mel said. "So I'm out of practice, but I can do better than this for conversation."

"For example?"

"You look so good in that dress I can easily convince myself to forget you're my best friend's sister."

June smiled. "Nice. I like this conversation. What else do you have?"

"You should say something about how

charming and irresistible I am, especially in this shirt and tie. The collar itches, you know. You have to throw me a bone."

"Every other woman in this restaurant is jealous and hoping I screw things up so bad you'll offer yourself to the next available woman in the room."

"Very nice. But I don't recommend it."

"What?" June asked.

"Putting me at the mercy of the expensive-jewelry-fancy-boat crowd."

"You might be just what they're looking for."

Mel laughed. "I got all the grease out from under my nails, but there's still a pair of work boots under my bed and a toolbox in the back of my truck."

"I like that about you."

Mel shifted in his seat. He wondered if she also liked the fact that he had an ex-wife, was currently married to his job, and came as a package deal with a boy who considered corn dogs a food group and had a drawer full of Lego in the kitchen.

He picked up his iced water and took a long drink. "New topic. My son has a birthday coming up this summer and I could use some ideas. What is the best birthday present you ever got?"

June sipped her wine, smiling at him over the rim, taking her time. "Dance costume when I was ten. It was black, so I thought I was really sophisticated. And it had matching shoes."

"Sequins?"

"Of course. You could see me from the space shuttle. I wore it constantly until I grew six inches between the ages of eleven and twelve and couldn't squeeze into it anymore."

"Too bad."

"Yes, but I like being tall, so hey." She leaned closer and lowered her voice. "Sometimes I worry that I'm too tall for a dancer. I maybe look a little goofy out there with the five-foot-seven crowd. I think I've lost a few parts because of my ridiculously long legs."

Mel leaned out and took a long, dramatic look under the table. "I see no problem there."

June slapped him lightly on the forearm. "People are staring."

"So?"

"Why don't you tell me about your favorite birthday present?"

"Best I ever got was last fall. My parents got me a game system."

June rolled her eyes. "Video games?"

"Hey, winters are pretty long. Plus, they got me and Ross some fun games we can play together. We build cities and knock 'em down. Sometimes we're superheroes. Sometimes we race cars. We race a lot of cars."

"You and Ross?"

"No fun playing alone. One of the best things about having a son. Never alone. That's sometimes the worst thing, too, but not often. Always have someone waiting for you after work, happy to see you just because."

June's teasing smile faded. She refolded the napkin in her lap. Mel was afraid he'd said too much, painting a picture of his life that lacked all the sparkle June was looking for in hers.

"Do you ever wonder," she began, but she was interrupted by the waiter delivering steaming dishes that smelled like heaven. Mel was hungry, but nervous. Wishing for all the time in the world, but feeling rushed like a summer day destined to end, no matter how beautiful the sunset.

He wanted to hear the end of June's question, but he needed food to clear his head and build his courage. He half hoped June would be distracted by her shrimp and pasta long enough for him to down his food or change the subject.

No luck.

June picked up her fork and paused. "Do you ever wonder if life is passing you by?"

"No."

"Just no? You never think maybe you're working and working toward something, but you're not sure what you'll do when you get there? Or even how you'll know if you've gotten there?"

Mel forked several mouthfuls before answering. A man would starve to death if he didn't fuel up for a conversation like this.

"I don't want to miss out on anything," June insisted.

"You've always been like that. I remember you—even when we were in elementary school—always wanting in on everything." He chuckled. "In high school, you auditioned for all the lead parts in the musical, and I think you were disappointed when you only got one. You were good, too. I showed up at two out of three performances."

"You're changing the subject and avoiding

my question. You seriously don't worry that your life isn't going where…where you always thought it would?"

"I used to. Used to worry about moving up the food chain and what I was going to be when I grew up."

"And now?" June asked.

"I'm all grown up and at the top of the chain at Starlight Point. At least as far as someone outside your family is going to go. Thought about throwing myself at Evie and marrying into the clan, but she's too tall for me," he said, grinning.

June wasn't giving up. "So you're living for the present."

"Yep. At present I have everything I need and something beautiful right in front of me."

June smiled and her shoulders relaxed. "Do you mean me or that big plate of seafood?"

"Yes."

AFTER DINNER, THEY walked along a paved path in front of the inn. Far across the bay, they could barely make out the lights on top of the coasters at Starlight Point. They paused by an old railing to watch the water.

When a breeze off the lake lifted goose-flesh on June's bare arms, Mel pulled her tight against him, just holding her for a few moments—long moments in which she breathed in his clean soap smell, her nose picking up the slight mint of shaving cream.

"The summer will be half-over before we know it," he said, his voice a low rumble against her. "I hate to see it go, but what I really hate…"

She waited. Suspecting but afraid of what he was going to say. He hated to see her go.

Did she have to go?

June's brain flooded with images. Mel in swim trunks diving into the lake in front of her parents' house. Mel, shirtless, playing catch with Jack in the backyard. Mel in a tux taking her to prom so her parents wouldn't worry. Mel in maintenance blues that brought out the color of his eyes.

It would be so easy to stay.

There were twenty years of reasons why the man whose scent, warmth and arms enveloped her should be hers.

And she would belong to him. To their shared past and future. To Starlight Point.

What about herself? Without her dreams

leading her on, would she still know herself, be herself? For an instant, she didn't care.

And then a vision of the stage, the lights, the huge crowds, the city, the life she'd imagined for herself flashed before her and eclipsed the quiet lapping of the lake on the dark shore.

"I think it's time to go home for the night," she said.

"I hate to argue with a beautiful woman, but are you really sure you want to go home?"

Being in Mel's arms made it nearly impossible to be sure about anything. Which was one more reason she needed him to let her go.

"I'm sure."

Mel hesitated a moment, and then very slowly released her and let the cool breeze burrow a path between them.

JUNE WAS SURE the low rumble of Mel's truck woke the whole household. If she was lucky, her mother was still out. She could deal with Evie, but Virginia was a wild card.

"I'm a little disappointed to see you so early."

June spun around, nearly shutting her finger in the heavy oak front door. Evie held a finger over her lips. "Mom's in bed so I'm the only one seeing you come home way too early from your date."

Heading quietly for her room, June heard Evie right behind her.

"Details," Evie said, closing June's bedroom door. "The price of my silence."

"What if I don't care about keeping you silent?"

"Then consider it bragging and tell me everything." Evie sunk into the chair in the corner of June's room and steepled her fingers, waiting, as if she were at a board meeting.

"Another time. I'm supposed to be helping at Mel's STRIPE class before park opening tomorrow morning. Although now I wish I hadn't said I would."

Evie groaned. "Any chance Mom will give up on that wonderful tradition?"

"Senility is our only hope. She'll forget about it one of these years. Until then, I'm going to keep dodging it."

"Except for tomorrow. When you're helping your boyfriend, the electricity professor."

June threw a pillow at her sister. "He's not my boyfriend."

"How would I know that if you won't make

a full date disclosure?" Evie asked. "I want to hear about the sparks flying tonight."

"No sparks. I think it would make a pretty disappointing story." June sat on her bed, torn between wishing Evie would leave and wishing she was brave enough to tell her the whole story. A little part of her knew Evie had probably connected all the dots herself, anyway.

"Sorry you waited up for nothing."

"I'll keep hoping," Evie said. She looked as if she would pursue the conversation for a moment, but she heaved out of the chair and headed for the door. "There's still plenty of summer left."

Not for her. Time was running out, and the New York stage wouldn't wait.

CHAPTER FOURTEEN

THE NEXT MORNING, June watched, fascinated by the Mel Preston she'd never seen before. She was used to funny Mel—the mischievous sidekick to her brother, Jack. Accustomed to handyman Mel, who'd fixed a pane of glass in junior high and watched over every circuit board, gear and yard of coaster track at the Point. Lately, she'd acknowledged another aspect to Mel. Steady, family man Mel who still hated spinny rides but sent her world and carefully laid plans spinning. *Or he would if she let him.*

The man standing in front of ten dozen employees in the echoing Starlight Point ballroom was a Mel she had not seen in action. Of course she knew he was confident, competent and a strong leader. The park's safety and mechanical record testified to his talent since he'd become head of maintenance four years earlier.

What was different about him this morning? He reminded her of particularly capable directors or producers she'd seen work a stageful of performers in New York. A man in his domain who exuded masculine power.

June's eyes raked the crowd. She wondered how many of the female summer employees were enthralled by the neutral and hot wires or by the hot instructor. He was irresistible.

But it was in her best interest to resist. His magnetism threatened to root her here, at Starlight Point. Tempted her to say goodbye to Broadway. She was not ready to give it up, no matter how easy it would be to sink into a life at Starlight Point.

"Never touch anything you suspect could be hot," Mel was saying, pointing to sample pictures and graphics. "Even 110 volts— a common household current—can kill you. Amperage—amps you've probably heard it called—is something different."

Leaning against a column in the ornate old ballroom, June half listened to Mel's lecture as she daydreamed about couples who had danced here. Going back generations, wearing lovely dresses and dashing tuxedos. Summer romances leaving a whispered impression.

This ballroom always meant romance to her, but today it had another purpose.

The gleaming wood floor had been invaded by classroom tables and dozens of folding chairs. Dancing would be more fun. She'd missed the chance to teach ballroom dancing three summers ago when it was the STRIPE lesson. Away dancing on Broadway, she'd missed a lot. Especially the last few years of her father's life.

A young man in the front row raised his hand. When Mel acknowledged him, he asked, "Where'd you learn all this stuff?" His tone was more admiration than rudeness.

"Some at the local college," Mel said, "but mostly from the apprenticeship program here at the Point. I started right out of high school ten years ago. You could do the same if you want."

June mentally left the dance floor and its history of happy couples and returned to Mel. She was supposed to help at one of the tables when people split into groups. She should probably pay attention to the lesson so she didn't electrocute herself in front of her employees. Thinking about electricity was far less painful than thinking about the things she'd missed at home and the things she *would* miss if she stayed. She sighed, wishing decisions came more easily as she got older.

Her cell phone buzzed in her pocket. She pulled it out and glanced at the caller ID. It was Megan, her theater manager, calling at eight o'clock in the morning.

Not a good sign.

June stepped outside and answered the call.

"Are you in labor already?" she asked.

Megan laughed. "Don't even think it. It's Brooke. She had to go home for her grandfather's funeral. She got the call last night. Her roommate just called me."

"Oh. I'm sorry to hear that," June said. "Poor Brooke."

"I'm sorry, too, of course. And I understand why she left last night," Megan said. "But it gives us a problem for four days. We already sent Sarah to fill in Christina's spot, so now we're down two dancers in the Broadway show. Any suggestions?"

June had only one. She knew the routine like she knew every ride at Starlight Point. Her knee was strong and rested after weeks with almost no dancing. *She hoped.* Was she ready to test her knee? She had to know if it would hold up under pressure, just in case she got an offer or audition. This was a perfect opportunity.

And she wanted to dance.

"I'll do it."

"You?"

"Of course. I made up all those dance steps, I can certainly do them. I'll just need Gloria to make a slightly taller costume for me, and I'll put on my dancing shoes."

"That's not what I thought you were going to say," Megan said. "But it's a great idea if you're willing."

"Very willing," June said.

"In that case, you better hurry. Your first show is in three hours."

June went inside and caught Mel's eye. He had finished his lecture and the attendees were moving to various tables. Mel covered the space between them with long, quick steps.

"Problem?" he asked. "You look upset and excited at the same time. Was it my teaching? I told you I was no professor."

June laughed. "You were really good. I can't believe you claimed to be a lousy teacher—you had the audience in the palm of your hand."

Mel flushed, color and a smile lighting his

face. *Irresistible. Again.* Good thing she had something else to occupy her mind right now.

"Are you ready to help me out and captain one of the tables?" he asked.

June shook her head. "Sorry. I have to back out on you because of a problem with our show in the Midway Theater. One of the girls had to go home for a while and we need a replacement right away."

"Do you have spare dancers waiting in the wings?"

"No."

"So what will you do?"

"Call in a professional."

"Let me guess," he said, pointing at June.

She smiled. "I have no idea why I'm so excited about dancing here. It's not Broadway or even close."

"But it's where you started. And the shows this summer are all you." Mel touched June's upper arm as he spoke. "Don't worry about the STRIPE classes. I've got it under control." His eyebrows drew together and his usual smile was absent. He drew a long breath. "When dancing calls, I know you have to go."

June took a deep breath. This was nothing like her leaving their summer romance. They were grown-ups. And she wasn't leaving the state. She was going across the midway to do her job.

"I have to go. The show is in a few hours and I'm six inches taller than the girl I'm replacing. I hope Gloria is in the mood to make an emergency costume for me."

"I could put in a good word for you," Mel said, his smile returning. "I haven't ruined a shirt this week, so I might be on her good side."

JUNE GOT TO the Midway Theater an hour before the first show. She put on the soundtrack and ran through her part. *Why am I so nervous?* The eleven o'clock show would probably draw a crowd of eighty-five people. She'd danced in front of thousands, night after night.

But this was her show. Expectations from her dancers and herself were higher than the lights over Broadway. Because June's knee would get a good test. It was strong, she knew that. The summer had been good for her knee. *How would it feel after twenty shows?*

"This would be a whole lot easier if you weren't taller than the average man," Gloria said, bustling through the stage door with costumes draped over her arm. "Some of these seams aren't perfect, but you take what you get when you give a gal two hours to make six costumes. Lucky I had patterns and material ready and plenty of help."

Gloria held out an arm draped with costumes.

June hugged her. "Thank you. I haven't been this excited since you made my prom dress when I was a senior."

"I'd rather be making you a wedding dress. Pretty girl like you ought to get married before you get much closer to thirty."

June laughed. "When I'm thirty, I'll come see you about that."

Gloria scrunched her lips. "You better try these on. Time's running short."

ON THE SECOND day of June's substitute dancing position, Mel picked up Ross from the hotel day care in time to catch the five o'clock show in the Midway Theater. Because June had been performing during the parade, Mel had personally picked up and delivered his son to and from his job as parade grand marshal. He sure would be glad when June was back on the parade route.

"I'm hungry, Dad," Ross said.

"Me, too. Can you wait until after the show? I thought we'd see if Miss June would like to have dinner with us."

"Okay."

"I'll get you some M&M's in the lobby. You can eat them during the show."

"Awesome!" he said, smiling.

If only it were that easy to please everyone.

They got there early enough to grab seats in the front, where Ross wouldn't be stuck behind someone tall with a big head. Mel had no trouble seeing over everyone, but he didn't want his son bobbing back and forth in his seat and driving the person behind him nuts.

"I didn't know Miss June was in the show," Ross whispered as the curtains split and June was front and center, only a few feet away from them. "I thought she was the piano player."

"Shh," Mel said. "I'll explain after the show."

He sat back, transfixed. He'd seen part of this show while other dancers were practicing. But other dancers were not June Hamilton.

There was something magical about her

performance. Her sureness, grace, energy and smile were like the other dancers, but beyond.

She was a professional.

Her love of dancing was obvious in every step. When she took the microphone to sing, Ross elbowed his dad and whispered "Wow" loud enough for people two rows back to hear. Mel knew June saw him and Ross in the front section. She smiled at them, making eye contact with each.

Mel recognized some of the music. Although not an expert on musical theater, the songs were part of the popular culture. He'd heard them before, but listening to June sing was like hearing the songs for the first time.

The show ended, and Ross stood up, clapping enthusiastically.

"Can we eat now?" he asked when the curtains closed and people around them started heading up the aisle toward the entrance.

"Almost. Let's go around back and see if Miss June is available."

Mel waited until the theater emptied. He knew there was one more show but hoped June had time for dinner. He took the side steps and pushed aside the curtain. He'd been on the stage dozens of times, checking the wiring and doing other maintenance, but now he felt as if he was intruding. Maybe it was the closed curtain, the aura left by the show. This was a performer's world, not his world.

"The Preston men," June said when Mel and Ross came through the curtains. She was in the wings, almost hidden by the dim lighting.

"I hope we're allowed back here," Mel said.

"We're hungry," Ross said.

June smiled. "I'm hungry, too."

"She said yes, Dad."

Mel ruffled his son's hair.

"What have I said yes to?"

"Do you have time for a quick dinner before your next show? It's Ross's night to cook so we're cheating and eating out."

June grinned and nodded. "I could use something to eat. Can you give me five minutes to change?" She slipped out of her dance shoes and took off her silver vest as she spoke.

"Sure," Mel said, swallowing hard. The sight of June, her cheeks and eyes still alight with excitement, was a test of his resolve. "Want to go to the Midway Buffet?"

"I only have about forty-five minutes," June said, "but the buffet is fast. Does Ross like the food there?"

"Garbage disposal, remember?"

Ross smiled. "They have mini corn dogs."

Ten minutes later, the three of them navigated the buffet line. June had her own plastic tray, but Mel juggled his food and his son's on one tray.

"I'm buying," Mel said as they slid their trays along the silver grooves in the counter at the register.

"Thank you. This is the nicest date I've had in a long time."

Mel raised one eyebrow and grinned.

"Almost," June whispered so Ross wouldn't hear.

Mel smiled.

They found a table by the front window where they could watch people go by on the midway.

"We loved the show," Mel said. "You're an amazing performer."

"Can you believe it was my first time dancing?" June asked, winking at Ross.

"Right," Mel said. "I searched the internet for some of the shows you told me you were in. Watched videos on YouTube."

Mel felt his heart slow down and almost stop. He had not planned to confess that. She glanced up from her soup and salad, an un-readable expression on her face. If he had to describe her look in one word, it would be *caution*.

"Really?" she said. "I didn't know you were interested in musical theater."

"He did," Ross confirmed. "We watched a bunch of videos. You looked like a cat in one of them."

"That was the idea," June said. "We all dressed like cats. What else did you see?"

"You were a cowgirl in the one show. You even had a fake gun."

"How do you know it was fake?" June asked.

Ross's eyes rounded with excitement. "They let you use a real gun?"

"Just kidding."

"It's amazing what you can find on You-Tube," Mel said. He thought he should get in on the conversation before his five-year-old son took it in the wrong direction.

"So you saw *Cats* and *Oklahoma!*," June said. "How about *Hello, Dolly!*? There are huge dance numbers in that one, but it was probably hard to spot me."

"You wore a pink dress," Mel said. *Crap.*

His mouth betrayed him before his brain remembered to tread easy.

June's face colored and she put down her spoon. "I'm going to refill my drink," she said.

Maybe he'd gone too far.

"Is she mad we Googled her?" Ross asked after June walked to the beverage counter.

Mel shook his head. "I don't know, but we should probably talk about something else when she comes back."

June returned with a full glass of iced water. "Thirsty," she said. "All that dancing."

They ate in silence for a few minutes. Ross went back for a fresh plate and another stab at the kids' buffet area.

"So you stalked me online," June said, a forkful of salad poised in midair. "Did you watch any videos of my favorite show, *Pippin*?"

Mel nodded. "Are you mad?"

Her eyebrows drew together as if she was thinking about her answer. Mel held his breath. "No," she finally said. "Just surprised. It's nice and I...didn't expect it."

Mel glanced over to the kids' buffet area and noticed Ross carefully using the tongs to put more mini corn dogs on his plate. He was well trained.

He turned his attention back to June. "I tried watching *Pippin*. I liked the music, but I couldn't understand what the heck was going on," Mel confessed.

"Here's the thirty-second summary. A young man thirsts to see the world and whatever is out there for him. He doesn't want to settle for the life his parents have planned for him. So he goes on a journey and discovers—"

She stopped.

"What does he discover?" Mel prompted.

Ross careened back to his seat, flopping down with a full plate of corn dogs and Tater Tots, some of which rolled onto the table.

"Looks like you're getting your money's worth," June said.

Mel laughed. "Ross is eating your share. Are you sure you only want soup and that tiny salad?"

"I have one more show tonight, and I don't think I can dance on a stomach full of heavy carbs."

Mouth full, Ross nodded agreeably. "One time I ate too much and threw up in the car on the way home."

Mel reached across the table and took Ross's plate. "Maybe we should cut you off."

"I should go," June said. "It's not long until the next show."

"Want me to empty your tray for you?" Ross asked.

"Sure."

The boy picked up June's empty tray and headed for the trash and tray station.

"He doesn't sit still for long, does he?" June asked.

Mel shrugged. "He's a five-year-old boy. I have no idea how school is going to go this fall. He's just starting kindergarten since he has a July 29 birthday. I could have pushed him to go last year, but I wasn't ready to give him up yet."

"I can understand that," June said.

Could June really understand what it was like to love someone so much it was like sharing one heart? That's how Mel had felt the moment he held his son for the first time. If June hadn't left seven years ago...if Ross was their son...

That line of thinking was so tempting, but so pointless. Dangerous.

"I know you're booked solid tomorrow and

the next day with five shows," Mel said, "but when the dust settles, would you like to do something together? Adults only?"

Living dangerously...

June stood.

She was going to say no.

"Sure. We'll talk in a day or two when I can breathe again."

Maybe June didn't feel what he felt—that he could only breathe when he was with her.

CHAPTER FIFTEEN

IT WAS BITTERSWEET, getting ready to dance her last show. Brooke was due back tonight and would step into her role tomorrow, just two days ahead of the big July Fourth holiday. As far as June knew, this show would be her last time taking the stage at Starlight Point.

She felt wonderful. The audience would be close enough to touch. The familiar stage, worn by time, was every inch a part of her. June almost hated to hand the spotlight back to Brooke, but it was time she took up her other responsibilities. The parade, managing the theaters and helping her siblings run Starlight Point had suffered as she'd danced five shows a day for the past four days.

Fifteen minutes before June went onstage, Megan found her backstage. "There are three people out front who say they know you. Friends from New York."

"Really? Did they give their names?"

"Cassie, Macy and Ian."

What? Her three best friends, the only solid ones she had in New York, were all doing off-Broadway work for the summer. *What are they doing here?*

"Are they seated in the audience?"

"Front row," Megan said. "When I told them you were subbing in for a dancer, they said they wanted to see the show and they'd meet up with you after."

Okay, now she was nervous as a first-year dancer. She loved her friends, but just thinking about having them in the audience raised her heart rate. What if they thought her show was amateurish and small town? Compared to Broadway…well, it wasn't fair to compare summer theater in the Midwest with the shows on Times Square.

They were her friends. They were not going to judge her. *But why are they here at Starlight Point?*

The curtains opened, the music started, and June took the stage with the other ten dancers. Although she tried not to look, she saw her friends in the front row. Smiling and watching her every move. Of course they would know the music, recognize some of the dance steps even. June had been in *Cats* with Macy, *Oklahoma!* with Ian, *Hello, Dolly!* with Cassie, and they were all in the recent revival of *Pippin* as troupe dancers. They shared the same talent agent, which was probably the reason they often ended up in shows together. In the crazy competitive world of Broadway, they'd become friends, watching out for each other. June shared a small apartment with Cassie but hadn't talked with her in weeks.

As soon as the show ended and the audience cleared, June peeked out the curtain. They were waiting near their seats. She rushed out and hugged them all.

"What are you doing here? I didn't think any of you had ever been west of Manhattan," June exclaimed.

"Research," Macy said. "Guess what show just announced a casting call?"

"Carousel," Ian gushed.

"You were supposed to let her guess," Cassie admonished him.

June laughed. "I already knew. Our agent called me. He seemed to think I was a shoo-in for a musical that involves an amusement park."

"But?" Ian asked. "I hear a *but*."

"But the casting call is next week and rehearsals start in a month," June said. "I can't do it. I've committed to being here through September."

Cassie put her arm around June. "We're here to talk you out of that."

"I thought you were here for research."

"That, too," Macy said. "How about a ride on the carousel and then you come over to the hotel for drinks? We only have two days off from our off-Broadway *South Pacific* and we want to have some fun."

"What hotel are you staying at?" June asked.

"Yours. The old fancy one on the beach," Ian said.

"The Lake Breeze? I happen to know the bartender there and he'll take good care of us. You guys can stagger back to your rooms and I'll find my way home somehow."

"Home?" Cassie asked.

"My parents' house is just across the main parking lot. It's my home for the summer. Don't worry," June said. "I'll be back on Times Square in the fall."

Guests strolled the midway on the hot July evening. Because most of the park patrons who stayed late were adults and teens, the line for the old-fashioned carousel contained only a handful of people.

"We can ride twice," June suggested.

"Once will probably be enough for me," Ian said. "We're just trying to get the flavor."

He mounted a painted horse next to June.

"You could have gotten the flavor a lot closer to New York City. There's a carousel in Central Park," she said. "You had to fly into Detroit and rent a car to get here."

Cassie took a horse on the other side and shrugged. "Summer vacation. And we get to see you."

June suspected there was more to the story. After a few drinks at the hotel lounge, she imagined her friends would try convincing her to give up Starlight Point for an early return to the city. The carousel lurched into action and June and her friends filled a row going up and down on their fancy horses. It was the first time June had been on the carousel in years even though she heard the music all day, every day. It was fun holding on to the shiny pole and getting a cinematic view of the front midway.

Perhaps it was the lights and the movement

that made her heart lurch when she thought of leaving in eight weeks.

MEL SUPERVISED BATH and bedtime, making sure Ross put on clean pajamas and brushed his teeth. He shut out the light in Ross's room and headed to the small kitchen for a cold beer to keep him company while he mellowed out in front of the television.

He sunk into a recliner and picked up the remote, hoping he'd recorded his favorite home-renovation series. Before he even found the recorded shows, shrill ringing from the kitchen interrupted him.

Rats. The stupid cell phone was on the metal table, a table that amplified the noise. If Ross was already asleep, it would wake him. Mel shot out of his recliner and grabbed the phone, silencing the ringer. He didn't want to answer it, but the caller ID told him it was his right-hand man at the Point. Galway wouldn't call unless something major was going on.

"Hello," he said. *Don't make me put on my shoes and come over there.*

"Sorry to bug you. False fire alarm at the hotel, and the damn thing won't shut off. I think it's an electrical spike triggering it. Or something electrical."

"That's too bad. I just took off my shoes and opened a beer," Mel said.

"Very funny. My wife will come and sit with Ross so you can get over here. I already called her," Galway said.

Mel blew out a breath.

"As soon as she gets here, I'll get on the road."

Galway lived three blocks from Mel, and this wasn't the first time his wife, a retired nurse, jumped in to help with Ross when Mel got called to an emergency. Mel's parents would also help, but he hated to run them over when they were probably side by side in matching recliners watching PBS. Ross probably wouldn't wake up, and if he did, he knew Mira Galway and liked her.

Mel pulled on his work boots and laced them. He didn't bother to change into a Starlight Point maintenance uniform. His loose jeans and T-shirt were good enough to go behind the scenes and check the electrical panel at the hotel. He even skipped the company name tag.

He switched on the outdoor light for Mira

and waited until she was safely in the house and he heard the lock click. Another late night for him. Even if it was a quick fix, he'd stay on scene at the hotel for at least an hour to make sure he'd knocked out whatever was triggering the alarm. Hotel guests outside in their pajamas was not part of the customer service package the Point wanted people to remember.

At least it was a hot night. He drove straight to the hotel, taking the curves on the Old Road as quickly as he could without compromising the safety of oncoming cars. The lights of the coasters and rides flashed and chased on his right as he rounded the peninsula.

Parking in the loading dock area, he strode quickly to the control panel room. This had happened before, last year, so he knew where to start. Galway had the panels open, a look of satisfaction on his face.

"Called you too soon," he said. "Think I got it—"

The fire alarm mounted on the wall pierced the room with noise and strobe lights.

"Maybe not," Galway shouted.

Mel opened the battery backup panel and motioned for Galway to shine a light inside. In less than five minutes, Mel found the faulty electrical circuit that triggered the alarm. The system was set up to default to battery in the event of power loss, but a faulty switch wrongly attributed a loss of power to an actual alarm.

"Got it," Mel said. He jumpered the switch and the alarm silenced. "Have to make a more permanent fix after we get a new switch, but it should shut this thing up for the night. Hope we have one in maintenance."

"I'll go look," Galway said. He peered at the switch, took a quick picture with his cell phone and headed for his pickup also parked in the loading zone.

Mel wandered over to the lobby, original to the century-old hotel. Gleaming hardwood floors, wicker furniture, a carousel horse in the center. Jack, in his usual business suit, stood at the check-in desk talking with the night manager.

Soothing ruffled feathers among the hotel guests. Not a fun job.

Mel gave Jack a thumbs-up but didn't approach the desk. Not wearing a uniform or a name tag, he didn't have to listen to complaints or officially represent the company tonight. He could hide out on the patio and hold his breath, hoping the alarm was finished for the night. When Galway texted, he'd meet him in the control room and fix the problem for good.

Guests milled through the doors, some of them in bathrobes and bare feet. The hotel lounge had also been evacuated with the fire alarms, and guests were strolling back in from the beach with glasses of wine and beer in their hands.

One of the guests was tall with long brown hair. She held a glass of wine and walked so closely with her friends they bumped hips and shoulders as they headed inside.

Who were those people with June Hamilton? He'd never seen them around Starlight Point. They didn't look like summer workers. Their clothing and hair was too…flashy and fancy—even the man in the group who had his arm around June.

Would June take her eyes off her friends long enough to see him as he stood by a pillar just off the lobby?

Laughing, June set her wineglass on a table for four and sat with her friends. The two women with June were blondes in two shades, very slender and pretty. The man was average height and rail-thin. His tight red jeans were rolled at the ankle and he wore loafers with no socks.

Mel glanced down at his faded Levi's and boots. Maybe he should go back to the control room and wait for Galway.

Just as he resolved to slink through the lobby and hide, June glanced up and saw him. She stopped midsentence and stared, wineglass in hand.

She crooked a finger and beckoned to him, inviting him to her table.

Bad idea.

He did it anyway. As he approached, he noticed June's friends turning to look at him. They probably wondered who or what June was staring at.

June stood. "Hi, Mel."

"Hello."

"I'm guessing you're here because of the fire alarm," she said.

"Almost fixed. Galway went to the shop for a part and then we'll get it done for good."

"Thanks." She gestured to the other people at the table. "These are my friends Cassie, Macy and Ian." She pointed them out individually as she said their names and Mel shook hands with each. "They're from New York

City. We became friends working together on Broadway."

"You're all dancers?" Mel asked.

They nodded.

"We're here to drag June back with us," the man, Ian, said. "She's burying her talent here."

Mel turned to June. "You're leaving?"

"Of course not," she said quickly. "I'm staying all summer. Just like I said."

It sounded like she was protesting a little too much. Maybe he was just afraid to follow this train of thought. Letting himself get close to June the past few weeks, he'd told himself he still had two months before she left.

Not if she changed her mind and left early. There was, technically, nothing stopping her.

"Now that your knee is better," the blonde to June's right said, "there'll be nothing stopping you from getting a great part."

June's face flushed even brighter, uneven spots coloring it, and she gave her friend a look that said *shut up.*

She had a knee injury? She'd never mentioned that. The other two people at the table looked surprised, too. What else had June not shared with him? His mind flashed to that painfully thin dancer they'd driven to the hospital. What kind of world was Broadway?

A world where he obviously didn't belong.

"Have a drink with us," one of the blondes offered. *Is she Cassie or Macy?* Didn't matter. He wasn't going to get to know them. Especially after they bundled June off to Broadway and never looked back.

"No, thanks," he said. "I have to get back to work."

"You work here?" the other blonde asked.

Cassie or Macy must not have followed the earlier part of the conversation.

Mel nodded. "Head of maintenance at Starlight Point."

"The whole thing?"

"Yes."

"So that's how you know June," Ian said.

Like he needed to explain to these strangers that he'd actually known June since he was seven. But how much water would that hold when compared to Broadway and the fancy life this trio seemed to represent?

Mel crossed his arms and tried to paste a friendly expression on his face. "How long are you staying in the area?"

"We're staying in this hotel right here two

nights," the other blonde said. "And then we have to get back to our show."

"I'll try to make sure the fire alarm doesn't disturb you anymore tonight," Mel said. Even though he wasn't sure he meant it. "Enjoy your visit. Good night."

He turned to walk away.

"Mel," June said behind his back. "Are you headed home in a little while?"

"I hope so. Hour or so."

"Would you drop me off at home on your way?"

He should say yes. She was a friend. More than a friend. And he wanted her to get home safely. But he didn't have space for drama in his life right now. Did he want to fight the appeal of her friends and her dream from the big city?

Not tonight. He had a job to do and a son waiting at home.

"I saw your brother in the lobby," he said. "He'll be going your way in a while. I'll tell him to find you before he leaves."

June set down her glass and drew her eyebrows together. She looked like a little girl who wasn't having a good time at her own birthday party.

Whatever was going on with June and her friends, Mel reminded himself it was really none of his business, no matter how much he wanted to pull the fire alarm and run away with June while no one was looking.

CHAPTER SIXTEEN

THE FOURTH OF JULY was an explosion waiting
to happen. Weather forecast calling for scorch-
ing heat and humidity, presale tickets off the
charts and a June flame under his collar had
made Mel stand in a tepid shower a long time
before putting on his uniform. As the head of
maintenance, he could give himself the holiday
off, but he never did. Anything could happen
with that many people, that degree of heat and
that drain on the park's power systems.

Last year's fireworks show had been re-
duced, saving money but not making much
of a dent in the celebration. Mel had carefully
avoided taking sides with the Hamiltons over
this year's expenditure. Jack wanted to go big
with the fireworks and spend the same kind
of money Ford Hamilton used to. Evie wanted
to be conservative, as always. He had no idea
what June wanted, if she even had a say.

The Starlight Point fireworks show was a

huge draw and a local tradition, with people already staking out their chunk of shoreline over at Bayside Park for a great view across the bay. But a few extra mortars and minutes didn't mean life or death to Mel. Decisions like that reminded him he was glad he wasn't in charge.

From a practical perspective, he could see why June didn't want to be tethered to Starlight Point.

But he couldn't imagine how she could leave.

Or what he was going to do when she did.

With an hour to go before the park opened to the flood of July Fourth guests, heat saturated the midway and sent trickles of sweat down Mel's back.

In front of the Star Spiral, in a relatively open and quiet part of Starlight Point, June had dreamed up a Fourth of July live show. Summer crew mixed with year-round carpenters had built the stage in sections, waiting until this morning to haul it over and set it up. Throughout the day, June would oversee its decoration while Mel's electricians set up lights and ran wire for sound. It was an insane plan for an insane day, but Mel had to admit it would be a firecracker of a show.

The fireworks would be set off right behind the stage, on the beach. He had no doubt the singing and dancing would draw a crowd, and who could argue with fireworks for a grand finale?

"Busy day," Jack commented as he leaned against a light post near the temporary stage.

"Lots of presale, I hear."

"Thirty thousand. And I'd guess that's about half of today's total."

"Hot weather."

"But dry. No rain, no storms. Wall-to-wall people and sun."

Mel flipped some switches on the temporary breaker box he'd set up on the stage. He shielded his eyes from the morning sun, straining to see which lights came on. Satisfied, he switched them all off and sat on the edge of the stage.

"We'll be ready," he said.

Jack sat next to him, drinking coffee out of a white paper cup.

"Too hot for that stuff," Mel said, leaning back on his elbows and crossing his long legs at the ankles.

"Yep, but Gus made it for me, so I couldn't turn it down."

"Newlywed," Mel said, chuckling. "As I recall, July Fourth is some kind of anniversary for you two."

"Rumor has it."

The rumors had flown like fireworks last year when Jack and Gus finally surrendered to the sparks between them. His invitation to a fireworks viewing on the Star Spiral had spawned plenty of jokes about their long private ride.

Jack polished off his coffee and crumpled the cup. "You got any special plans for the fireworks tonight? Bringing Ross?"

Mel shook his head. "Too much chaos here. I'm taking a few hours off this afternoon. Bringing Ross to a picnic at my parents' house. They'll take him downtown Bayside to watch the fireworks tonight."

"Better view from there anyway," Jack commented.

"And it keeps him out of the crowds and traffic. I'll come back and be on duty tonight. With the heat and thousands of people, you never know what could happen."

"Party in the lot afterward?"

"Why not? Ross is staying the night with my folks, so I have no reason to rush home."

Jack leaned back on his elbows, mirroring Mel's relaxed posture and crossing a long set of legs—just a little longer than Mel's.

"Notice how I have carefully avoided grilling you about my sister."

"Uh-huh."

They exchanged a quick uncomfortable glance.

"Not sure how things are between you, and I'm not going to ask," Jack said.

"Appreciate that. I'm not sure what I'd tell you, if I was going to say anything about it."

"Glad her friends from the big city didn't stay long," Jack commented. "I gather they were disappointed when she refused to go back with them."

Mel shrugged. "June can make up her own mind about her future." Mel watched one of the food vendors shoving a big cart with a bad wheel and made a mental note to have someone fix it later. He turned to Jack. "Did June hurt her knee a while back?"

Mel knew his best friend well enough to know the look of surprise was genuine. "Not that I know of," Jack said. "Why?"

Mel shrugged. "I must have misunderstood something."

It was strangely reassuring that June's own brother didn't know about it, either. Trusting June with his heart—even a tiny bit of it—was the most dangerous thing Mel had done in a long time. He knew he was playing with fire.

They were both silent a minute, watching dozens of summer employees scattering around the midway, preparing to take up their posts for a busy day. Mel wondered where Jack stood on the whole issue of June's leaving. Had he and Evie asked her to stay? What kind of partner could she be from hundreds of miles away? All the Hamiltons were tight, Mel being the only outsider who'd ever been roped into the family circle. But there were still things he wasn't going to ask.

"Glad we talked about it." Jack stood up, towering briefly over his longtime friend. "If you need to know anything, I'd recommend asking Evie. That's where I get all my information."

Jack walked away and Mel turned his attention back to the electrical panel.

Today's heat would tax air conditioners all day long. Mel had the prickling fear that some of the older transformers wouldn't be able to handle the load. Even if only one of them blew, it would cause a massive diversion to the others and they could fall like dominoes.

"Maybe this wasn't such a great idea," he muttered, eyeing the huge lights and speakers on the stage.

"Why not?" June asked, surprising him by ducking out a hidden entrance on the side of the stage.

"Too much to handle," he said, smiling at June.

"Too much electricity?" she asked, laying a hand on his shoulder and standing much too close.

"Uh-huh."

"And heat?" she asked.

"Way too much."

"My show will be totally worth it."

"I'm sure," he said. "Are you sad your friends didn't stick around a few more days to see it?"

June's face clouded and Mel wanted to kick himself for taking a piece of sandpaper to a raw nerve. Why had he brought them up?

June removed her hand from his arm and took two steps backward.

"The friends I care most about are going to see it," she said.

Mel swallowed. *What did that mean?*

THE SHOW WAS a success. June knew it from the first number, and the energy kept the crowd totally jazzed until the end. It was hers. Totally hers. There had been years of summer theater at Starlight Point, but this was different.

The fireworks scheduled to go off in only five minutes would be icing on the cake. June hated to see the show end. The red, white and blue sparkly costumes with a little gold and purple thrown in were pure magic from Gloria and crew. The live musicians drawn from the best of the shows played like they owned the place. And they did. Until the dancers came on stage and stole the show.

It wasn't just June's opinion. The crowd gathered in front of the stage had plenty of opportunity to leave and take advantage of a hundred other diversions. They weren't in seats in a darkened theater where leaving would be rude and obvious. They stood under the stars on a hot night on concrete that still clung to that heat. And from their faces and enthusiastic applause—they loved it.

"No way to top this," Megan said. "Glad I had a three-hour nap this afternoon or I wouldn't have survived even watching that show."

June smiled sympathetically at her stage manager. "I can't imagine being eight months pregnant and on my feet."

"I'm actually fifteen months pregnant. I just wear it well," Megan said.

"Are you staying for the fireworks? They'll start any minute."

"Nope. My husband is waiting just outside the employee entrance with the car. If we figure it right, we'll be pulling in our driveway just as everyone else is lining up for the traffic jam on the bridge."

"You'll be missing a great show."

"I've already seen one tonight. And I can't stand much more excitement. I'll watch the fireworks next year. There's always next year."

Megan slung a small bag over her shoulder and waddled toward the employee gate tucked behind the Scrambler. June watched her go, wondering where she would be next year and if Megan was right. Was there always next year?

"That's a pretty serious expression for a

woman who just pulled off the show of the century."

Mel's familiar scent—Dial soap mixed with a little bit of sweat and motor oil—tingled her senses even with a hundred other distractions. Of course he was hard to ignore. He was standing so close their clothing touched.

"I was just worried about Megan. Hope she gets home okay."

"Her husband is right outside the gate. I saw him a few minutes ago. Windows rolled up in his car, air conditioner on blizzard mode."

"True love."

"My work truck has air-conditioning and it's parked at the gate," Mel said. "We could go sit in it and watch the fireworks through the windshield."

June trembled despite the heat. Even though she'd just pulled off a show worthy of Broadway, Mel made her forget everything outside of the here and now.

"I'd go to blizzard mode for you," Mel said. "Even though the condenser doesn't really work unless you get the RPMs up on the motor. We could still try."

"I have no idea what you're talking about."

"Shoot. Thought I had you at 'blizzard.'"

"Absolutely. But the fireworks should start in about thirty seconds. Especially if Evie is in charge of the timing."

"Evie has a license to fire off pyrotechnics?" Mel asked.

June laughed. "Nothing about my sister would surprise me. I'm starting to think she won't be happy being an accountant forever. Like there's more out there for her."

And me.

The first of the shells exploded into the dark sky over the lake, raining red, white and blue streams of light in a huge arc. June leaned back against Mel, and the cooling night air combined with his body heat in a perfect combination—like sugar mixed with cinnamon on toast. Sweet, a little spicy, delicious.

Snappy white sizzlers followed the initial graceful arcs of color and light. Unlike the waterfalls of color, the screamers plunged toward the lake like they were on a noisy mission. People clapped and yelled, the intoxicating noise taking them along for the ride.

"You like those?" Mel asked, close to her ear.

June shook her head slightly, not wanting to move from her position folded into Mel's body. "Nope. Too loud and they're over too soon. I like the ones that fall forever until they disappear."

"I like the blue ones," Mel said. "Just-before-twilight blue. Like this outfit you're wearing."

"How can you tell in the dark?"

"Saw you in it earlier. Memorized the way you look."

June wondered if anyone had ever memorized anything about her before. It was one of the most wonderful things she had ever heard.

"What else do you have memorized?"

"Wiring schematics for most of the park. How many steps to the top of the Sea Devil. Dates we changed the oil on the old-fashioned cars. And everything I know about you."

"I hope you don't have that on a chart in your office."

"Don't need to," Mel said.

A volley of shells streaked up, exploded into huge weeping willow shapes that took ages to fall sparkling through the sky. June counted to ten before the last of the colored sparks disappeared. In less than two months she would be far away from the scent of the lake, the sounds of the Point, the touch of Mel.

She'd be closer to her dream, but far from here.

Red fireworks shot into the sky followed by an army of white screamers.

Where would she be next Fourth of July? Summer hiatus from a Broadway show? Home for a long weekend? Watching fireworks with someone else?

June never wanted to see fireworks again unless they came with a pair of warm arms smelling like the maintenance garage—the heart and soul—of Starlight Point. But she'd made her choice.

"Ready for the grand finale?" Mel said, his lips brushing her ear. "Want me to make hand-muffs over your ears? I have to do that for Ross at fireworks and loud movies."

"I'll tough it out," June said.

"Good," he said, releasing her and putting his hands over his ears. "I get my own earmuffs for once."

June laughed, leaning against Mel and watching the furious explosions of the grand finale. She could get used to this. In fact, she already was.

She turned into Mel's body and pulled his hands from his ears. "It's over."

"Far from it. The traffic is a better show than the fireworks. Especially with a sunburned, dehydrated crowd like this. There's an hour's worth of horn honking and hot tempers out there."

To prove his point, the mass of people around them began to move in a messy human wave toward the front gates.

"Want to escape out a back entrance and walk on the beach while everyone else races to their cars?" Mel asked.

"Very tempting, but I promised Evie and Jack I'd meet them at the front. Mostly out of curiosity. We think today might be a park record. Curious to tally up the gate receipts and see what we've got."

"Can I tag along or is it a Hamilton family secret?"

"Like we have any secrets from you." June caught his hand. "Come on. We'll slip through the games warehouse and then go to the parking-lot party after that."

Despite the dark, Mel's wide grin lit up June's night like stars, coaster lights and sparklers. He followed June to the small glass-walled office of the front gate ticket manager. Usually called "the bank," the area was the front line for guests and ticket sales. It was also guarded by at least one Starlight Point police officer during operating hours and until the last guest exited the turnstiles. June joined her siblings near the corner desk, but Mel stood just outside the door talking to the guard.

"Forty-seven thousand five hundred," Jack said. "An official record."

"By just a little," Evie said.

"Still counts. We can take that to our bankers. One more sign Starlight Point is on the right track."

Evie scrolled through the calendar on her phone. "We meet with them next week. They'll want to know what the reasons are for our success and if it's sustainable."

Jack sat at the desk and propped his feet on it, watching people stream out the gates. "Right now I'm just glad today's over. We can do math tomorrow after a good night's sleep and a half dozen doughnuts."

"What do you think, June?" Evie asked. "What accounts for the extra sales this year?"

"Weather and fireworks."

"How about live shows?"

"Hate to grab too much credit," June said, "but my show was a real crowd-pleaser."

"I saw it," Jack added, closing his eyes and rubbing them. "From a distance mostly, but even I could tell how good it was. Very good. But I don't think it sold tickets."

"Maybe not, but it kept people here longer," Evie said.

"Fireworks did that," Jack said. "Just like every year."

"Hey," June said, slugging Jack in the gut while his eyes were closed. "You're hurting my feelings."

"Sorry," he said, doubling up and clutching his midsection. "Just trying to think like a banker and not a big brother."

"I like you better as a big brother."

"When did you start thinking like a banker?" Evie asked. "You've been hiding that talent. I had no idea you had any business sense."

Mel finished his conversation with the police officer, came through the glass door and sat on the edge of the desk.

"Good," Jack said. "I need backup. My sisters are picking on me."

"Can't help you there. I'm afraid of one of them," Mel said. "Not saying which one."

The police officer jerked open the glass door and leaned in.

"Fire. Games area by the temporary stage," he said quickly, radio in hand.

"We were just there," Mel said, instantly on his feet.

"Report of explosion, lots of smoke," the officer continued, holding the door as Jack and Mel raced through it with Evie and June right behind them.

"Transformer blew, I bet," Mel said, running alongside Jack, long legs flashing.

They passed several food stands, swimming upstream against a fleeing record crowd. Negotiating a sharp turn just before the Kiddieland motorcycles, they encountered smoke and confusion.

The four of them ground to a stop, struggling to see the source of the fire through the smoke. Security guards all around them forced onlookers back.

"Transformer right behind the big sign for the games strip," Mel said, his breath coming hard and fast. "Bet it went up, that's the explosion people heard. Sparks hit those awnings, set 'em on fire."

Whining sirens approached. June pictured the firefighters on duty back by the maintenance garage making the quick decision to drive on the rapidly emptying midway instead of taking the narrow road outside the gate along the beach. She hoped they'd hurry.

The entire strip of games—Skee-Ball, ringtoss, steeplechase—was alive with flickering lights illuminating the hanging prizes. Teddy bears, dragons, crazy hats, inflatable toys and plastic Starlight Point drinking cups swung from their hooks, ready to entice people out of their money, one or two dollars at a time. The games strip curved around and connected with a string of souvenir shops which then attached to the front gate area. A fire in any of the buildings threatened all of them.

June stood, paralyzed with fear. She flashed back to her six-year-old self tossing balls at bowling pins to win a stuffed dog, her father smiling as she knocked a whole array of pins off a table taller than she was.

The agony constricting her heart was a grim reminder of how dangerous it was to let herself fall in love with Starlight Point. It had such a powerful hold over her that she had only two choices: surrender or run.

This was not what she intended when she came home for the summer.

It was agony.

And there was only one thing that could make it worse.

"Got to hit the main breaker in there, shut it down, or we'll never get the fire out," Mel said. "I'm going in."

"I'll go with you," Jack said.

"No, you won't," a voice behind June and Evie said. June turned, wondering who was arguing with her brother and Mel.

A firefighter in full turnout gear looked absolutely huge in the flashing lights from the fire truck he'd just stepped out of.

"You—" he pointed at Jack "—stay out here and take charge of the scene. You—" he continued, pointing at Mel "—put on a helmet and help me shut this thing down."

Mel grabbed a helmet from the other firefighter who was busy pulling hoses off the truck. He jammed it on his head and headed straight for the building with only half its lights flashing now.

"Wait," June said. She grabbed Mel's arm. "It's too dangerous. I don't want you to go in there. You could be hurt or killed. It's not worth it," she pleaded.

"It'll be okay," the firefighter interrupted. "Flames mostly on the south side, and we're going just inside the north where the panel is. I'd do it myself, but I could use an expert."

Mel gave June a long, searching glance and then went into the chaos.

June crossed her arms over her chest, trying to stop shaking. Jack draped his arms over both his sisters.

"Trucks from Bayside will never get here with the traffic mess. Hope those two can knock out the power so we can put this out," Jack said.

"They shouldn't be in there," June said, her voice quivering.

"I think they know what they're doing," Evie said. "Ten seconds. Just count to ten and they'll have it shut down and be back out here."

"You love numbers too much," June complained.

But it was good advice. June started with ten and counted slowly backward. When she got to three, the whole building went dark. Only a faint orange glow came from the south side. She strained to see Mel and the firefighter come out. *Where were they?*

"Grab a hose," the firefighter on the truck yelled to Jack. "Power's out, so it's safe to hit it with some water."

The firefighter trained a searchlight on the building, and finally Mel and the other firefighter walked out together, shielding their eyes from the bright light.

June ran to Mel and crushed him against her, only letting go to kiss him. Mel circled her with his arms and returned her kiss with equal passion. Until he suddenly stepped back and coughed into his shirt sleeve.

"Sorry," he said, his voice raw. "It was smoky in there."

"Are you all right?"

He nodded. "Fine. Just need some water."

"I'll get you some," she said, pulling back to run and find him a drink.

"Wait." Mel pulled her close. "One more kiss. I've waited seven years for that, and I don't want to let you go now."

CHAPTER SEVENTEEN

"I DIDN'T THINK the *Roller Coaster Times* would do a story on us this year," Evie said. "Since we don't have any new rides."

"They loved the shows," June said. "And they called my parade a 'glittering new addition.'" The approbation meant more to her than she thought it would. After all, it wasn't a Broadway review magazine or a *New Yorker* article. It was just a magazine devoted to theme parks that happened to send a reporter who happened to see both her shows and appreciate them.

The article would run in the magazine's August edition, but the reporter had sent a preview of the story and a link to the magazine's website which ran a teaser.

Evie stood over June's shoulder and read the screen on her sister's smartphone. "Fresh and professional," she said. "Those are nice things to say about the theaters. True, too. Plus they mentioned you. Look at that. The article says Starlight Point is lucky to have a co-owner with real Broadway experience."

June felt another rush of pride. *And they didn't say she was formerly on Broadway.*

"I'm going to have to start being nicer to you," Evie said.

"Thanks."

"They gushed about the steampunk show, which I admit I was afraid was too much for our usual audience. According to them, it evokes passion and emotion," Evie continued. "Wow."

"That's what I was going for when I came home this summer. Passion and emotion."

"Just to be clear, we're still talking about the theaters, right?"

June pocketed her phone. "Of course."

"Because I saw that kiss last night," Evie said.

June felt her cheeks burning. "It was the heat of the moment."

"Sure," Evie said. "It was a tense night. A holiday and a major fire causing thousands of dollars of damage. I kissed at least three firefighters and one security guard."

"Very funny. Maybe you should have a fling. Then you'd stay out of my business."

"As your favorite sister," Evie said, "I think you should talk to me about Mel."

June sat on a bench by the midway fountain and watched summer maintenance and security staff set out poles and ropes to cordon off a large area where last night's fire had occurred. The state fire inspector was due any moment, and June and Evie were waiting for their brother while he scammed coffee and doughnuts from his wife's bakery. They knew from experience Augusta would send enough for all of them. Last summer there were some tough times with the food vendors, but Augusta's leadership had helped solve it. Marrying Jack in a Christmas ceremony had forged a permanent peace accord.

"I'm sure it'll officially be ruled an accident," June said, viewing the scene of melted plastic overhangs and half-burned game prizes. The poor stuffed monkeys and gorillas. They were missing parts, still soaked from fire hoses, or charred.

"You'd officially rule kissing your old boyfriend an accident?"

"You know what I mean."

"Not really. I never ditched my summer boyfriend to dance on Broadway and then came back seven years later and worked him over again."

June swiveled to face Evie. "I'm not working him over. I've been totally honest about my plans."

"Just like last time," Evie said. "But I think he never really believed you'd leave all those summers ago."

"I imagine he's learned from his mistake. Besides, he got over me then. He has a son to prove that. He'll survive me leaving again."

"I never understood why he married that girl," Evie said.

June cleared her throat. "I believe she was pregnant. See? He'd obviously moved on."

"After a year went by."

"You could look up some insurance reports or metrics or something. It might take your mind off my relationship with Mel," June said.

Despite her cavalier tone, June felt like her sister was stabbing pins in every tender place in her body. Everything was practical to Evie. Accounts, ledgers, numbers. She couldn't possibly understand how complicated things were with Mel.

Evie crossed her arms and stood over June. "You think I don't get it, but I see what's going on. You want Mel, again, but not enough to give up dancing on Broadway."

June blew out a breath and stretched her legs. "It sounds awful when you put it that way. Romance is a total flop when you try to look at it practically."

Evie gave her sister a long look. "This reminds me of last summer. You were off tap dancing while I had to watch Jack fall in love with Augusta long before he was willing to admit it." She sighed. "It was a real pain."

"I'm not in love with Mel."

She wasn't. *Was she?* No. This feeling was… complicated. She loved her family. And dancing. And carousel music. It was perfectly fine to love things. It was not the same as being in love with them.

"Well, good," Evie said. "That's much simpler. So what are you planning to do?"

"I said I was staying until September, and I'm sticking to it. My friends wanted me to go back early and join the *Carousel* cast. It's a great opportunity, but I turned it down so I could fulfill my commitment to the family circus."

"Don't act like a martyr," Evie said. She flopped onto the bench next to her sister and put an arm around her shoulders. "You're too shiny for that role."

June closed her eyes and soaked in the sunshine. Despite the smoky and musty smell emanating from the games area, it was a beautiful morning.

"My agent called while I was in the shower."

"I know you're dedicated to your career, but you don't take your phone into the bathroom, do you? I think it voids the warranty."

June laughed. "No. He left a voice mail."

"Good news?"

She nodded. "The show I'm hoping for, *White Christmas*, has auditions in a few weeks. He got me a good audition slot."

"There are good and bad ones?" Evie asked.

"This slot is for one of the major roles. Not just a chorus dancer. Have you ever seen *White Christmas*?"

Evie nodded. "I've seen the movie about a hundred times. Mom loves it. She always cries at the end when they sing the song."

"Me, too. The stage show is similar. The role I'm hoping for is Judy, the sister of the main character. Since I can sing and dance, my agent thinks I have a shot."

"That sounds like a major opportunity," Evie said.

"It is. It's what I always wanted, where I always hoped I'd end up."

"So," Evie said. "Why don't you sound thrilled about it?"

June turned and studied her sister. Evie was only twenty-two. Smart and beautiful, she had a world of opportunities. But she was here. "What would you do if there were two things you wanted but you couldn't have both of them?" June asked.

Evie pulled her glasses and a slim laptop out of her bag. She perched the green-rimmed glasses on her nose and opened the computer. "I try to only want one thing at a time," she said. "Right now I want to know where our brother is with my coffee."

JUNE HEADED TO the hotel day care after it became clear the state fire inspector wanted to walk through the damage with only one person to minimize the risk. Lucky Jack. As the CEO of Starlight Point, he got the honors. June and Evie didn't mind missing out on burned plastic, charred stuffed animals and soggy everything on an otherwise perfect July morning. Evie had already pulled up their insurance policy and declared they should be all right. The fire was clearly an accident and unavoidable. That part of the park would be off-limits for at least a month, even with crews working throughout the night. But they would survive.

Instead of touring charred wreckage, June would spend the hour before the front gates opened at the day care, which would already be lively with kids. And kids are morning people.

June loved dancing, even if it was just in front of her bedroom mirror. Being on the Broadway stage as part of a group or even featured in a coveted solo spot had filled the corners of her heart for years. This summer, her heart was getting crowded. The theaters at Starlight Point, her family, her coworkers, Mel…especially Mel. And Ross. There was standing room only in her heart right now, and spending time at the day care only made it worse.

The kids were delightful. They danced with happy abandon, not caring who was looking. Never comparing themselves to others.

No negative body images, no competition. It couldn't have been more different from the Broadway stage.

Everything about this summer, including the strength in her knee, was healthy—her whole environment was healthier than it'd been in a long time.

"Miss June's here," Mrs. Nelson, the teacher at the day care, announced. "Put on your dancing shoes."

June smiled. "We could go barefoot if you want. No rules in dancing. Although cowboy boots would probably be best for today's lesson."

"Are we cowboy dancing?" one of the girls asked.

"Square dancing," June said. "Partner up while we clear a big space."

"I wish we could use one of the empty rooms on this floor," the teacher said.

The hotel day care was housed in a closed wing of the hotel. The historic building was due for a major renovation, but because the money for such an extensive project was a shimmer in the distant future, they had opted last year to close the oldest wing most in need of renovation. It wasn't up to snuff for hotel guests, but the rooms and restrooms were functional. With fresh paint and carpet in four of the rooms, it made a nice day care for infants up to ten-year-olds.

However, each of the rooms was full. Cribs, toy boxes, or tables and chairs. Coatracks, puzzles, a plastic slide. The space was cluttered with the trappings of kids.

"I don't have a key to the other rooms," the teacher said. "And I hate to bother the front-desk staff. I know they're probably busy with holiday guests checking out."

"I don't, either," June said. "I didn't want to haul around eighty-five million keys, so I only have the ones I typically use."

"My dad has a key to everything," Ross volunteered. "We could call him."

Mrs. Nelson looked to June, eyebrows raised in a silent question.

June shrugged. "It's a good idea, but only if he happens to be close by." She pulled a cell phone from her pocket and dialed.

"Do you want me to ask him?" Ross said.

June smiled. "I'll do it. That way if we're interrupting him, he'll be mad at me and not you."

Mel answered on the second ring.

"World's greatest kisser," he announced instead of saying hello.

June covered the phone and stepped into the hallway. "I'm at the day care, and I'm pretty sure fifteen children just heard you say that."

"Well, I'm glad I didn't say world's worst kisser, then. I have some pride," Mel said. His tone shifted to serious. "What's up at the day care?"

"Dancing lesson. But we're out of room. Do you have a master key that'll unlock the empty rooms down the hall?"

June heard Mel's hesitation. "They're probably damp and smelly. Maybe even mold. They've been closed for over a year."

"We could check. If you have a minute to run over here."

"I'm on my way up front to meet with Jack and the fire inspector. I guess the guy wants me to do a report, come up with inspection records, wiring schematics, stuff like that."

"Thank you. That'll help our cause considerably."

"It should be okay. I'm just getting in my truck. I can stop by the hotel on my way up front. But if those rooms are black-mold city, I'm nailing the doors shut."

True to his word, Mel arrived five minutes later jangling a huge ring of keys.

Ross hugged his legs and followed him down the hall with June right behind them. "Don't get your hopes up, these closed rooms might be pretty gross."

"This is cool," Ross said. "I wondered what was down this hall."

Mel started with the first room beyond the day care and shoved his key into the lock. He opened the door just enough to peek in. Musty air stole out through the crack.

"Are you sure about this?" he asked June.

"We're square-dancing. We need a big space."

"Wait here," he said and went in. June and Ross stood in the doorway. She kept her arm around his shoulders in case he was tempted to stray in before his dad gave the thumbs-up.

From her position at the door, the ancient room looked like she remembered it from her childhood. Dark blue carpet, beige walls, popcorn ceiling. The carpeting had seen better days, but the sun shone brightly through bare windows. All furniture and curtains had been removed, and the room seemed to be waiting for its chance to shine again. Maybe she should talk to Evie and Jack about doing the hotel renovation sooner rather than later.

"It's not bad," Mel declared. "Safe to come in."

June and Ross entered, and Ross ran around the perimeter as if it were a baseball field and he was running the bases.

"Kids love empty rooms," Mel said. "One time I moved everything out of Ross's bedroom so I could repaint it, and he didn't want me to put things back in. Must be the novelty of it."

"Life gets too crowded," June said.

Boy, is that true.

"I'll open the window for some fresh air, and then I don't see why you can't use this for your do-si-do-ing," Mel commented. "Just remember the water is shut off to these rooms, so the bathroom is off-limits."

"Got it," June said.

"Ross," Mel said, catching his son's collar on his third time around the room. "Why don't you go down the hall and tell everyone to use the bathroom if they have to before they come on down for their dancing lesson with Miss June."

Ross darted out of the room.

"We have thirty seconds," Mel said. He pulled June close and kissed her until they heard voices and footsteps approaching. She remembered him being a good kisser, but time had improved Mel in more ways than one. When he kissed her now, it was deeper, more meaningful. Less experiment, more experience. "It's even better when I don't have to wait seven years," he said, his voice deep and husky.

June loved the children who were fast approaching, but if they'd taken several minutes to get there, she wouldn't have complained. Being in Mel's arms, his lips on hers, his scent still fresh from the shower but with a touch of maintenance garage, made her wish dancing could wait. Just for a while.

He pressed one more quick kiss to her lips and released her just before the first child burst into the room. A dozen kids ran around the perimeter just as Ross had done.

"I don't get it," June said.

"I told you. Kids love big empty spaces. Soccer fields, empty swimming pools, unfinished basements. They all have the same magic. Maybe adults should learn to be so easily satisfied."

"Big empty stages," June said, suddenly realizing she *did* understand. "I love it when there are no props or sets, just dancers. I like the empty theaters, too, before everyone gets there."

"But you also love the crowds," Mel said.

She nodded. "Of course. If it weren't for all those people buying a ticket, I'd be out of a job."

"We better get them started before they burn off all their energy," Mrs. Nelson said.

"Not much chance of that," Mel replied. "I swear Ross is like a battery-operated toy sometimes. Just keeps going."

June smiled at Mel and turned to the room. "Dancers!" she yelled. "Find a partner and line up."

Mel leaned against the wall in the musty hotel room. June felt him watching her every move.

"Ross," she said, motioning for him to join her. "Will you take your dad back to the other room and show him where I keep the CD player? Have him unplug it so you can bring it back here. Okay?"

Ross, happy to have an important responsibility, grabbed his dad's hand. "Come on, Dad, we have to get the music."

They were only gone two minutes, but June missed them. When Mel had nodded a good-bye while she was putting the dancers through a grand right and left, a devastating realization washed over her.

She was going to miss all of this when the Starlight Point season ended and her time under the Broadway lights began. *If only she could have them both.*

CHAPTER EIGHTEEN

STORM CLOUDS GATHERED and dispersed before
the afternoon parade, defying the prediction
of thunderstorms. But it was only temporary.
The heavy dark clouds moved back in with
surprising speed as soon as the parade ended.
With a Saturday crowd spilling out of every
queue line, souvenir shop, restaurant and show,
Starlight Point was no place for a thunderstorm. Its position on a peninsula thrust into
the lake made it especially vulnerable to wind
and lightning. Growing up, June had once seen
a waterspout, a tornado over the lake spinning
viciously. It had dissipated before touching the
Lake Breeze Hotel, but she'd never forgotten
it and its remembrance fueled her healthy respect for summer storms.

It was the middle of July, and they'd been
lucky so far. Good weather had brought record crowds. But June knew from experience
they were overdue for a major summer storm.

The kind that would rearrange the sand on the beach, close the rides and wash over the docks in the marina. Depending on the time of day, major storms caused traffic jams on the Point Bridge as a mass of vehicles tried to escape the peninsula. Because it was only midafternoon and guests would likely want to salvage their ticket price, June expected them to wait out the storm indoors in restaurants, shows and the hotel lobby.

The air held the tension of coming rain, but it had been like that off and on all day, and the thirty-minute parade rolled out as scheduled. She'd already texted Mel and offered to return Ross to the hotel day care after the parade. June grabbed a scooter so she could get Ross settled and drive Megan straight to her car instead of making her walk on swollen feet in bad weather. Ross climbed in the open back and sat on the floor as instructed. Keeping a close eye on the weather, June drummed her fingers on the wheel and waited for Megan to finish talking to one of the dancers from the Western show.

The hotel wasn't far, just a quarter mile down the outer loop, across an access road and a parking lot punctuated by rows of young trees and a few huge old cottonwoods no one had the heart to cut down. Not a lengthy trip by scooter or car, but it was a long way in wind and lightning.

The breeze off the lake shifted again, swaying the trees and casting shadows with the clouds and branches. June shivered in the sudden shade. And she felt an awareness of another kind, signaled by a pickup truck sliding up next to her scooter. She was not at all surprised to see Mel only five minutes after her text reached him.

He got out of his truck and jogged over to the scooter.

"Hi," he said, running his fingers down her bare arm. June's pulse responded, electricity sizzling in the air. Mel was thrilling, confusing, questioning—a present she'd finally opened that would never go back in the box, even if she wanted to put it there.

"Your son is in the back," June said.

"Hey, Ross."

Ross smiled. "Hi, Dad."

Thunder rumbled across the lake and Mel turned his head, listening.

"The storm's coming for real this time," June said.

"I'm hoping it goes out over the lake," Mel answered, watching the wind whip the trees along the road, "but I think it's coming our way."

June's phone beeped and she dug it out of the small shoulder bag on the seat next to her.

"Weather alert," she said, scrolling with her finger. "Severe storms, damaging wind, possible hail." She held up the small screen so Mel could see the radar. He cleared his throat and looked again at the darkening sky over the lake.

"Better batten down the hatches," he said.

Lightning crackled and a raindrop splashed on the dashboard of the open scooter. Megan waddled over and hoisted herself onto the seat next to June.

"The sky's ugly. I don't like it," Mel said. "You take my truck. I'll take the scooter."

Raindrops—huge ones—bounced off Mel's head as he leaned over June.

"You'll get soaked."

"Don't care. Get in the truck, Ross," Mel said, raising his voice over the noise of the wind. "You, too," he added, nodding to June and Megan.

June swung her legs out of the scooter and

climbed into Mel's truck. The keys were already in the ignition. Mel shut the door, but the window was rolled down.

"This is your personal truck," June said. "Where's your work truck?"

"Dead battery. No big deal. You better go."

He ducked out but was back a second later, shoving her purse through the window before she could roll it up against the wind and the steadily increasing rain.

From inside the truck, June watched Mel race down the access road in the open scooter, shoulders hunched against the pounding rain. He disappeared around a curve in the road, heading for the maintenance garage. She felt guilty taking his truck, but as far as she knew, Mel had been thinking of Megan and his son as much as her when he shoved her into the dry truck.

When he did gentlemanly things like this, it made her never want to leave him. The men on Broadway, her friends in the dancing troupe, didn't even hold open doors. It was a dog-eat-dog world. June sighed, putting the truck in gear.

THE CELL PHONE deep in his pants pocket rang mercilessly, but Mel ignored it. One thing at

a time. In the fifteen minutes since he'd sacrificed his dry pickup truck, he'd reset electric
breakers at three locations in the Wonderful West and gotten so wet his socks were
sponges.

"You look like a drowned cat," Jack said.

"And you look just as pretty as the day I met
you," Mel grumbled.

Jack, his suit coat gone and white dress shirt
soaked and sticking transparently to his skin,
slugged Mel. He leaned out the open garage
door, getting rain in his face and eyeing the
dark greenish-gray sky.

"Think we ought to shut down? Use our
emergency weather plan?" he asked.

Mel shrugged and pulled out his phone.
"June had an app for weather on her phone.
I swear I used to have that, but this is a new-
ish phone. Forgot to have Ross update all my
stuff on it. Kids," he added.

"I'll call Evie. She's up front in the office,"
Jack said.

Mel nodded. "Maybe it's sunny up there and
we're crying over nothing."

A loud crackling across the sky interrupted
him and he and Jack both took a step backward into the garage.

"Crap," Jack said, pushing a button on his smartphone.

The speakers mounted in the ceiling hissed. They were tied into the Starlight Point Police Department's radio traffic, occasionally alerting the maintenance department to a hazard or situation requiring tools. Maintenance guys were used to listening with half an ear, usually only being called into service when guests returned to dead batteries or lock-outs in the parking lot. On a day like today, anything could come over the radio and it would be all hands on deck.

"Tree down in hotel lot, possibly on a vehicle," the dispatcher intoned. "Possible wires down. Fire service, you copy?"

Mel swore. "Tell me you have a car of some kind back here."

"Bicycle," Jack said.

"You're an idiot."

"Where's your truck?"

"Gave it to June," Mel said.

"Who's the idiot now?"

"Still you."

Mel grabbed a chain saw from an equipment locker and hoisted a bag over his shoulder while Jack talked to Evie on his cell phone.

He stowed the gear in the back of an open scooter and got in the driver's seat as Jack slid his phone in his wet pocket.

"Well?"

"One ugly band coming off the lake and then just rain, according to the radar," Jack said.

"How ugly?"

"Tornado ugly. Shutting down all rides and having the ride operators scuttle guests into storm shelters." Jack's expression was dark, serious. "Heading to the hotel lot?"

"Uh-huh," Mel said. "Got to see about that power line. Get in. You can secure the hotel. Tornado off the lake will hit there first."

"Major crap," Jack said.

Wind lashed the scooter as Mel tore down the brief stretch of road leading to the hotel lot.

"Hope security already got there," Jack shouted over the rain. "And no one's hurt."

"Power lines, rain, wind…" Mel commented, not bothering to finish his thought.

They edged the parking lot of the Lake Breeze Hotel. A massive cottonwood at least a century old hadn't fallen on one vehicle. It was on at least three. And its long branches reached out, raking a half dozen more.

The rain kept onlookers inside the hotel but several Starlight Point police officers formed a perimeter around the scene, an arcing power line keeping them several yards away from the only vehicle clearly visible.

Mel's pickup truck.

His heart dove down to his belly and his chest tightened. One heavy branch lay across the hood, crushing it, while another imprisoned the bed. Although the cab was untouched, the power line lay over it.

Jack gripped Mel's shoulder wordlessly as they barreled out of the scooter and breached the line of police officers.

"Anyone hurt?" Jack asked, his voice shaky even over the wind and rain.

"Don't think so," a local cop who worked part-time at the Point said. "But we've got two people trapped."

Mel didn't need to hear his next words. He was close enough to see for himself.

"Your sister and a boy," the officer finished, unnecessarily because both Jack and Mel were an arm's length from the truck.

Mel leaned close, peering through the rain and the water-streaked glass. June, Ross on her lap, sat in the middle of the truck's only seat.

She stroked Ross's hair, not noticing Mel until he shouted her name.

Immediately, she scooted behind the wheel and reached for the door handle.

"No!" Mel shouted. "Don't open the door!"

She sunk back and snaked both arms around Ross, holding him tight. Mel's throat was so thick he didn't think he could speak. But he had to.

"Power company's on the way," Jack said. "What do we do?"

Mel ignored him, focusing on June and his son. He was never so afraid in his life but never so glad he knew what to do. If the wind and swaying trees didn't throw any more chaos his way.

"June, do *not* step out of the truck," he shouted, clearly chipping off the words. "Do *not* get out," he repeated. "Understand?"

June nodded once, twice, to say she heard him, but her expression was strained with fear.

"Trust me," Mel yelled. "Where's Megan?"

"I dropped her off at her car before this happened." June pointed across the hotel lot.

Wind whipped branches overhead and lightning struck close enough to raise the hair on the back of Mel's neck. He couldn't even think about what might have happened if he hadn't traded vehicles with June.

"You know what you're doing?" Jack asked. "We gotta get them out of there."

"Not yet."

"Are you crazy?" Jack yelled.

"Right now, the truck tires are grounding that line. As soon as anyone touches that truck—or steps out of it—they'll be the ground," Mel said grimly.

"We can't just leave them," Jack protested. "Who knows how long the power company will be?"

Mel nodded, his eyes following the power line as it snaked through the wreckage. It was still attached to the pole several rows over, a massive transformer clinging to the top.

"Are you listening to me?" Jack shouted. "This storm could get worse. And my sister's in there."

Mel turned on Jack. "My son is in there," he said.

Jack squeegeed water off his face with both hands, exasperation in every movement.

"Tell me what to do," he said.

Mel pulled him as close to the truck as he dared and motioned for June to unroll the window a crack. She obeyed, her whole face a question mark.

"Jack's going to stay right here and talk to you," Mel said. "Hey, Ross."

At his dad's voice, Ross uncovered his eyes and almost jumped off June's lap.

"Don't move!" Mel shouted. "Stay right there with June. Listen to everything she tells you."

"Are you gonna get us out of here?" he asked, his face puckered and tear-stained. Mel's heart clenched at the sight of his son. He needed to focus. *Stay calm.*

"Daddy will get you out. You have to be very brave and stay still. Understand?"

Ross nodded. Mel locked eyes with him and tried to smile, but he couldn't. He moved his gaze to June, willing her to be okay, hoping he wouldn't let them down. In a flash of raw honesty and emotion, he realized he wished June was his wife. The mother of his son. What if he had waited for her years ago…?

"What are you going to do?" June shouted through the wind and rain coming through her open window.

"Shut off the power."

Worry and relief flooded her face.

Jack held his position near June's door, but he didn't touch it.

"Be careful," he said. "You sure you know what you're doing?"

"Yep," Mel said. "Just need some equipment. What I really need is in my work truck, but—"

A blue Starlight Point maintenance truck pulled up right by his scooter.

"There's what I need," Mel finished.

Galway jumped out of the truck and speed-walked over. "Nuts," he said. "Radio traffic says the bridge's tied up with an accident. No power trucks from the city are getting through unless they drive all the way around and come in the Old Road. Who knows how jammed up that is."

Mel shoved past him and stepped into the bed of the newly arrived truck. He rummaged through the bins, making a racket even over the rising wind. He finally jumped down, wearing heavy protective gloves and holding spikes and a long pole.

"Bad idea, Boss," Galway said. "In this wind and rain, you'll kill yourself."

"My son's in that truck."

"I'll help you," Galway said, grabbing the

pole and matching Mel's stride as they clambered over downed branches on their way to the pole housing the transformer.

THROUGH THE RAINY WINDSHIELD, June watched Mel climb the power pole two rows of cars over. Lightning flashed and the wind rose impossibly higher.

Ross trembled. Although he sometimes seemed mature beyond his years, right now he was a terrified five-year-old boy.

"Your dad will shut off the power," she said, straining to see what Mel was doing, but also afraid to look. She hugged Ross tighter. "He's very brave and he knows about electricity. We'll be out of here soon."

Ross said nothing, and June craned her head to see his face. His eyes were squeezed shut.

"Hanging in there, June?" Jack shouted from his position outside her window.

She tried to smile bravely, imagining that this was almost as scary for him as for her. And he was in the rain. And he had the rest of the Point to worry about. Her fear deepened as she thought about the guests, food stands, rides and theaters of Starlight Point. Her friends, her family, her whole life was wrapped up on one small peninsula that was in the path of a terrifying storm.

"Where's Evie?" June shouted. "And Mom?"

"Handling things up front and in the park. Storm shelters open, rides closed. They don't know what's going on here."

June nodded, knowing there was nothing she could do. Except watch Mel climbing a pole like a human lightning rod. She didn't even have to think about her complete faith in him. But she was afraid for him, for all of them. She closed her eyes. Maybe Ross had the right idea.

"We could sing a song," June suggested.

"I want my dad."

Me, too, June thought.

After several more minutes of waiting with occasional checkups from Jack interspersed with thunder, wind and some popping sounds like hailstones, a new sound reached June and Ross in the truck.

It was a slithering, grating, thrumming sound. The windows were so wet and foggy, it took June a minute to connect the dots.

"They're pulling the wire off the truck," she said.

Ross opened his eyes.

June leaned forward and rubbed a clear spot on the inside of the windshield. Mel and another man wore heavy gloves and used long yellow sticks to pull the thick cable away from the truck. The wire no longer snapped or sparked.

Just as she wondered if and when it would be safe to get out of the vehicle, the door flew open and Mel reached in, his long arms encircling them both. He pulled them to the edge of the seat and hugged his son tight, keeping one hand free to cradle June's cheek.

"You're not hurt?" he asked both of them, racing his hands over his son, checking him over.

"No," June choked out.

"Good," Mel said, again holding them both against him. "Because I was so scared I think I wet my pants."

Ross laughed, the sound a warm balm against the fear and the punishing wind.

"Hotel," Jack shouted. "Storm's not over yet." He draped an arm around June and hustled her toward the hotel while Mel hoisted his son and kept pace, heading for the safety of the century-old structure. His eyes met June's and the look that passed between them had nothing to do with storms or danger. It was something June was afraid to admit to herself. He'd just rescued her, adrenaline flowed through her veins like water through a fire hose.

But she could no longer deny it. She was in love with Mel Preston.

CHAPTER NINETEEN

THERE WAS NO rational reason for his feelings. June had said from the beginning that she'd return to New York at the end of the season. She would stay there and dance as long as the lights of Broadway shone for her. There were years, maybe more than a decade, left of professional dancing in her long legs. *Assuming the knee injury she had never told him about didn't flare up.*

He'd missed his chance. If ever there was a moment to tell her he loved her, it was after he'd rescued her and Ross from his storm-shattered truck. If he had told her…

She'd still be heading for the airport tomorrow for an audition.

At work, he was a take-charge man. With June, there was no taking charge. She was always looking past him toward something brighter. And she'd never lied to him.

"Ready?" June asked through the open window of her mother's car.

She was definitely in the driver's seat. Without a vehicle as he awaited an insurance decision on his destroyed truck, Mel had hesitated to ask June out for a farewell dinner before she left for a two-day trip to New York City. But he gave in to practicality when she offered to be his ride for the day. He'd been asking for rides for three days now and he was tired of asking his coworkers and parents.

"Ready," Mel said. "Thanks for agreeing to drop Ross at my folks' house. I feel like a teenager without a driver's license."

He slid into the passenger side and June touched his hand. "I wrecked your truck. The least I can do is give you a ride until you get a new one."

"You saved my son's life. I don't give a monkey's butt about my truck."

"But you still need a new one," she said.

"I was actually hoping you'd be my driver for the rest of the summer. You're much prettier than the guys in the garage."

June laughed. "And who will chauffeur you while I'm in New York?"

They were both silent as she pulled onto the

outer loop for the short drive from the maintenance garage to the hotel day care.

"I meant for the next few days," she said quietly. "Not, you know, after…"

"I know what you meant."

He thought he did. But it wasn't any easier to go through with the plan he'd formulated instead of sleeping last night. And the two nights before that.

Have fun. Enjoy what time you have with her and accept the fact she's not staying. Accept it. It's not like he was turning down other dates left and right. With a more than full-time job and a five-year-old son, women were not lining up to fill his empty hours. Maybe he owed himself a summer flirtation. It would keep him going long into the cold winter ahead.

A winter in which June would be far away.

He knew he was making a mistake. Risking his heart. And his son's. For the first time in his life, Mel had lied to Ross. Told his son that his plans with June tonight were work related. A big meeting involving other Starlight Point employees.

He wasn't brave enough to admit to himself that he was giving in to his feelings instead of doing the smart thing and guarding his heart.

Admitting it to a five-year-old boy would be a big mistake.

"Be right back," he said when June stopped at the side entrance of the hotel.

As they drove across the Point Bridge to Mel's parents' house in downtown Bayside, Ross chatted about his day and his excitement about starting school in the fall. Mel wondered when it would hit Ross that Miss June wouldn't be around on the Tuesday after Labor Day when the Bayside schools officially started. He didn't want to break his son's heart. *Just one more reason it would be smarter to keep June at arm's length.*

He was being selfish, wanting something he couldn't have. And his life wasn't entirely his own. His decisions were Ross's, too, and the boy was too young to understand and decide for himself.

"I'll just be a minute," Mel said when June pulled into the driveway of the neat brick ranch-style house he'd grown up in. He should ask her in to say hello to his parents. But Mel didn't want to give them a reason to worry about him, and he was afraid of their inevitable questions.

They wanted him to be happy. And they'd

already seen him give his heart to a woman who couldn't wait to get out of town. He hated admitting he was making the same mistake again.

Even though June was not Sandi. He'd known her almost his entire life. Knew her family. Knew her heart…he thought. And in the two months since June had met his son, she'd shown more interest in the boy than his own mother had. *Maybe this isn't a huge mistake.*

"Next stop, my place, so I can change into something better for dining out. I'm always afraid someone will ask me to fix something if I wear my uniform outside work."

"Occupational hazard," June commented.

"And we could leave your car at my house," he added as June backed out of the driveway and turned toward Mel's place without even asking directions.

She sent him a questioning glance, both eyebrows lifted slightly. "We won't need the car anymore?"

Mel wished he'd planned a romantic dinner. A tablecloth and candles, a meal he'd put some thought into. Was that what June wanted? Intimate time alone with him at his place? He thought about the toy truck under the tiny kitchen table and the building blocks and crayons on top of it.

No. His plan was definitely more romantic.

"We can walk to our evening destination," he said. He pulled out his cell phone and checked the time. "I'll change fast and then we won't have to hurry."

June made full stops at all the intersections between Mel's childhood home and his current one. She used her turn signal. Looked both ways twice.

"I had no idea you were such a careful driver," he commented.

"Living in New York scares you straight," she said. "Not that I drive much there. One of my friends keeps a car in the city that we use sometimes, but it's usually public transportation."

"You're saving yourself a lot of hassle. Maintenance, insurance, tires."

"But I miss the freedom of having my own wheels," June said. "Life is slower and freer here. Not so much competition and pressure from every angle."

Mel reached over and put one hand on June's leg.

"Why didn't you tell me you had an injury when you came home?" He hadn't meant to ask, had told himself to let it go and not read too much into it.

She stiffened. Tightened her grip on the wheel.

"Sorry," he said. "None of my business."

"You have no idea how hard it is to perform at that level," June said. "One sign of weakness and you're out. They'll replace you like a dead lightbulb."

"You can show weakness in front of me," Mel said, his words barely above a whisper.

June took her eyes off the street and looked at him, lips parted, eyes wide. Her grip on the wheel loosened just enough to make him hope she understood him.

Mel held his breath for the next block and a half until June turned into his driveway.

"Please come in while I clean up," he said. "I hope you don't mind kid clutter."

She smiled. "Not at all. I have clutter all over my half of my apartment in New York. It would drive Evie out of her mind."

"Who do you share the apartment with?" Mel asked as they walked up to his front door.

"Cassie. You met her when they visited a few weeks ago."

Mel laughed. "I couldn't tell her apart from the other one."

"Macy. She shares an apartment with Ian one floor down from me and Cassie."

"Are they dating?"

"Just friends like the rest of us."

"So you're a close-knit group?"

June shrugged as Mel found one key out of the many on his ring. "All the dancers are close. When we're not competing with each other."

JUNE FOLLOWED MEL into his living room, which was much neater than he'd led her to imagine. It was also sparsely furnished with a big recliner, a smaller one and a table in between. Both chairs faced a wall-mounted television. A blue plastic bin next to the smaller chair overflowed with plastic blocks, wood blocks, magnetic letters, cars and trucks, and a large monkey.

"I'll take a superfast shower," Mel said. "Please grab anything you like from the fridge while you wait."

"I'm fine," June said. "I'll work on this puzzle while you change." She sat in the big chair and picked up the box of pieces with a picture of a red race car on the front.

"Just don't put in the last piece. Ross always gets the honor," Mel said.

June laughed. "I wouldn't steal the thrill from him. And I probably won't get that many pieces put in anyway."

While she listened to the water running just on the other side of the living room wall, June sat back in Mel's recliner. Breathing in his scent, burrowing into the comfortable chair, she imagined herself living there. What would it be like to come home after a long day of dancing at Starlight Point and put her feet up in this chair?

Just for experiment's sake, June pulled the lever on the side and popped out the footrest. She kicked off her shoes and settled her feet on it. *Just right.* She closed her eyes and felt an immense peace. She snuggled deeper into the chair and pushed the backrest into a reclining position. *Heaven.* Why didn't she have a chair like this in her New York apartment?

She had no idea how long she dozed in Mel's big comfy chair, but the next thing she felt was his lips on hers.

"This is like a fairy tale," he whispered. She opened her eyes and found Mel leaning over her. "I find a beautiful woman asleep in my favorite chair."

"Sorry," she said, struggling to sit up.

Mel laughed as she fought the chair into an upright position. "Don't be. That chair gets me every time. I hated to wake you up, but we have tickets on the sunset cruise leaving in half an hour."

June slid on her shoes. "I'm ready."

Mel shoved his wallet in the back pocket of his khaki pants and held open the door for her. It was a beautiful summer night.

"I decided on the sunset cruise because you won't get home too late," he said as they walked the short distance downtown to the public plaza and dock. "I know you're leaving in the morning for your audition in New York."

"Very thoughtful," June said. *It was.* "But I can always sleep on the plane. Unless I'm too nervous. Which I am."

Mel stopped and hugged her while they waited for the walk light. June didn't care who saw them. This was just what she needed. Wanted.

"You'll be wonderful," Mel said. "There's a

reason your agent was able to get you this audition. He obviously believes you can do it."

"I hope so."

They approached the dock and lined up with the other couples ready to enjoy a romantic evening. It was only a two-hour harbor tour, but it came with a bar and a spread of *hors d'oeuvres* as part of the ticket price. There were several older couples, some Mel and June's age, and a few teenagers on perhaps a first date.

They reminded her of the summer she was eighteen. The summer she left Mel and Starlight Point behind forever. Or so she'd believed. She swung Mel's hand and they walked across the gangplank onto the boat. She felt eighteen again. Although seven summers had passed since then…was it too late to go back and start over?

"We've never talked about it," she said aloud. Mel put his arm around her as they sat on a bench along the outer wall of the boat.

"What have we never talked about?"

"That summer."

"Oh."

"I'm sorry I hurt you," June said.

She tried to read the expression on Mel's

face. The years had been good to him. A handsome teenager and young man, age and maturity had made him more attractive. June wondered when he'd gotten those tiny lines around his eyes and realized with a wrenching pang of regret that she'd missed the last seven years with him.

By choice. She knew that.

"If you did hurt me, you're not to blame." He kissed her temple and looked out over the water. "You never lied to me. Never made me any promises."

His kiss seared her skin and sent waves of feeling from the spot.

"We were just kids then," she whispered.

"But we're not now," he said. He turned her face and kissed her on the lips, only breaking the kiss when the boat's horn blasted a warning that it was leaving the dock. They both jumped and Mel laughed, his broad smile making June wish the evening would never end.

TWO NIGHTS LATER, Evie pulled into the quick pickup lane at the airport. June was already on the curb, carry-on bag over her shoulder. It was a clear dark night and June had watched the moon on her descent into the metro airport. The same moon shone over New York, but it was brighter away from the city. No one stopped to look at the moon in New York. There were other lights so much nearer and brighter. *And more distracting.*

She climbed into the passenger seat of their mother's black car and barely had time to click her seat belt before Evie pulled away.

"Are we in a hurry?"

Evie nodded to the signs posted along the lane. "Five-minute parking only," she said. "Or they'll tow you."

June laughed. "New York would drive you nuts."

"Probably," her younger sister acknowledged. "When Jack and Mom and I came to your last three shows, I couldn't wait to escape the madness. Even though you were great, of course," she added, turning a quick smile on her sister before merging onto the highway. "So, did you get the part?"

June shrugged. "I don't know yet. I have to wait to hear from my agent. There will almost certainly be callbacks since I wasn't the only one who wanted that part."

"When will you know?"

"A few days, I think. I'm hoping for a call-back. Pins and needles until then."

"Good thing you have plenty of things to keep you occupied while you wait."

They drove in silence a moment.

"How is your knee?" Evie asked.

June's breath caught. "What makes you ask that?"

Evie shrugged. "You left your laundry in the dryer. I hauled it to your room and put it away for you."

June didn't say anything. What was the harm in confiding to Evie now that it was better?

"I'm nice like that," Evie continued. "You're welcome. So, anyway, there was a knee brace and one of those microwave heating pad things. In addition to being angelic in nature, I'm also perceptive."

"My knee is fine," June said. "Now. I'll admit it. One of the reasons I came home this summer was to rest my knee. All that dancing takes its toll."

"Full-disclosure time," Evie said. "How bad was it?"

June watched streetlights out the side window for a moment. "I saw a specialist in New

York. The same one who sees all the dancers. Knee problems are as common on the stage as blisters are at the Point. He said I should take it easy for a few months. And then see how it is."

"So you didn't come home to revive the theaters totally out of the goodness of your heart," she said.

"I never said I did."

"True, but I wondered. Either way, it's been good to have you home. The theaters are amazing. And your knee is apparently ready to take you back to Broadway."

"It is. Filling in for Brooke a few weeks ago was a big test for me."

"I'm glad you passed the test. If you ever decide to come home for good, I want it to be because you want to. Not because you have to."

"Me, too," June said without thinking. Did she really just say that?

Evie glanced at her but didn't say anything.

June cleared her throat. "Anyway, if my knee can survive the miles of walking at the Point every day, I believe I'm good to go for another season on the big stage. Starlight Point is a one-hundred-day marathon every summer. I don't know how you do it."

"I plan to hibernate all winter and store up

my energy," Evie said. "I don't know why I didn't think of it last year."

June pictured herself hibernating in Mel's dangerously comfortable recliner. She might climb out of it every now and then to build a snowman with Ross or drive him to school.

What was she thinking? She'd just flown in from her audition and she was dreaming about settling down back where she'd started?

She had to get a grip.

"What's the news on the insurance situation from the fire?" she asked, hoping a practical matter would slap some sense into her.

"Good news," Evie said. "The state fire marshal took a few weeks to make his official ruling and do the paperwork, but the fire was judged accidental. Just like we knew it was."

"So this means we can go ahead with re-building?"

Evie nodded. "Jack and I are meeting with the planners next week to talk about the design. Since we have to rebuild it anyway, we have the opportunity to change it a bit."

Something about changing Starlight Point made June's heart sink. "I liked it the way it was," she said.

"Since when do you want things to stay

the same? Aren't you the one who wanted to change the theaters at the beginning of the season?"

June shrugged.

"The games area is tacky," Evie declared.

"You just hate the games in general," June said.

"Absolutely. People throwing money away for a chance at a cheap toy. I swear I'll never understand it."

"It's the thrill," June said.

Evie scoffed.

"Taking chances is exciting and dangerous." She should know.

"Foolish," Evie said. "People are too anxious to toss away what they have in hopes of something better."

Even though June knew her sister wasn't directly talking about her, the words cut deep. She stared out the window as the road took her closer to her hometown.

CHAPTER TWENTY

TEN DAYS AFTER the summer storm, the ballroom was ready for hundreds of employees anxious to blow off steam—thanks to Virginia Hamilton's exuberance and touch of eccentricity. July 25. Christmas in July.

"You like it?" Virginia asked.

"It's sparkly," June said, an approving smile lighting her face.

"And on budget," Evie added.

"The snack tables look fantastic," Jack said. "Gus has been busy, and so have the other vendors." He bent low, kissing his mother on the cheek. "You're amazing. And people are going to have a great time."

"Beginning with dance lessons," June said. "Party starts at ten thirty as soon as the park is clear, but lessons start at nine for anyone interested and available. I hate seeing bad dancing, people just flailing their arms and shuffling around the floor."

"Are you teaching?" her sister asked.

June nodded. "Me and some of my summer crew. Their last show is at seven, so they can be here."

"I heard you've been giving private lessons to Mel Preston," Virginia said.

June rolled her eyes.

"Maybe I just assumed that's what you've been doing those…uh…three late nights you were out in the last week."

"Two."

"Maybe the other one was just past my bedtime," her mother said.

Jack stuck his fingers in his ears and looked at the ceiling.

"Back to the dance lessons," June said.

"That's what I was talking about," Virginia said. "Teaching Mel some excellent moves. Makes me wonder what you two are going to do about your…tango."

June hated the way this conversation sounded in the cavernous ballroom with her whole family standing there. Evie was grinning and Jack was still studying the overhead lights.

"I think Mel's looking for a permanent instructor."

"And?"

"And I'm still leaving at the end of the season. Just like I've said all along. Nothing's changed."

Virginia raised her eyebrows. "It seems like something's different to me."

June blew out a sigh and her siblings abandoned her by slinking off to supposedly check out the rest of the decor and tables.

"Your father and I fell in love in this ballroom," Virginia said. "Long time ago now."

"I know."

"I know you know," her mother said. "I'm just bringing it up for myself. It's a happy memory I want to keep with me tonight."

June nodded, unsure of what to say.

"Life is short," Virginia said. "I know you know that, too."

June waited for the lecture she'd been expecting all summer. The one where her mother reminded her that things were different now that her father had died and she should come home and help out.

"I've always been proud of you, June. Your talent is one thing, but what I really love about you is your ability to go for what you want. If you want the starring role in any show, I believe you can get it."

Her mother hugged her while June fought tears.

"You're my shining star," Virginia said. "I want you to have whatever you want."

TWILIGHT SOFTENED THE lines of the ballroom and sharpened the contrast of the lightbulbs outlining and illuminating the grand old entrance. Mel had enjoyed dinner at his parents' house and supervised Ross's bath and pajama ritual. His son would stay there tonight, freeing Mel to spend a precious evening with June Hamilton.

He found her leaning against a pillar on the edge of the dance floor. Several couples were attempting some moves, awkwardly holding each other and counting steps aloud under the direction of some performers from live shows. June wore a deep green dress with no straps, her bare shoulders glimmering in the soft lights.

Something about the way she bumped one trim hip against the ornate post made her seem like part of the architecture. He'd been in this room countless times for staff meetings,

STRIPE lessons, but tonight, the ballroom was a ballroom. Pillars edged the parquet floor, refreshment tables and chairs waited in the wings, starlight would be visible through the tall Art Deco–styled windows.

June was beautiful in the knee-length dress and strappy high heels.

"Got time for a lesson?" he whispered, his lips brushing her ear from behind.

Goose bumps rippled across her shoulder despite the warmth in the ballroom.

She turned into him, placing them both behind the pillar and partially hiding them from sight.

"Depends on what talents you bring to the table," she said. "Some students catch on faster than others."

"I'm good with my hands," he said, facing her and settling both hands around her waist.

"I know, but you have to dance with your feet."

"Seems to me that hands are an important part of the deal."

She smiled. "If you do it right."

June took Mel's right hand and moved it to her left shoulder. Goose bumps again, he noted when his fingers met her bare skin.

She left his other hand at her waist and moved away from the pillar, giving them a shadowy, secluded dance floor behind it.

June took a small step backward with her left leg. "Follow me. Pretend your thighs are glued to mine."

"I think I can remember those directions," Mel said, swallowing hard.

June stepped back with her right leg, forcing a small turn. "Like a square," she said. "Basic math. But you'll have to lead."

Heat collected under his shirt collar and he wanted to tear off his tie.

"I think I'm going to need a drink." He closed in on her, keeping his hands where she'd placed them. "Or a bucket of cold water."

"This is just a ballroom step. Wait until we get to the tango," June said. "You might incinerate."

Trying to cool his thoughts, Mel looked over June's shoulder and concentrated on the smooth and simple steps. He had danced before at weddings and thought he knew the basics.

Having a good partner made a difference the size of the peninsula Starlight Point sat on. June was light and graceful, her love for the movement clear in every step and sway. Leading her as a dance partner was like being behind the wheel of a Ferrari. The only way he could go wrong was if he lost control.

Like he hadn't already. He paused, kissing June's cheek and just holding her, loving the electricity of her touch, the small sparkles at her ears. He felt her straining to move, to keep dancing. He would be happy holding her in his arms all night without negotiating a single square foot of the dance floor.

But she loved to keep going, keep the dance steps thrumming. More than standing still, more than…anything? This was it in a nutshell. He wanted to hold on tight, but June was a bird trying to decide how to use her wings. Spread them and protect the thing she loved, or use them to soar to some distant horizon.

June placed one palm on his cheek. "You're hot. Maybe we should get a drink before the crowd pours in and the real dance starts."

She took his hand and led him to one of the refreshment tables. They passed Jack, who was lugging a big box at the direction of his mother. Virginia caught Mel's eye and gave him a nod that seemed like it was supposed to mean something. Evie was behind a table organizing cups into neat rows that would be decimated when the summer and year-round employees energetic enough to dance started streaming into the ballroom.

"You look like you're burning up," Evie commented. "Too much sun today? I saw you on the track of the Silver Streak."

"Hot in here," Mel commented. "Maybe you should squeeze your spreadsheet a little and air-condition this old place."

Evie grinned. "I don't think it would help you."

June had been watching the practice dancers finish a round but turned back to her sister and Mel now that lessons were over. "What was wrong with the Silver Streak?" she asked.

"Down almost all afternoon. Alarm kept tripping on the first set of brakes. Turned out to be a computer chip causing the problem, but it took us a while to figure it out. That whole system is due for an upgrade next time you feel like putting some money into an old ride."

"Worth it," June said. "The Streak is part of the skyline here and it was probably the first coaster for half the people in the county." She sipped the drink Evie handed her. "Sentimental value. Just like this old ballroom. Mom and Dad fell in love here."

"Since when did you become so sentimental?" Evie asked.

"I'm allowed," June said.

"Sure, but you're always making fun of me for being married to Starlight Point. I think you're having a secret affair," Evie said. She waggled her glass at Mel. "And a not-so-secret one."

June set her half-finished drink on the table. "You'll have to write all about me in the company newsletter." She attempted a casual tone, but even with his limited powers of interpreting nuance, Mel could see that Evie had touched a nerve.

"I bet I could learn the tango," Mel blurted out, desperate to say something guaranteed to distract June.

"I bet I could teach you," she said, rewarding him with a smile—although that smile did not quite reach the guarded look in her eyes.

Party guests began arriving as the stars appeared over the point. With the front gates finally closed, employees were free to enjoy the Christmas in July event that had become a tradition. Mel, and the other year-round workers, saw the ballroom decorated for Christmas twice a year. The winter party was a much smaller group, and it was far more intimate because the year-round employees had known each other for years. The summer crowd at the July event was younger and livelier.

Trees sparkled and lights flashed as Mel waltzed past with June in his arms. He credited her excellent teaching for his respectable performance. And the fact that she had enough talent for both of them.

Around eleven o'clock, Virginia made a speech wishing a happy half Christmas to the Starlight Point family.

"And now for a fun diversion," Virginia continued, "our head of live shows has a Christmas song prepared."

Mel still had one arm around June at the foot of the stage. He glanced at her and she smiled. "I'm singing 'White Christmas,'" she said. "I had it prepared for my audition anyway."

June stepped onto the low stage and took the microphone from her mother. Virginia draped a red coat with white fur trim over her daughter's shoulders.

Mel listened as June sang the classic "White

Christmas" for the assembled crowd, unable to look away for an instant.

"YOU LOOK VERY SERIOUS," Mel said as they danced together close to midnight. "I know my tangoing was hideous, but at least I gave up before anyone realized how hard I was actually trying. Now I know my limitations."

The DJ was playing a popular slow song. June didn't want to look at the young couples around them clutching and swaying with no skill whatsoever. She focused instead on the man who happened to be doing a decent job of leading her in a slow dance. She couldn't even see his lips moving as he counted steps. Maybe she should give him more credit.

"I was thinking about Evie."

Mel tightened his hold on her. "Don't let her teasing get to you."

"And I was thinking about Jack."

"Now you're killing my dance mojo."

"I just don't want them to hand over their lives to this place like our father did."

Mel stopped dancing, took June's arm and guided her onto the patio behind the ballroom. The raised outdoor deck had a view of the lake.

Right now, the water was a stretch of blackness under a half-moon.

He leaned against the rail and pulled June close. With her ear against his chest, she felt the rumble of his voice.

"What happened to your father was terrible. And it should never have happened. He needed help running this place, and he needed to open up about the problems. If he'd shared the burden with someone else, maybe things would've turned out different."

June shook her head, a tiny movement against the wall of Mel's chest.

"I know how much you love your family. I know you're afraid they're going to work themselves to death. But it's what they want to do, what they love. And things are different. They have each other. It's lousy doing everything yourself."

Mel smelled like shaving cream, shower soap and laundry detergent. For a moment, June pictured him putting Ross to bed and then hauling the laundry basket downstairs to start his full-time father and homemaker job. Trying to do everything himself.

"I could help," she whispered.

"You have. You made the theaters new again

and set them up for a great season. Maybe you'll be a distant partner for Jack and Evie, but you're still a partner. That makes a big difference, and it's a luxury your dad never took."

June had a vision of her father, shirtsleeves rolled up, holding her hand as she walked to work with him when she was a little girl. They always walked across the wide parking lot separating their home on the Old Road from the front gates. In the summer, she walked with him almost every morning, following him around as he made the preopening checks, met with the lease vendors, said hello to employees. She had done it for so many years, she knew each step he would take and exactly what he would say.

Of course, he always had Jack by the other hand, but June never considered him competition. She didn't know exactly how old she was when she'd started to realize that she had a choice in life and maybe nailing her feet to the midway at Starlight Point wasn't in her best interest.

Little by little, the lure of the stage and the magic of the audience had replaced the man with rolled shirtsleeves. Starlight Point had begun to seem like an anchor keeping her ship in a narrow harbor when she wanted to see the whole ocean.

Now she wished she could have even five more minutes holding her father's hand and walking through the front gates.

"I know you're leaving," Mel said quietly. "And I understand. You have to pursue your dreams. You've got the gift. I felt it tonight when we were dancing."

Her head still on his chest, June heard Mel's heartbeat. Despite his calm and deliberate words, his pulse raced, each ragged beat revealing how hard the words were for him to say.

The night air smelled like cotton candy mixed with freshwater lake. It was a scent she could summon up even far away in her city apartment. The ballroom lights laid a pattern on the decking at their feet and a tall cottonwood, like so many of the trees that lined the beach, rustled nearby. Even if she left Starlight Point, it would never let her go.

CHAPTER TWENTY-ONE

"Last night's party was a success," Evie said. "But now I have Christmas hangover. I hate the letdown after the holidays."

June laughed. "I could cheer you up with news."

"Is this good news the reason you took me out to lunch on a Friday? If we skip out during the workday, people will think we own the place."

"You have to eat. And it's good to get away from Starlight Point every once in a while," June said. "I promise we'll only be an hour and I'll return you to the tower before the guards find out you escaped."

The two sisters sat at an outdoor table at the Bayside Grille. The long docks housed pleasure boats, and the city dock was the departure point for the Starlight Point ferry. For fun, June and Evie had taken the ferry across the bay. Evie turned it into research, counting the minutes the ferry took and the number of guests who rode it on a sunny Friday in late July.

They'd already placed their lunch order at the window, picked up their drinks and sat down to wait for the grill cook to call their number.

"Well?" Evie asked. "Are you going to toy with me or are you going to tell me you got the part in *White Christmas*?"

"I didn't get the part," June said. She turned up one corner of her mouth, stalling for effect. "Yet," she continued. "But I got a callback this morning which is the best news I could expect."

Evie jumped up and gave her sister a hug. She bumped the table and sloshed diet soda over the rim of the plastic cups.

"Are you sure you're happy for me?" June said. "If I get this part, I'll leave September 1 and you'll be stuck with Mom and Betty."

"Of course you'll leave. This is your big break. Not that you were floundering before."

"I know," June said. "But I thought you were getting used to having me around."

"Are you kidding? When you leave, I'll get to take over the entire bathroom between our rooms. I'm thinking of investing in an arsenal of cosmetics to get me through the winter."

June laughed. "I can't picture you dropping a fortune at the cosmetics counter at Macy's. Not much return on investment if you're planning to hibernate."

They sat down again and Evie meticulously soaked up the spilled soda with her napkin.

"Can you take me to the airport Sunday afternoon? I want to have plenty of time to prepare for the audition, so I'm going the night before."

"Didn't I just pick you up at the airport five days ago?"

"Sorry."

"Just kidding," Evie said. "I don't mind. I'll even borrow Mom's car instead of Jack's so we know we'll make it."

"He should get a new one."

"I should probably get something, too, instead of borrowing all the time. Speaking of new cars, did you see Mel's new truck?"

Mel had a new truck?

"No."

"He picked it up while you were in New York a few days ago."

"He didn't mention it at the dance last night," June said.

"He had other things on his mind."

"So what does it look like?"

"His truck?" Evie asked. She shrugged. "It's blue. Looks pretty much like his old one to me, just shinier."

June smiled, picturing Mel and Ross test-driving pickup trucks and buying one just like the one they had before. "Mel's a creature of habit. You know what you're getting with a man like that."

Evie raised her eyebrows but didn't say anything.

The teenager working the window yelled their number. "I'll get it," Evie said. She got up and headed for the counter.

June glanced at the water sparkling in the bay. Her thoughts turned to her agent's excited voice when he'd phoned with the news about the callback.

Evie put a plastic tray laden with food in the center of the table.

"For a person who has a shot at her dream role, you don't look happy. Is it your knee? Are you worried about it?"

"No. This summer has been so good for it. I swear I feel five years younger."

Evie gave her a skeptical look.

"Okay, maybe three years younger," June said.

Evie took a big bite of her grilled sandwich and chewed, giving June time to think about confiding in her sister. June picked at her salad.

"It's the date," she said.

Mouth full, Evie drew her eyebrows together in a questioning look.

"July 29."

Evie tilted her head, clearly unaware of the problem.

"Ross's birthday. I was going to have a surprise party for him at the hotel on Monday."

She had already requested a cake from Augusta with a roller coaster outlined in blue icing.

"Oh," Evie said. "Maybe you could do something for him tomorrow or a different day."

June shook her head. "Birthdays are important to little kids. I feel like I'm letting him down."

"But it's not your fault you only got a few days' notice to get yourself to New York. And it's a surprise party. He doesn't even know about it."

June rearranged the lettuce, tomatoes and cucumbers on her plate.

"It's not him you're worried about," Evie said. "It's Mel, isn't it?"

At least I didn't tell Mel about the surprise party. It would be one fewer disappointment when she chose dancing instead of him.

"Ross already has a mom who puts her own artistic career ahead of him," June said. "Way ahead of him."

Evie leaned across the table and touched her sister's arm. "Listen. You are not Ross's mom. He doesn't even know you planned a party. You have to go to New York or you'll always wonder if that role could have been yours."

"You're right," June said.

They finished their food and returned the plastic tray and baskets to the pickup window.

"We just missed a ferry, so we have about twenty minutes to wait for the next one," June said. She was in no hurry. There was plenty of time before the three o'clock parade lined up, and the performers could easily do it without her anyway. She'd hired quality people and trained them. If she left for good, would anyone at Starlight Point even miss her?

"We never have time to goof off in the summer," Evie said. "We could take a quick walk downtown and look at the cute shops."

They crossed the street running parallel to the waterfront. A large plaza with a fountain and planters provided an outdoor venue for summer concerts. Beyond that, a boulevard divided the main street downtown. Augusta's bakery was just around the corner, and numerous boutiques and restaurants filled the street-level floors of the historic buildings. Colorful planters overflowing with flowers and elegant awnings gave downtown Bayside an upscale vibe.

June stopped in front of a business, obviously closed, with brown paper covering the tall windows facing the street.

"What used to be here?" June asked, something about the shop triggering a memory.

"The dance studio," Evie said. "Your old instructor from when you were a kid finally retired. She's moving to Florida. Mom told me about it."

June faced the empty windows and found a small space uncovered by brown paper. She peered in, leaving a smudge on the glass. It looked just like she remembered. Open floor space for dancing, mirrors along one wall. She pictured herself in her favorite dance clothes lining up with the other girls. Her life in a nutshell.

"It's available for lease," she said aloud.

"Uh-huh," Evie said. "I bet it'll end up being a bar or a microbrewery. A few of those have already gone in downtown and I hear they're doing well."

"A bar in my old dance studio?"

"You haven't been inside there in almost ten years," Evie said. "Who knows what it's like now?"

"Looks the same," June said, still straining to see inside.

"Okay," Evie said, glancing at the time on her cell phone. "We should head back to the dock so we don't miss the ferry."

June pulled her phone from her purse and took a picture of the front of the store.

"Are you getting sentimental?" Evie asked.

"No. I'm taking a picture of the Realtor's number."

Evie crossed her arms over her chest and looked at her sister as if seeing her for the first time. June shrugged and started to walk away, then glanced back at the building.

As she and Evie walked along the sidewalk back toward the ferry docks, her phone rang.

"Hi, Mel," she said, checking the caller ID before she swiped the phone to answer.

Evie shot her a grin.

"I hope you don't mind having your cover blown," Mel said, "but Augusta told me about the cake you ordered Ross."

June's shoulders sank. So much for not disappointing Mel.

"I was walking by her bakery on the midway and she called me in to check Ross's age," Mel continued. "She had sixth birthday written on the order form, but she thought Ross looked too tall and it must be his seventh."

"He is tall," June said, finding her voice. "Takes after you."

"Anyway, I just wanted to say it's really nice of you to have a little party for him at the day care."

"He's a great kid," she said, unwilling to tell Mel over the phone that her plans had changed.

"My parents are having dinner and cake on Sunday night at their house. It's the day before his birthday, but it works better having it on a Sunday with my crazy work schedule," he said.

June could hear the excitement in Mel's voice. He spoke a little fast as if he was speed-walking and talking at the same time. Maybe he was. He could be dashing off to fix a ride for all she knew.

"Anyway," he continued. "I wondered if you'd like to come to the party Sunday night."

"Sunday night?"

Evie shot her a look as they lined up for the ferry.

"Yes," Mel said. "Dinnertime."

"I'm just getting on the ferry," June said. "I'll talk with you when I get back to the Point."

Evie shoulder-hugged her sister and steered her toward a bench seat on the front of the ferry.

"Maybe it'll all work out," Evie said.

June sighed. "I have no idea how."

"We'll be back in plenty of time for the parade," Evie said. "I'll bet that will cheer you up."

FOUR O'CLOCK ON a Friday afternoon and the Fates were against him. No stage lights in the

Starlight Saloon, and the clock was ticking on the five o'clock show. Megan, the theater manager and second in command, sounded panicked on the phone, so Mel called the hotel day care and told them he'd be late. They were used to it.

Mel had no idea where June was. Something sounded off when he'd talked with her just after lunch. Maybe she was disappointed he'd found out about her surprise party for Ross. He'd caught a glimpse of her when the parade went by. Mel made it a habit to be somewhere on the parade route every day so he could wave to his son. It was their game, and Ross watched for him all along the route.

"Thanks for coming here so fast," Megan said as she met him at the back entrance. "I flipped on the lights, there was a popping sound and then nothing."

She followed Mel to the breaker panel.

"Do you think I should cancel the next show?" she asked, sounding breathless.

Mel put down his toolbox, grabbed a chair from a stack by the back wall and placed the chair in front of Megan.

"Sit," he said. "Take a break while I look at the box. Might be just a breaker."

Megan eased herself onto the chair.

"How much longer?" Mel asked.

"I'm due in three weeks," she said.

"And you're still on your feet all day?"

Megan laughed. "I can't see or feel my feet, so it's not so bad."

Mel flipped a switch in the panel and the lights came on.

"Oh," Megan breathed. "Thank goodness."

"I wonder what tripped the breaker in the first place," Mel asked. "I'm going to check a few things while you remain in that chair where I can find you if I need you. Give me five minutes and I can tell you whether or not I'd cancel the show."

Mel followed the path of a group of wires, checking for heat in the walls or power-hungry things plugged into the line that had overloaded. He was on the other side of a flimsy partition wall when he heard Megan talking to someone.

June.

"Mel has it fixed already." He heard the relief in Megan's voice.

"He's a lifesaver," June said.

"So, are you excited about your callback?"

Callback? June hadn't mentioned that.

"Very. It's the break I've been waiting for. My agent said there were only three performers called back for this role, so my chances are decent."

"When do you leave?" Megan asked.

June was leaving?

There was a pause. Mel didn't move. It was wrong, crouching and eavesdropping, but he had to hear the answer.

"Sunday," June said. She didn't sound happy...did she? "The audition is Monday."

Monday. Ross's birthday. The day she was supposedly throwing him a surprise party.

Mel dropped his flashlight and it knocked against the wall before landing on his foot. He cursed.

"Is Mel still here?" June asked.

He didn't hear a response. Megan was probably nodding and pointing, unaware that he and June had things to clear up. At least they did now.

He heard footsteps and didn't have to look up to know the quick, light steps were June's, not Megan's.

"Hi," she said.

Mel picked up his flashlight and shoved it in his tool holster. He should make this easy on her. Just tell her he overheard the conversation and wish her good luck on her audition. *Have a nice life.*

"You heard," she said.

Mel nodded. He ran his hand down the length of the wall and checked the electrical outlet near the eye-level light switch.

"What are you doing?" June asked.

"Just checking things." It was baloney. He was stalling and avoiding eye contact. Avoiding the inevitability of June's departure. Something she had never lied about.

So why did it feel like a betrayal?

"I'm sorry I'll miss Ross's party," June said quietly. "Both of them."

"That's all right. He's used to having just me and his grandparents."

He wanted to add that the boy's own mother had missed his last three birthdays. Ross had experience being chosen last by the women in his life. But never by his dad. Ross was Mel's first priority. Always. And that was why this summer whatever-it-was with June had to end. Now.

"I didn't have a choice on audition times," June said. She followed him along the wall and stood too close.

Mel risked eye contact and saw tears glisten in her eyes, even in the dim light of the backstage area. He hated seeing June's tears. Wanted to kiss them away. But he was already in too deep. She was leaving. She'd have to dry her own tears in the big city and she might as well start now.

"Speaking of time," he said, "Megan's waiting to find out if it's okay to run this show."

"I don't care about the show right now," June said, her voice trembling.

"Yes, you do. It's always about the show with you."

June drew in a sharp breath and flushed. "That's rotten. You're being rotten." Tears spilled over and ran down her cheeks. "I never promised you anything. I told you from the start—"

"I know. You're not staying past summer." Mel flipped the light switch off and on. He looked at the overhead lights for no reason except to change his focus.

He stalked back to the electrical panel. Megan was no longer sitting on the chair, and he didn't care how much of their conversation she might have overheard.

"Would you listen to me?" June asked, following him.

"Why?" Mel said, turning to her, arms crossed over his chest. "So you can tell me how great the city is, how that's where you have to go to pursue your big dream?" He swallowed, anger making his chest tight. "I've heard all that before."

The color drained from June's face. She stared at him for five seconds. Ten seconds.

He'd gone too far.

"Are you kidding me," she said, her voice low like the rumbling of a distant train. "Are you actually comparing me to your ex-wife?"

He swallowed again. "That's not what I said."

June advanced on him and put one finger on his chest. "It's what you meant. How dare you. How dare you make me feel guilty for doing something I've always said I would? Always wanted. I'm *not* your ex-wife walking out on you. Walking out on *our* son." She took her finger off his chest and pointed it at him. "If you can't tell the difference, maybe it's a good thing I'm leaving."

"I looked it up," Mel blurted out. "The end of *Pippin*."

June's expression turned from fury to confusion.

"You never finished telling me what the main character found out in the end. That he searched the world and discovered what he really wanted was right at home where he started."

Mel waited for June to say something. He watched her swallow. Bite her lip.

"But I guess that's not everyone's idea of a happy ending," Mel said, his voice flat with defeat.

He had been a fool for thinking it was.

CHAPTER TWENTY-TWO

JUNE STOOD ALONE on the stage. The director of *White Christmas* waited in the first row of seats and June's agent sat several rows back, watching.

"Sing 'Count Your Blessings,'" the director said. "And then we'll have you sing 'Sisters' with the girls who got called back for the main part."

The sound technician turned on the music and June counted, waiting out the introduction. It was a piece she knew by heart.

Last night, as she lay awake in the apartment she shared with Cassie, she thought about her blessings. She opened her eyes and watched the city lights dapple her bedroom ceiling. She closed her eyes and saw the lights of Starlight Point. Her sister's blond hair as she walked down the midway in the sunshine. Her brother's hopeful expression as he watched the front gates open. Even her mother with her dog sleeping in the wagon.

Starlight Point used to seem like a curse instead of a blessing, but this summer had reinvented June's opinion of her childhood home and family livelihood.

When she'd closed her eyes and counted her blessings last night, she also saw the faces of Ross and the other children as they danced with happy disregard for style and rules. Who knew teaching children to dance could be so much fun? She thought about Ross's birthday party that was probably going on right at that moment. She hoped they would dance. At least a conga line.

Most of all, when she counted her blessings she saw Mel's smile. His blue uniform. Disheveled hair. Eyes, hands, lips.

Long ago, a music coach had told her to think of someone she loved and sing to that person. Sing as if the song were only for that person's ears.

As June auditioned for the part of a lifetime, she smiled and let images of Mel roll through her mind like a film reel. He could be as angry and unreasonable as he wanted, but she knew why he'd reacted as he did when the reality of her leaving hit him.

He was in love with her. There was no other reason. It wasn't about his ex-wife. It wasn't even about this show. It was about love.

She poured all her love for Mel into her audition song, hoping for one of two things. It would burn clean through and leave nothing, or it would light her way.

When June finished singing and dancing to the satisfaction of the director and his staff, her agent signaled for her to meet him backstage.

"I think you'll get it," he whispered. Harold Summit had been June's agent for three years and she'd never seen him so excited. "You should stay in New York, to be here when they deliver the news."

"You can call me with the news," she said. "Like I told you, I'm staying back home until rehearsals start, assuming I get the part."

"If you get this lead, you may need to come back a week or two before the rest of the cast."

June kissed her agent on the cheek. "Thank you for everything you've done for me."

Harold frowned. "Plenty more to do," he said.

June smiled. "I have no plans to slow down. Call me when you get an answer, and we'll talk about the future."

MEL COULDN'T BELIEVE his son was six years old. He remembered the hot July day Ross was born and put into his arms for the first time.

"Do you want to do the honors?" Virginia asked. She handed him a lighter. "Or we could let your son play with fire. Kids love that, and it's his birthday."

Mel grabbed the lighter. "I've got this."

Augusta had delivered the large sheet cake just in time for the party and she stood by wearing a pink apron, ready to cut and serve. Jack, dressed in a business suit and Starlight Point name tag, leaned against one wall. Mel couldn't tell if his friend's eyes were on his relatively new wife or the cake. Either way, Ross would be happy Uncle Jack was there.

Mel leaned over his son and lit all six candles. "Make a wish," he said. "But it can't be a puppy."

Ross's shoulders fell and he frowned. "Kitten?"

Mel ruffled his son's hair. "How about something without fur?"

"A fish!"

"Now that," Mel said, "is a wish that might come true."

Mel remembered Ross's birthday wish two

years ago. At a nice dinner at his grandparents' house, Ross wished aloud for his mother to come home. Mel swore he could hear his own heart breaking for his son. At least that hadn't happened again last year. The poor kid had given up false hope at a tender, young age.

A shadow blurred in the door and Mel glanced up. Of course he knew June wasn't coming to the party. She was probably wowing some director in New York City right now. Starlight Point wasn't enough for her. *He wasn't enough for her.*

Maybe he should take a lesson from Ross about false hope. Especially after the way he'd left things with June.

Virginia led the group singing an off-key but enthusiastic "Happy Birthday." Augusta and Jack joined in, and Evie slid through the door just in time for the final notes. She held a wrapped gift with a large red bow.

The Hamiltons were practically family and they were all there for his son's party. Except one.

"This is from June," Evie said. She handed the gift to Mel. "I don't know if you want Ross to open it now or later."

Mel took the package. Judging from the

shape and size, it was a book of some kind. *Probably an atlas of all the places you can go that aren't here.*

"She wanted to be here," Evie said quietly, so only Mel could hear. There were at least a dozen kids helping Ross make a dent in the cake and ice cream. They wore party hats and kicked balloons around the floor as they dodged streamers hanging from the ceiling. Mel made a mental note to stop by later and help clean up. The day-care teachers already put in long days, and he preferred to stay on their good side.

He turned to Evie. "If she wanted to be here, she'd be here."

"Not fair," Evie said, shaking her head.

Mel shrugged.

Evie elbowed him. "I remember my sixth birthday. You and Jack threw water balloons at my girlfriends and wrecked my princess party."

Mel grinned. "You were just mad that I got your new cash register wet."

"Best birthday present I ever got. The drawer rang every time you opened it."

"You still have it, don't you?" Mel asked.

Evie laughed. "It still rings."

Virginia stuck around to play with the kids, but Jack, Augusta and Evie left. Mel tucked June's gift under his arm and debated if and when to have Ross open it.

He watched Ross play board games with the other kids, helped supervise a conga line down the long hallway and back, and was ready to call it quits on the party. He needed to get back to work for a few hours. He had plans to take Ross for his favorite drive-through food in their new pickup truck on the way home. Ketchup was going to get on the seat sooner or later anyway.

"Is that present for me?" Ross asked as he reached up to straighten his party hat. He pointed at the gift tucked under Mel's arm.

No choice now.

"It is." Mel decided to test the waters. "It's from June."

"Cool," Ross said. "I wish she could've come to my party. I kept hoping." He held out his hands. "Can I open it even if she's not here?"

Mel handed his son the gift and waited while he carefully peeled the bow and tape off the paper.

"Is it a book?" Mel asked.

Ross nodded and studied the unwrapped present. "I get it," he said. "It's a book to teach you how to play the piano." He handed the book to his dad. Mel flipped it open.

Ross sighed. "It would be more fun if she taught me. But the book is nice, too. I can mail her a thank-you card."

This is exactly what I was afraid of when I let us both get too close to a shooting star. "Look," Mel said, holding the page open so his son could see it. He wanted the sad look on Ross's face to disappear. "It's 'Twinkle, Twinkle, Little Star.'"

"I already know that one," Ross said, a small smile returning. "I can skip right to song number two."

"You'll be terrific." Mel closed the book. "I'll pick you up in a few hours and we'll get those chicken fingers you like."

Ross headed for the games and treats and Mel looked at the book in his hands. What did June mean by getting his son a piano workbook? If she didn't plan to stick around and teach Ross, it was a lousy substitute.

"SEE WHAT I MEAN?" one of the summer workers said, pointing at the marquee of the Midway Theater. From above, the black-topped marquee was a solid mass of white bird poop. "It doesn't look very nice and people always point and giggle. It's gross."

June was on the platform of the cable cars, where guests boarded for a trip above the skyline of Starlight Point.

Her phone rang and she answered it. "I got your message. What do you mean you need a day to think about it?" June's agent practically yelled into the phone.

June sighed and held up one finger, indicating to the summer employee that she needed a moment. She walked to the edge of the platform. "I mean I need a day, Harold," she said into her phone. "I just got back last night and haven't even unpacked."

"Why did you fly all the way here for callbacks if you weren't darn sure you wanted it? I heard you sing at the audition. Saw you dance. It was like you were inspired. It sure seemed to me like you wanted that part like you wanted your next breath."

"I did. Do. It's complicated," June said. "I'll call you tomorrow. I promise."

She clicked off and turned back to the problem at hand. Birds were crapping on her marquee and it seemed to be her problem to solve. *She was a long way from Broadway.*

June laughed. She was never going to change the birds' minds, but there was always another way. *I wonder if the painters have time to paint the top of the marquee bird-poop white?*

SOMETHING WASN'T RIGHT. Jack had called at half past seven and asked Mel to meet him and Evie at their office. Jack said he wanted Mel's help getting to the bottom of a box of doughnuts, but Mel didn't believe it for a minute. His best friend never voluntarily shared doughnuts.

He heard Jack and Evie arguing as he took the steps two at a time.

"She's being a fool," Evie said.

"So? It's her life."

Mel stepped into Jack's office. "Your wife divorcing you already, Jack?" Mel asked.

Jack glared at him.

Evie swished her lips to one side and narrowed her eyes.

"You look just like your mother when you do that," Mel said.

"Why did we call him?" Evie asked, looking at her brother.

"You're the one who wanted to. I wanted to mind my own business."

Mel dreaded asking what was going on, but a cool breeze down the back of his neck told him it was about June. And him.

Evie faced him, arms crossed. "June's planning to call her agent this morning and turn down the part she's wanted for a long time."

"She got the part she went back for?" Mel asked.

"You didn't know that?"

"No. I haven't talked to June in almost four days."

"See?" Jack asked. "Mel had nothing to do with it."

Evie rolled her eyes.

"I tried talking to her, but she says her mind's made up. For some reason," Evie said, turning her stare on Mel, "June is suddenly giving up a dream part on Broadway and planning to stay home permanently."

June was giving up Broadway and staying home? Mel felt like someone hooked a vacuum hose to his chest and sucked out all the air.

"She hogs the bathroom counter with all her junk," Evie continued, her lips curving into a small smile. "Who could blame me for want-

ing her to go back to New York?" She sat behind her desk. "Plus it's her lifelong dream,
blah, blah, blah."

Mel didn't move. Jack and Evie had called
him here to tell him he had a chance with June.
But that chance meant she was giving up the
opportunity of a lifetime.

"Did she already make the call?" he asked.

Evie glanced at the clock. "Her agent isn't
in the office until eight. June's backstage at
the Midway Theater fussing with something
before the shows get started."

The clock read 7:55.

CHAPTER TWENTY-THREE

MEL RACED DOWN the steps, dashed past Kiddieland and ran full speed to the theater. He
pulled on the front door. Locked. He raced
around the side. Also locked.

He unclipped the wad of keys from his belt
and speed-sorted to find the right one. He
didn't even know what he was going to say
when he found June. Why on earth would he
want to stop her from turning down her dream
role?

Because he loved her.

Which was also the reason he wanted her
to stay.

These infernal keys...

Mel finally found the key, unlocked the door
and shoved his way onto the stage. Only a few
lights were on and he was momentarily blind
after being outside in the morning sunshine.
He tripped over a drum set and knocked over
a rack of costumes. He rolled to a stop in a

pile of glittering vests, shimmery skirts, dancing shoes and at least one top hat. Which was now crushed. The crash was deafening in the silent theater.

Desperate to disentangle himself, Mel kicked off the sparkly costumes and unhooked the frame of the clothing rack from his foot. Static electricity glued a sparkly vest to his cotton uniform sleeve and Mel jerked at it and tried to fling it away.

"June!" he yelled. He thought he heard a voice getting closer.

Finally free of the clothing pile, Mel rushed toward the voice. It was June, cell phone to her ear. When she saw him, a huge smile lit her face.

Definitely better than the reaction he'd expected after their argument.

She covered her mouth with her free hand and smothered a laugh. Her eyebrows rose in a question. Of course he looked ridiculous, but was that the only reason she looked so happy?

And was she happy because she was taking the part on Broadway…or turning it down to stay here working the theaters. Or—*and this was the great* or—was she just that happy to see him?

June approached Mel and stood so close he could pick up the voice of the other person on the phone call. It was a man's voice, but Mel couldn't hear a word he was saying. June reached for Mel and plucked a sequin off his forehead. She held it on her finger so he could see what she'd done.

June continued holding out her sequined finger as she nodded slightly and said, "I'll take it. I'll call you later and we'll discuss the details."

Mel's heart, already racing from his mad dash across the midway and his flailing fight with the clothing rack, jerked to a sudden stop.

He knew his face must reflect the near-stoppage, because June's expression changed. She drew her eyebrows together and tilted her head.

"I'm excited, too," she said. "Thanks again. Bye."

She ended the call and tucked the phone in the back pocket of her curve-hugging jeans. Mel wanted to reach out and pull her into his arms so she wouldn't have a chance to leave. He closed his eyes, trying to control his feelings.

Eyes still shut, he felt June's arms slide around him. "Are you all right?" she asked.

Mel cleared his throat. He opened his eyes.

June ran her fingers through his hair and pulled out more sequins. "What happened to you?" she asked. "You're covered in sparkles and your shirt's missing a button." She touched the place on his chest where the button should be. Mel didn't move. Having June's finger right over his heart was a problem he'd been fighting for months.

June glanced over his shoulder and saw the trail of wreckage.

"What did you do?"

"It was dark. I tripped."

"You could have turned on a light."

"I was in a hurry."

June stepped back slightly but kept her finger on the missing button. "Why?"

"Because I had faulty information. I heard you were going to call your agent and turn down the part you desperately wanted."

June opened her mouth, but Mel touched her lips with one finger.

"I didn't want you to turn it down. It's your dream, June. You're the most talented and beautiful person I know." Mel looked up at the darkened ceiling and then returned his gaze to June's face. "I love you. And loving you means I have to let you go. I'm glad I got to hear you tell your agent you'll take the part. I'm glad I got to see the joy on your face when you said it. That's how I know for sure this is the right thing."

"Mel," June said. "Listen—"

"I don't know where we go from here. I've racked my brain trying to figure it out."

He was talking too fast and he knew it, but he couldn't stop.

"I thought about following you to the city. I could find a job there. Ross could start school someplace nice. Or maybe we could stay here and wait for you. You could come home on the weekends, holidays—"

"Stop talking, Mel," June said. Her eyes filled with tears.

"I'm sorry. I don't even know if you feel the same way about me. Maybe you don't and you can't wait to unload me and my son—"

June kissed him on the lips. A long, deep kiss. Mel held her close, unwilling to let go until she said the final words that would make him. *Is this a goodbye kiss?* If so, it was the most incredible goodbye he'd ever had.

"I WANT TO SHOW you something," June said, finally breaking the kiss. The last thing she wanted to do was stop kissing Mel, but there was something he needed to know.

She pulled her cell phone from her back pocket and handed it to him. "Look at my call history."

Mel took the phone in one hand and scratched his forehead with the other. "I'm not good with these things. I don't even know what I'm looking for. Ross handles complicated electronics at our house."

"You're an electrician," June said.

"That doesn't count."

"Did you hit your head when you crashed through my costumes?"

"Maybe."

June swiped the screen on her phone as it lay in Mel's outstretched hand. "There's the number I just called. The person I was talking to when you came thundering in here."

Mel frowned. "It's a local number. Is your agent in town?"

June laughed. "No. I called a Realtor." She let her words sink in for a moment, but Mel's confusion showed in the twist of his mouth. "I called the man who has the listing for a dance studio in downtown Bayside. The one I used to go to when I was younger."

"You want to lease a dance studio?"

"Yes. It's where I learned to dance. And I discovered this summer just how much fun it is to teach. The studio needs to be modernized. I know it needs work, but I can't wait to get started."

"So you're not taking the part?"

June shrugged. "I haven't called him yet to tell him the bad news. I was more interested in seeing if the Realtor could get me the lease on that place downtown."

"You're turning down the part and staying home. And you're leasing a dance studio."

June felt her smile stretch her cheeks. "I am."

"But why? What changed your mind?" Mel reached out and plucked a sequin off June's neck. "These look great on you, by the way."

"Of course they do. I was born for the stage."

"But you're giving it up."

She shook her head. "I'm not giving it up. I'm changing course. Don't get me wrong, I'm glad I went to the city. Glad I was on Broadway for several years. I'm proud of my performances and I wouldn't trade those years. But this summer has changed me. For the better."

Mel's look was pure hope. Eyes huge, a smile beginning to dimple his cheeks.

"I fell in love," June said.

Big smile now.

"With Starlight Point," she continued. The smile dipped a little. "With the theaters here. With the people I've worked with. I fell in love with choreography, the parade, teaching the kids at the hotel day care. I fell in love with a boy who turned six while I was away doing something else, a mistake I won't make again."

"And?" Mel asked. He ran a gentle finger down her cheek and the hope returned full force to his expression.

"I fell in love with you."

Mel crushed her against his chest, holding her tight as if she would fall off a cliff if his grip failed. His cotton work shirt scratched her cheek, and his lips pressed into her hair. Finally, Mel loosened his hold and gently pushed her away from him, holding her at arm's length.

"I love you, June, so much it hurts. But if you really love me, I want you to prove it."

"I do love you," she said. What more did he want? She'd decided to stay home, took out a lease on a local studio and gave her heart away.

"I believe you. But I still have to ask you to do something."

"What?"

"Take the role in *White Christmas*. The one you earned."

June felt her breath catch. Her heart lost its rhythm. He loved her but he wanted her to leave?

"It's only for a few months, right? The show ends right before Christmas?"

She nodded, totally flummoxed. "The last show is December 23."

"Perfect," he said. He drew in a long, deep breath. "Ross and I will work on your studio while you're gone. And we'll be there to watch your last show and bring you home for Christmas."

"Why do you want me to do this, Mel?"

He pulled her close again. "I want you to know I trust you. After what happened with my...well...you know, I found it very hard to trust and let someone into my life. Especially hard to trust someone with my son's heart." Mel laughed. "Whether I wanted him to or not, Ross fell in love with you before I could stop him."

"I love him, too. I hope he liked my birthday present."

"He loved it. And I'm so happy you'll be here to teach him to play. In a few months." He planted a quick kiss on her lips. "I believe in you and us. And I don't want you to finish this phase of your career with any doubts, any regrets. Please. Do this one last show for me, but also for yourself. And then you'll be the best Christmas present I've ever gotten."

June's heart kicked back into a rhythm. A fast one. This was the most incredible moment of her life. Better than opening day on a big show, better than a standing ovation.

Clapping erupted from the other side of the curtain.

"Am I hearing things?" Mel asked.

June slid out of his arms and crossed to the side of the stage. She pulled the ropes to open the curtains. Jack and Evie sat in the front row.

Mel stood center stage and waited for June to cross to the middle with him.

"You're just in time for the grand finale," Mel said. He dropped to one knee and took June's hand. "Will you marry me, June? I can't guarantee it's the most glamorous part you've ever had, but I'll always be your biggest fan."

June smiled, tears racing down her cheeks. "I love you, Mel. I can't wait to come home at Christmas and marry you."

Her brother and sister stood and clapped enthusiastically.

"Where's the ring?" Jack called out.

June shook her head. "There's always a heckler in the audience."

Mel got to his feet and they took a bow together. "If you'll come over to the arcade, I'll try to win you a nice shiny ring from one of the machines. It'll work until I get you a more permanent one."

"Perfect," June said.

"Those things are all rigged," Evie yelled.

June laughed, took a quick bow and danced off the stage with her fingers laced through those of the man she loved.

EPILOGUE

IN THE GLOW of the towering Christmas tree, June held hands with her fellow performers and walked to the front of the stage. They sang the final bars of "White Christmas" with the orchestra swelling and audience members already rising to their feet to sing along. She smiled and lifted her eyes to take in the theater, alive with thousands of guests enjoying the holiday classic.

She loved it. Truly loved the music, the lights, her floor-length red dress with white trim. But in her heart she was ready for the next stage of her life. When she sang about twinkling lights and snow-covered Christmases, she thought of Starlight Point. The glittering tree behind her was stunning, but she couldn't wait to see the tree Ross had described in detail over the phone.

Ross and Mel. They were in the audience, somewhere, tonight. She wished she could have been there when they cut down their tree, but she'd get to decorate it with them as soon as they all got home.

The curtain closed, the cast members said goodbye and June headed for her dressing room to take off the sparkling costume for the last time. Two men waited for her at her door. A six-foot-three man who'd been part of her life almost as long as she'd been dancing. And a boy with bright eyes who'd recently stepped into her heart, but she'd never let him go.

Mel and Ross each held out bundles of flowers, their gestures and smiles identical. June hugged them both, crushing the roses and releasing a summery scent that took her back to Starlight Point.

"Let's go home," she said.

* * * * *

Don't miss the next book in
Amie Denman's
STARLIGHT POINT STORIES
miniseries, available
December 2016!

LARGER-PRINT BOOKS!

GET 2 FREE LARGER-PRINT NOVELS PLUS 2 FREE MYSTERY GIFTS

Love Inspired®

Larger-print novels are now available...

LILP15

LARGER-PRINT BOOKS!

GET 2 FREE
LARGER-PRINT NOVELS
PLUS 2 FREE
MYSTERY GIFTS

Love Inspired®

SUSPENSE
RIVETING INSPIRATIONAL ROMANCE

Larger-print novels are now available...

WESTERN (WP) PROMISES

YES! Please send me **The Western Promises Collection** in Larger Print. This collection begins with 3 FREE books and 2 FREE gifts (gifts valued at approx. $14.00 retail) in the first shipment, along with the other first 4 books from the collection! If I do not cancel, I will receive 8 monthly shipments until I have the entire 51-book Western Promises collection. I will receive 2 or 3 FREE books in each shipment and I will pay just $4.99 US/ $5.89 CDN for each of the other four books in each shipment, plus $2.99 for shipping and handling per shipment. *If I decide to keep the entire collection, I'll have paid for only 32 books, because 19 books and gifts are FREE! I understand that accepting the 3 free books and gifts places me under no obligation to buy anything. I can always return a shipment and cancel at any time. My free books and gifts are mine to keep no matter what I decide.

272 HCN 3070 472 HCN 3070

Name	(PLEASE PRINT)	
Address		Apt. #
City	State/Prov.	Zip/Postal Code

Signature (if under 18, a parent or guardian must sign)

Mail to the **Reader Service:**

IN U.S.A.: P.O. Box 1867, Buffalo, NY 14240-1867
IN CANADA: P.O. Box 609, Fort Erie, Ontario L2A 5X3

WPBPA16R